From the *Essence* bestselling author of *Hiding in Hip Hop* and an entertainment insider— a juicy debut novel about the down-low life of one of New York's most beloved Hip Hop producers.

AFTER THE SUDDEN DEATH OF HIS FATHER, A RENOWNED JAZZ musician, Aaron "Big A.T." Tremble clings to music as an escape. Making Hip Hop beats becomes his life. His love for music lands him at the estate of Larry "Pop" Singleton, a retired and respected Hip Hop music mogul who sees something special in Big A.T., and also knows the truth about his sexuality. With Pop's blessings and nurturing, Big A.T. is on the path to becoming the next great Hip Hop producer in New York.

With the help of Pop and "the family," a network of secretly gay men in the Hip Hop world, Big A.T. finds success and starts his own music label. He's signed and worked with some of the biggest Hip Hop artists in the country. One of them is Brooklyn native lyricist "Tickman." Together they make sweet music. But Tickman and Big A.T.'s relationship goes beyond producer and rapper—they become secret lovers.

Nothing can stop Big A.T. All of the radio stations play his music. He has money, fame, and Jasmine, his girlfriend who doesn't know about his secret love for men. However, at the pinnacle of his career, compromising photos of Big A.T. land on the desk of a national news program—and in the hands of his girlfriend. Big A.T., for the first time, is at a crossroads: come out publicly with his secret or watch his music empire crumble.

# Advance Praise for MOGUL

"[Dean] writes with passion about the dual lifestyle gay men feel they must construct. His explicit and often tender descriptions of sex between men are bold moves for street lit. Urban libraries will do patrons a huge service by making this title available."

—*Library Journal*

"Taboo-busting portrait of a hidden world behind the music."

—*Kirkus Reviews*

"Dean has penned a page-turning scandal, a plot-explosive classic, and given life to taboo characters that leap off the page! A fast-paced novel that seduces you into the underworld of Hip Hop and never ever lets you go!"

—Tu-Shonda L. Whitaker, *Essence* bestselling author of *Millionaire Wives Club*

"I enjoyed reading this book. It kept my attention from the first page to the last. I know it will provide readers that missing link since E. Lynn Harris's death . . . Bravo Terrance. You are da man."

—J. L. King, *New York Times* bestselling author

"*Mogul* is where fame, secrets, and sexuality meet. If you loved E. Lynn Harris, check out newcomer Terrance Dean."

—Tananarive Due, *Essence* bestselling author of *Joplin's Ghost* and *Blood Colony*

"With the sensuality of E. Lynn Harris, the flare of James Earl Hardy, and the classiness of Ricc Rollins, Dean has cooked up a well-crafted masterpiece that is sure to have readers glued to the pages. Get ready. You're about to be taken on the ride of your life."

—Anna J., bestselling author of *Snow White: A Survival Story*

"Terrance Dean's debut novel *Mogul* is a cautionary tale in the tradition of E. Lynn Harris. It enters the secret world of Hip Hop and gives new meaning to the word 'family.' Fast, suspenseful, and eye-opening, *Mogul* will make you take a second look at everyone you thought you knew."

—Donna Hill, author of *What Mother Never Told Me*

"With his novel *Mogul*, Terrance Dean continues to make words simmer on the page, with insightful character development, dramatic plot twists, and explosive dialogue. Terrance uses his rebellious keyboard to add to his sizzling body of accessible, page turning, jaw-dropping fiction. Sure to be another bestseller! Read it!"

—Sabrina Lamb, bestselling humorist of the satirical novel
*A Kettle of Vultures . . . Left Beak Marks on My Forehead*

"Terrance has creatively crafted the perfect storm of a novel: a fiery, fast-paced plot, intriguing and dynamic characters, and a deliciously edible scandal. Strap yourselves in and hold on tightly—it's one hell of a ride!"

—Lee Hayes, bestselling author

"With *Mogul*, you get an inside look—though fictional—at the entertainment industry, the making of a Hip Hop star, and the secrets those stars must keep in order to keep their fame and fortune. I couldn't put it down."

—Frederick Smith, author of *Down for Whatever*
and *Right Side of the Wrong Bed*

"When I heard this book was underway, I awaited it with bated breath. Terrance Dean did not disappoint, either. *Mogul* is 'unputdownable'—just what the doctor ordered. The literary webs he has woven with this titillating tale about the down-low and low-down deeds within the music industry kept me at the edge of my seat. I didn't want this book to end. It is many, many things and a must read. With this debut novel, I can pay

Terrance Dean only the highest of compliments and christen him as the E. Lynn Harris of the Hip Hop generation."

—Karu F. Daniels, digital media producer, journalist, and author

"Nobody else could have written this book. Terrance Dean broke new ground with *Hiding in Hip Hop* and now he does it again with *Mogul*. For the first time ever we are given an exclusive red carpet and backstage pass into the mind of a rap mogul living on the down low. Whether the industry is ready or not for an openly gay exec in Hip Hop, Terrance Dean brings his journey straight to us along with a secret world and sizzling tale of sex, sensuality, and self esteem."

—Abiola Abrams, TV personality, author, and lifestyle maven

# MOGUL

A NOVEL

TERRANCE DEAN

**ATRIA** PAPERBACK
New York   London   Toronto   Sydney

**ATRIA** PAPERBACK
A Division of Simon & Schuster, Inc.
1230 Avenue of the Americas
New York, NY 10020

First Atria Paperback edition June 2011

**ATRIA** PAPERBACK and colophon are trademarks
of Simon & Schuster, Inc.

For information about special discounts for bulk purchases,
please contact Simon & Schuster Special Sales at 1-866-506-1949
or business@simonandschuster.com.

The Simon & Schuster Speakers Bureau can bring authors
to your live event. For more information or to book an event
contact the Simon & Schuster Speakers Bureau at 1-866-248-3049
or visit our website at www.simonspeakers.com.

Designed by Esther Paradelo

Manufactured in the United States of America

10   9   8   7   6   5   4   3   2   1

Library of Congress Cataloging-in-Publication Data
Dean, Terrance.
    Mogul : a novel / Terrance Dean.—1st Atria Paperback ed.
      p. cm.
    1. African American sound recording executives and producers—
Fiction.   2. African American bisexual men—Fiction.   3. Sound
recording industry—Fiction.   4. Hip-hop—Fiction.   5. New York
(N.Y.)—Fiction   6. Musical fiction.   I. Title.
    PS3604.E1545M68   2011
    813'.6—dc22   2010044570

ISBN 978-1-4516-1192-2
ISBN 978-1-4516-1194-6 (ebook)

*For my son, Ramelle Quinn. I love you more than you could ever know. I am so proud to be your father.*

PRESENT DAY
EVERY STORY HAS A BEGINNING . . .

# ONE

I hear my breathing. It's loud, hard, and fast. I don't know why I'm doing this, but I have to go through with it. I've summoned every entertainment reporter and photographer to the Ritz-Carlton this morning for a news conference. Hell, every media outlet across the country received the press release.

The media generally doesn't send out reporters to cover breaking news stories related to the music industry, let alone Hip Hop. But when I called, it was something they knew they couldn't miss.

Who am I?

I'm Big A.T., government name Aaron Tremble.

I have a record label, clothing line, real estate properties, and television and film deals. And oh yeah, I just signed a licensing agreement with a liquor company to use my name and image.

It's been documented in every notable magazine from *People* to *Newsweek:* "Big A.T. *is* the entertainment industry. He *is* Hip Hop."

It's even been stated, if I am quoting accurately, *"He's suave. Debonair. Charming. Enticing."*

I'm not one to toot my own horn, but like my man Kanye West put it in his song "Stronger," "Bow in the presence of greatness."

I'm a mover and shaker. Moves aren't made without me. I am invincible. A power player. Superman. And, I'm a winner.

I make everyone around me feel like a champion, and that can't be bought anywhere.

Yet, right now, I'm not feeling like a winner. As a matter of fact, I am feeling like shit, pure shit.

As much as I may want to think I'm Superman, what I'm dealing with is my kryptonite. 'Bout to kill my career . . . might as well kill me.

I've been pacing back and forth for over an hour in my thirty-second-floor Ritz-Carlton presidential suite. The sun is trying to pierce through the drawn curtains, fighting to be revealed. My freshly manicured fingers fidget with my diamond-encrusted Rolex watch.

In the room with me is Kenya, the head of A&R of my record label, and my publicist, Tracey Chambers.

Tracey is the publicist for almost every major celebrity in Hip Hop. She is a smooth bitch. Tracey is petite with a plump ass. Her tiny body carries attitude and confidence that makes her seem larger than life. With a few nip-and-tuck jobs here and there, Tracey looks like a black Barbie doll. So beautiful she can make a brother lose his religion and forget he ever had one.

Other industry insiders, including myself, often wonder if she has her own agenda of being a celebrity.

Tracey is good. No. She is phenomenal. She can turn a gun-toting, drug-dealing, pistol-whipping, hard-core thug into a charity-giving, save-the-children, the-black-church-needs-you, the-community-loves-you superstar.

Tracey helped to convert Big Bad Mamma, a hard-core ghetto-pimping rapper, into a primped princess darling. Once Big Bad Mama's image changed, she landed movie roles starring opposite of some of Hollywood's biggest names. She even got nominated for a few awards.

Tracey now has a daunting task ahead of her. The news I am about to break will create one of the most challenging moments of her career. Tracey is tough. Not afraid to break new ground. But, this is going to put her spin-doctor skills to the test.

My feet are not keeping up with my racing heart. Everything feels like it's in slow motion. I pace from the bathroom to the window, from the window to the living room and back to the bathroom. Kenya and Tracey are sitting quietly on the double-seated red leather sofa. Every now and then they check and respond to their ringing BlackBerrys.

Everyone in the entertainment industry is calling or sending text messages to get the scoop. The entire music industry is waiting to hear the news.

As I make my way back to the living room, I stop. I run my hands across my fresh-shaven face. I gaze at my Rolex, studying the time. I am lost in a daze . . . lost in the sweeping movements of the seconds that turn into minutes.

I turn toward Kenya. "Baby girl, this is it. It's ride-or-die time. You got my back?"

Her innocent black doe eyes gaze at me. Her nose crinkles as her pouty lips curve up into a smile. Her deep-set dimples indent her smooth brown cheeks. "I got your back," she says and smiles.

"Tracey." I glance at her. "I'm trusting in you to handle this with all you got. So, work your magic."

Tracey leans forward. Takes her right hand sporting the three-quarter diamond ring and tosses her long weaved black locks behind her back. "I got this," she says.

I look at my Rolex, again. I say to no one in particular, "It's showtime."

We make our way to the elevator down the hall. I let out a deep sigh when the doors open on the first floor.

I step out and look left. I see a short dark-skin man with gleaming white teeth. "Welcome to New York City. The place where *your* dreams can come true and celebrities are made," he says into the camera. "This is Scott Jaredson with *City Access* and we have a huge breaking story about to take place right here in the heart of the entertainment capital. It's an exclusive announcement and everyone's on edge waiting to hear what top music executive Big A.T. has to say."

My heart starts its rapid pace again. Thumping. I walk faster, trying to keep up with the beats.

As we move toward the conference room I see my reflection in the mirror next to the big gold doors. I give myself a once-over. My dark skin is glowing. My hair is shaped and lined up by my man, T-Money, the best barber in New York City. My slim six-foot frame looks impeccable in my own clothing line, A.T. Wares.

I run my fingers across my black cashmere blazer and smooth out the sleeves. I brush my shoulders. I snap the collars on my crisp white button-down oxford shirt. And then, we enter the frenzied room of awaiting photographers and journalists.

I cross over to the podium and adjust the microphone. The photographers' flashes are nonstop. I squint, adjusting to the glaring lights.

I reach inside my blazer's left pocket. I fumble with the piece of paper that is my scripted speech. I am scared. Scared shitless. I am about to do what no man in Hip Hop has ever done. Rattle the cages. Deliver a punch like Joe Louis. Hip Hop is about to be knocked out with a sucker punch in the first round.

I begin to perspire. My palms are sweaty. My mouth is dry. I need water.

I attempt to look out into the audience, but the flashes are unbearable. I put my head down and take a few deep breaths.

*You can do this,* I say to myself. *You got to do this.*

The room falls eerily silent. Then someone breaks the air. "What's this about Big A.T.?" I don't respond. I wipe my dry mouth with my hand. I lick my lips to moisten them. I glance toward Kenya. She smiles at me with those beautiful soft eyes and nods her head.

I look at Tracey standing next to Kenya. She is cradling her cell phone between her shoulder and ear. She is rummaging through the big Chanel bag dangling from her wrist.

*What the fuck am I doing here? I am not supposed to be here. This shit is crazy.* I stare at everyone. *I need some water. Can't they see I need some damn water!*

My knees begin to buckle. My body starts to shake. My hands tremble.

I take another deep breath and begin. "Ladies and gentlemen of the press, I wish to thank you for taking the time to come out today." I swallow hard. "Some of you have known me since I was in diapers, and some of you have changed them." I laugh, trying to lighten the tense mood of the room as well as shake my own nervousness.

A few chuckles infiltrate the room.

"I first would like to say 'Thank you very much,' as some of you have followed my career and have treated me favorably in the press. I am here today because something has me in turmoil with myself, family, and fans."

I take another deep breath.

"I am a very loyal person, as many of you know. I am extremely loyal to the fans of Hip Hop and in their interest in hearing good music and having good role models."

I see a few journalists scribbling on their pads. Others are sitting on the edge of their seats, hanging on every word.

Perspiration forms on my head. It is a cold sweat. I reach for my handkerchief in the front lapel of my jacket to dab my forehead.

*I need some water. I really need some water.*

"Can someone please get me some water?" I blurt.

Kenya rushes over to the two tables on the side of the room, where an assortment of fruits, bagels, and beverages are provided for the press as a complimentary breakfast. She grabs a bottle of water and races to the podium.

I start to have second thoughts. I feel I am making a big mistake. *What the fuck am I doing? Am I really ready for this?* The thoughts race in my head. *I wish this was a dream. I need to stay King of New York. I can't throw it all away.*

My sweaty hands grip the podium. Kenya thrusts the bottle of cold water in front of me. I snatch it from her.

"Thank you." I take a big gulp.

My legs feel as if they can no longer sustain me.

"Are you okay?" Kenya leans in and whispers.

My fingers are trembling. I close my eyes and whisper, "I'm fine."

I take a deep breath and start again.

"As I was saying . . . it is with good intentions and with much love to my family, friends, fans, and the music industry that I announce . . ."

My eyes roll into the back of my head.

My body goes limp.

I fall backwards onto the floor.

*THUMP!*

I hear people in the room scream. Someone yells, "Oh my God!" Footsteps are scrambling near me. I am fading in and out of consciousness. A few journalists rush to the podium.

Kenya kneels next to me and frantically starts fanning me with her hands. My eyes are fluttering. I turn my head from left to right.

I see Tracey, my publicist extraordinaire, fling her Chanel bag over her shoulder and rush her tiny frame toward me. "Someone call an ambulance!" she screams. Tracey pushes her long black mane from her face. "And for God's sake, stop taking pictures," she orders and shoos at the photographers standing over me.

# TWO

I am in the hotel for the news conference. It's crazy. There are about fifty journalists here, from everywhere. I mean, come on now, it's Big A.T., giving an impromptu press conference.

That doesn't happen every day. Not with someone like him.

Everyone is sitting, waiting and waiting, and in walks Big A.T. The room becomes eerily silent. There is this look on his face, like you can see something is heavily on his mind.

As he starts talking, I notice him shaking. His body is twitching, sweat is on his forehead, and then he just falls. He drops right in front of all of us. Faints.

It happens so fast that people think he is faking it. At first no one moves. It's like everybody is suspended in stuck mode, but I know something is wrong. I run to the podium as fast as I can. Then everyone starts screaming and shouting.

When I get on the stage, I think for a moment, *Should I take some pictures?* And without hesitation I pull out my camera and snap a few shots, right before Tracey starts pushing everyone away. I have to get these photos. They will make my career. I will have the scoop. The pictures will see to just that.

# THREE

"It's seems like anxiety got the best of you," the doctor says. He removes his cold wrinkly freckled hand from my forehead. "You'll be fine, but take a few hours to rest before doing anything strenuous."

I grit my teeth and shake my head as I lie in the hospital bed.

This absolutely can't be happening. Not right now.

*I'm up in the hospital because a powerful nigga like myself fainted. What the fuck is this really about? I deal with stress on the daily. Running a record label. Investing in properties from the East Coast to the West Coast. A multimillion-dollar clothing empire. Working with rappers. Singers. Wannabe rap stars. Wannabe divas. I deal with real stressful shit every day.*

I just stare up at the ceiling, counting the tiny holes in the tiles. I got to do something to distract my mind. I hear Kenya's and Tracey's heels clicking as they step into the room with me. I glance toward the door and see a few burly security men standing guard outside my room.

"The paparazzi followed us to the hospital," Tracey says. "You know this is an exclusive story. It is the scoop of the day."

"Yeah, I can see the headlines now. **Big A.T., Hip Hop's Impresario, Faints**," I say. "They are going to capitalize off this moment."

"It's going to be all over the Internet and on every blog within minutes," Tracey says.

"No, make that seconds. Especially MediaTakeOut and Bossip. Fucking technology," Kenya adds.

"Hey, Doc, I got a plane to catch in a few hours, so do you mind if I get out of here?" I ask.

"As long as you are not doing anything to cause another anxiety attack, I don't see a problem with it. Just call me when you arrive where you're going and let me know how you're feeling."

"I think I can manage that," I say with a feigned smile.

"Make sure to drink lots of fluids. Your body needs to be hydrated." The doctor walks to the foot of the bed.

"Got it."

"I'll go and let the hospital know that it's okay to release you."

"We have to arrange an escape out of here, because the paparazzi are piled in front of the hospital," Kenya says.

"Don't worry about it," Tracey tells her. "I'll go out and distract them. I'll make a few statements. That will allow security the time to escort Big A.T. out of the hospital undetected."

"Let's get one of the security guards to put on a hospital gown as if he's me," I say. "We can get one of the nurses to wheel him to another part of the hospital. Then I can slip out through the back entrance and get to the airport."

"Fabulous," Tracey says. "Let's be ready to rock 'n' roll in five minutes. You don't want to miss your flight, and I have a lot of damage control to tend to."

Tracey pulls her compact mirror from her bag. She checks her face, teases her hair, and puts on her Chanel shades. She is now ready to handle and answer all the questions like the diva press maven she's become.

The smaller-build security guard changes into a hospital gown and gets into the wheelchair. A nurse comes in and wheels him out.

I see nurses and doctors running past my room. A fury of security guards and hospital police rush through the halls. I hear the chattering voices screeching through the walkies as they haul the press off the hospital's premises. "They are coming in the front entrance. We need some more security here, now!"

I hear patients screaming they want medical attention. "I don't give a fuck about no damn celebrity—I got an emergency, too!" one big black woman shouts while she holds the hand of a frightened little boy.

"Fuck this shit! Y'all motherfuckers wrong," an elderly man yells. He is waving his cane at a nurse scurrying past him.

A few giddy nurses come inside my room while I am waiting for my moment to escape. They want to get autographs. "This is for my son. He loves your music." One of the bright-eyed nurses giggles. "I'm a fan, too." She blushes. I don't mind. I know it is my fans that got me to where I am.

Kenya and two burly bodyguards are ready to take me to the airport. It's part of the original plan. I was to make my announcement, then head to the airport. And then go off to the Dominican Republic to let it all die down.

I sit on the edge of the bed and stare at my feet. I fidget with my watch. I feel empty on the inside, yet filled with so much confusion as to what to do now.

The room is quiet. No one is saying anything.

Tracey and the doctor are in the hospital lobby doing their thing. They are distracting the audience. Tracey is informing the press that due to me being overworked with the many projects I am producing, I am suffering from exhaustion. She lets them know I will be fine and that my fans should keep me in their prayers as I recover and regain my health.

Yes, distraction. Just like I learned early on in this entertainment business, a business full of illusions.

You have to keep the fans distracted.

LIGHTS! CAMERA! ACTION!

"Let me get some paper and a pen," I tell Kenya. She reaches into her Louis Vuitton carry bag and pulls out a notepad with a Montblanc pen. I quickly start writing.

A tall lanky white orderly wearing green scrubs rushes in. "We have to leave now," he says. "Follow me."

One muscled bodyguard is following directly behind him. Kenya and I are in the middle. The other tall muscular bodyguard is behind us. The orderly whisks us past the nurses' station and then the janitors' closet. He makes a quick right turn where there are a few doctors talking with some nurses.

He glances behind him, then gently opens a side door that leads to a stairwell. Once inside, we go down two flights of stairs to a locked door marked *Emergency Exit Only.*

"When you exit out of here your car will be right outside waiting for you." The orderly smiles. His crooked teeth are large and bucked.

"Thanks, man, I really appreciate it," I say and give him a handshake.

He unlocks the door. The bodyguards shield me with their bodies as Kenya and I climb into the waiting black Cadillac Escalade SUV.

The SUV speeds through traffic. Dipping and dodging between cars. We are on our way to Kennedy Airport with no press in tow.

I sit quietly, staring out of the tinted window. The city's skyline is fading behind me. New York City is all I know. It is all mines, and now I feel like it is slipping away from me.

Everything I worked so hard to create seems so minuscule.

# FOUR

My BlackBerry is ringing nonstop. I hand it to Kenya. She turns it off and gently caresses my hand. She doesn't have to say anything. Kenya knows this is the type of comfort and support I need right now.

I met her five years ago while I was at a lunch meeting in Chelsea at Maroons Restaurant. Anyone who was anyone was seen at this restaurant.

Kenya and her three girlfriends were dressed in their finest. I noticed them when they came in. The host seated them near the front of the restaurant at one of the huge windows. I was at a back table and had a full view of the young ladies.

I saw Kenya's reaction when she spotted me. She put her hand over her mouth and squealed. I kept watching them as they chatted loudly, giggling and falling over one another and pointing toward me.

I shifted in my seat and continued with my meeting. Then I saw Kenya push her curly hair away from her smooth oval face and slowly make her way to my table. "Excuse me, Big A.T.," she said.

"Do I know you?" I asked.

"No, you don't," she said, clearing her throat. Her dress was hugging her body in all the right places. "My name is Kenya Ross and I'm a big fan of yours." She pushed her brass bracelet up her arm. "I was a little disappointed with the album you just did for Caeser Jones. I hope that you don't call that music and expect us to support it!" She continued a little more confidently. "You have produced some of the biggest names in the industry like Shawty Mike, Crazee Black, Cee Cee, and of course Ms. Freeda. Those albums are bananas—I mean, they are hot!" she corrected herself.

Taken aback, I listened. I was surprised by her candor, and impressed by her boldness. I looked her up and down. Her cocoa brown skin glistened under the dim lights. Her dimples winking each time she spoke.

"Look, I don't mean to bother you, but I love music," she continued. "Music today is disposable and it's only about what's hot now. Real music fans, like me, we want something more. We want to hear something new, fresh, and innovative." She looked me directly in my eyes. "Can you produce something like that next time?"

I jerked my head back. "Wow, I'm speechless," I said. "For the first time I got a real person to tell me something really real about me. I guess my shit *does* stink." I laughed out loud.

"How old are you, Ms. Kenya Ross?" I asked.

"Now, you know you're not supposed to ask a woman her age," she quickly replied, putting her hands on her hips. "But, it is my twenty-first birthday." She sucked her teeth.

"Well, look at that." I raised my glass and tipped it toward her, then took a sip of my drink. "Are those your girlfriends over there staring and smiling at us?" I waved at her friends. They all started giggling and waving back.

Kenya nodded yes.

"Okay, check this out. Are they all over twenty-one?" I asked.

Kenya nodded yes again.

"Now, don't lie to me, because I don't need any trouble," I said.

"I don't have to lie to you," she quipped and whipped out her ID from her purse.

"She's snappy and bold. I like that. Okay, I'm going to send over a bottle of champagne for your table, and the celebration dinner is on me. How about that?" I smiled at Kenya.

"That sounds real cool to me." She smiled back, her dimples becoming even more prominent. "Thank you so much, Big A.T. This is so nice of you." She reached over and hugged me.

"Also, I am going to need a big favor from you," I said, taking another sip of my drink.

Kenya's eyebrows furrowed. She squinted her eyes. "What is that?" she asked.

"I'm looking for an assistant. Someone who can handle a few phone calls, set up some meetings, and be my eyes and ears on some new ventures," I said, handing her my business card. "How about you give me a call so we can set up an interview and talk a little more?"

Her mouth dropped open as she took the card. She quickly pulled herself together. "Let me think about it and get back to you."

I laughed and said, "No problem." I wished her happy birthday and told her to enjoy the rest of the evening.

Kenya called three days later. I loved that about her: She was not quick to jump into anything. She needed a little training on business etiquette, but she had the tenacity for the industry, and was willing to work her ass off. She was also someone I could depend on. She became a confidante. She let me know early on that no matter what, she loved me and would always have my back.

As the SUV approaches the American Airlines international terminal, I focus on what my next move will be. I have to play it smart. The entire entertainment industry is about to explode with my news and I know I will be hounded by the media.

I have a lot on the line. I am jeopardizing my life, music, and industry contacts.

When we pull in front of the terminal, Kenya and I get out of the car. The bodyguards get my bags and hand them to the curbside check-in attendant. I take out the pad and pen. I write down a few more sentences and hand it to Kenya.

"Give this to Tracey. It's my official statement that I want her to release to the media."

"You sure about this?" she asks, taking the note.

I hesitate for a minute. Thinking, *Is this really the best way?*

"No, I'm not. That is the coward's way out. I want you to video-record me from your BlackBerry reading the announcement."

Kenya pulls her BlackBerry from her bag and aims it toward my face.

"Let me know when you're ready," she says.

"How do I look?" I brush my hand over my hair. I smooth out my mustache and goatee.

"You look fine."

"Okay, I'm ready." I clear my throat. Kenya pushes the Record button. I steady the piece of paper and read my statement.

When I finish I feel the weight of everything gone.

Pressure.

Anxiety.

Shame.

All gone.

"You got it?" I ask.

Kenya turns the screen over and we view it.

"I guess that's it," I say when it finishes playing.

"I guess it is," Kenya says.

"There's no turning back now."

Kenya reaches over and gives me a big hug. A hug that seems to last an eternity.

"Everything is going to be fine," Kenya says. "This is going to blow over in a matter of weeks."

"I sure hope you're right." I pause. Then I say again, "I sure hope you're right."

Just as I am about to walk inside the terminal, Kenya runs over and hands me my BlackBerry.

"You're going to need this."

# FIVE

I check in with the ticket agent and go to the VIP section of the American Airlines passenger lounge. I plop into one of the cushiony black leather chairs and order a shot of A.T. Patron. One of the brands I promote with the liquor company.

I need a drink. It has been a long day, and it has just started. Then something on the television catches my attention. I glare at the screen. The news is showing footage of my press conference.

There they are. The photos. Photos of me lying on the floor, looking like a damn fool, flash on the screen.

I jump up, nearly spilling my drink. I grab my BlackBerry off the table. I rush toward the bar and strain to hear what is being said. The sound is too low—I can't hear the news anchor.

"Can you turn that up?" I yell to the bartender.

"I don't have the remote," the bartender says.

The boarding announcement is made for all first-class passengers traveling to the Dominican Republic.

Shit.

I'm trying to read the anchor's lips. Straining to hear the barely audible words, but the announcement comes again.

I gulp down my drink and rush to the gate. I hand the agent my ID and ticket. She glances at me, smiling. "Thank you, Mr. Tremble," she says. "I'm a huge fan of your music." I just nod and walk through the gate, wondering how long the media is going to run those photos.

# SIX

Of course I'm going to get paid for the photos. Every media outlet wants the pictures.

How much? Well, let's just say I stand to do really, really, really well in hitting the jackpot.

Don't make me out to be the bad guy. I am just doing my job. Thousands of people visit my blog on a daily basis. If I wasn't doing my job then my fans wouldn't support my work.

# SEVEN

As soon as I take my seat in first class I order another drink. "I need a glass of white wine," I tell the flight attendant.

I start searching the Internet on my BlackBerry for stories about me, the press conference . . . and those photos.

Moments later the flight attendant returns with the glass of wine on a platter. The plane is taxied onto the runway and we proceed onto the tarmac.

"Excuse me, but you're going to have to turn off your phone," the flight attendant says.

"Damn!" Just as I'd connected to CNN's website and saw the photo of me. I turn my BlackBerry off.

Within minutes we ascend into the clear blue skies. I glance out of the window. New York is slowly fading away. I'm not sure if I'll be able to bounce back after the blow I'll deliver to the entertainment industry.

*Is this the end of my career?* I think. *What is everyone going to say about me?*

*A lot of people don't know what's really going down in this place. Yeah, it's a city where your dreams can come true and celebrities are made. It's New York fuckin' City! Everyone comes here because they want to be famous or discovered.*

*It's full of glitz and glamour, but people really don't know what's going on behind the closed doors. They don't know about the deals being made and how those deals are being conducted. People have no clue that many of their favorite celebrities, stars, and top executives are part of my family. The family of down-low and gay men who actually run the entertainment industry.*

*Yes, the real "Family."*

*We run this!*

*I just wonder if the world is ready to accept the first openly gay black executive in Hip Hop.*

I emptied the glass of wine as soon as we took off, and now the flight attendant offers me another drink. When she returns I lift the glass from the silver platter, look out of the window, and make a toast. "Here's to a new life, or something or other. Shit. *Something* is going to happen. Or other: I find a new career," I mumble.

I recline in my seat. Close my eyes and let the buzz take effect.

THE PAST
HOW IT ALL BEGAN . . .

# EIGHT

In my junior year at Boys and Girls High School in Brooklyn I had it going on. I was popular. I had a fly girl and fly gear.

And I was on the basketball team . . . had a jump shot like you'll never believe. I was even recruited by some scouts to go to upstate New York to play ball at Syracuse University. That's how fucking good I was.

But, I will always remember the date: October third. I'll never forget it. It'll always stick with me.

After basketball practice, we were all pissed off as we headed to the showers. One of my teammates couldn't seem to make a basket to save his life, nor the team's ass. So Coach made us sprint around the gym ten times at full speed.

Generally, after a long hard practice the team would head out to get something to eat before going home. But, this practice was *hard* and *long.* My entire body ached. My muscles were throbbing. My feet were screaming for a relief from my sneakers, and my hands had begun to cramp.

We were sweaty and smelly. I was in desperate need of a shower. The gym reeked of musk and old sweat socks. Some players started joking around. We needed it. The mood was tense. I was, at least.

While showering, I caught a glimpse of my teammate George Rochelle's naked six-five, rock-hard body. George was a high school senior, captain of the basketball team. All-City and All-State power forward. And, the most popular male in my school.

His back was toward me and all I saw was George's bubble ass slowly being lathered by his massive hands. George was dark, like a chocolate Hershey bar. His entire body was the same color.

No imperfections.

His muscles rippled as he washed under his arms and reached around to his back and ass. Watching him, I started to get an erection. I couldn't help it. The sight of George's nakedness caused my loins to stir.

Then George turned around and faced me. His six-pack abs were on display, along with his long and dark dick.

He smiled and nodded at me before I could turn away. I was embarrassed. My dick was fully erect. I grabbed my erection, I fled the shower, and rushed toward my locker. I dressed quickly. George walked by and smiled at me. I put my head down and pulled on my sweater. I was trying to get out of there.

"Hey," George said, standing in front of me with his towel wrapped around his waist.

I stuffed my feet into my sneakers and stood up.

"What's up?" I said, avoiding eye contact.

"What you got up for this weekend?" he asked.

I glanced at him. Damn! He was fine. Smiling at me with his beautiful lips.

Pink.

Luscious.

Lips.

"I got a lot of studying to do," I replied.

"Oh, aight. Well, hit me up this week so we can hook up and hang out."

"Yeah, aight." I grabbed my backpack and rushed toward the locker room doors. My feet were tripping over each other. My head and underarms started to perspire.

"Yo!" he yelled as I was hustling through the doors. His deep voice startled me. I stopped and slowly turned to face him. My heart was pounding. He was still smiling. Standing with the white towel perfectly wrapped around his waist.

He pointed toward me. "You got your sweater on backwards."

"Thanks," I said, flustered. I pushed through the doors and ran toward the water fountain at the end of the hall.

That evening I couldn't stop thinking of George.

His smile.

His body.

Thoughts of his nakedness kept me awake the entire night.

# NINE

George had me yearning for some physical contact. I needed the touch of a guy. I kept tugging at my erection while I lay in bed thinking of George.

When I was around eleven years old there was this kid in my neighborhood I used to grind dicks with. He was two years older than me. We started messing around one day while we were playing in his room. He asked if he could touch my penis. I pulled it out and when he touched me my erection pointed directly at him. He pulled down his pants and we started dry-humping. It was funny as hell. Our little dicks sticking each other.

After that incident we would meet up in the vestibule of his building and do our thing. But I still liked girls. I figured my grinding with this boy was some sort of phase. Maybe it was just a passing moment. I read about it in sex education class. We even had a discussion about it. Sometimes members of the same sex have sexual thoughts of one another. It's normal. It doesn't mean you're gay. It's your hormones.

Yeah. Maybe it was my hormones. But I started to think about guys more. And more . . . and more . . . and more. I never acted on my urge, or erections. I only fantasized about being with a guy, wondering what it would feel like, what it would be like.

Masturbating was fulfilling. But now my body was screaming for a touch, yearning for male contact.

For an entire week I tried to ignore George. I ignored him like he was something deadly. Something that if I let seep into my life, as he had my mind, I would die an uncertain death. A death that comes looming and swallows your whole existence. I would be no longer.

So, whenever I saw his tall lean muscular body I walked the other way. I avoided his chocolate skin, rich like a true Africans. I ran from his beautiful darkness. That is, until practice. Every day.

There he was. Like God himself said, "Let there be light." I unwillingly, uncontrollably, and undeniably could not resist the darkness, for now it was my light.

And George, acting as if he was in cahoots with God, nodded his head and smiled at me. I needed to be strong and resist the tree of life. George's tree.

Coach paired us together during practice. We ran sprints, did layups and one-on-one drills. I couldn't run from him—his chocolate darkness, his sweaty glistening skin. His gorgeous smile followed me everywhere. And George made sure I noticed him. At every turn, there he was.

"I'll call you Saturday," he said to me as he took a three-point shot.

*Swish.*

Saturday afternoon my mom called for me to pick up the phone.

"What up?" the deep voice said on the other end.

"What up?" I replied.

"Yo, why don't you come to the park and shoot some hoops."

I wanted to say no. I wanted to tell him I didn't want to be near him. I was afraid of what my body would do.

"Aight. See you in twenty minutes," I said.

My heart was already at the park even before I walked out my door. I fidgeted with my watch as I counted each step I took on the sidewalk.

I took some deep breaths to calm myself. It didn't work.

He was already at the DeKalb Avenue playground shooting hoops. Damn, he was sexy. The sun was beating down on his bare chest. Small drips of sweat dotted his forehead. His lean body flexed with each shot he took.

I approached him like nothing had ever happened. Like I had never seen his nakedness and become aroused.

I gave him some dap and we began shooting hoops.

Two hours went by. We were tired, sweaty, and hungry.

And I was horny.

"Come to my crib," George said as he pulled me up from the ground. "My moms cooked before she went to work this morning."

This was my opportunity to leave. To go home. To leave him. To not be around him anymore.

"Aight," I said. I pulled on my sweatshirt, then dribbled the ball as we walked toward his apartment on Flatbush Avenue.

We devoured the food his mom prepared for him. Fried chicken, string beans, mashed potatoes, and corn bread. I was stuffed.

Then we sat on the sofa in the living room and played video games. After an hour George said he was going to take a shower and would be right back. Five minutes later he strolled out of his room naked. His dark, chocolate body was naked.

George walked in front of me. "You coming?" He reached out his large fat hand.

I hesitated. Not sure what to do. But my dick did. I immediately got an erection.

I stood up. Grabbed his extended hand and followed him into the bathroom. When he opened the door the hot water had already steamed the mirror. He pulled back the yellow flowery shower curtain and got in. I slowly stripped out of my clothes and followed.

I was nervous. My entire body was convulsing. I felt like I was going to pass out. The hot water hit our bodies and I was jolted back by the beautiful sight of George standing in front of me.

He placed his hand on my shoulder. Then my chest. We fumbled around, touching each other's nakedness. His long dick doubled in length. We hugged, and then caressed one another. Our lips finally met. We kissed like two clumsy fools having their first kiss. A peck here. A peck there. Then we found our rhythm. His lips parted and he forced his tongue into my mouth. He sucked my lips and my tongue. I sucked his.

The water pounded our bodies and we began to rock and grind on each other. George's hard body felt so warm, and so soft. I liked how he felt in my arms.

The pounding of my heart finally subsided and I went with the flow of our hands, searching for a place to hold, touch, and feel. My hand found his erection and closed around his throbbing dick. It was long and thick. I gently stroked him. His body shivered from my touch. George reached for my dick and held it in his hands, squeezing it.

George kissed me from my neck to my chest. He licked my nipples and then sucked them. I let out a soft moan. His soft lips on my body were an orgasmic feeling. He was exceptionally gentle.

His mouth explored my body.

Stomach.

Back.

Thighs.

Then he found his way to my dick. He opened his mouth and swallowed as much of me as he could. My head went back and I fell against the wall. My legs shook as he sucked and bobbed. I moaned louder. The louder I moaned the faster he sucked. George then grabbed my balls. He caressed and stroked them while he sucked my dick with his beautiful pink luscious lips.

I grabbed the back of his head. I was feeling myself about to release. Then he reached under me and grabbed my ass. When his huge massive hand grabbed my ass I let go. I erupted in his warm mouth. My body shook and I went limp. George's mouth was still wrapped around my dick.

George refused to let me leave after we showered. He wanted more of me. I needed more of him.

Somehow we finally got dressed.

Yearning for more, we fondled, kissed, and caressed each other at the front door. I didn't want to let him go. Each time I reached for the doorknob I found myself reaching for his dick. Stroking and kissing him with everything I had. George's mouth never left my body. I was under a spell, I was certain.

Why couldn't I leave?

Why couldn't I let him go?

## TEN

A month had gone by. But it seemed like a year since we began seeing each other.

"We have to keep this between us," George said. We were sitting on the sofa in his living room.

"Yeah, I know," I said.

"Cool. Maintain your girl and I got mine. Nobody will find out."

"No doubt. I'm not trying to get caught."

"That's what's up. I'm really feeling you." George leaned in and kissed me.

My body shivered when his lips pressed against mine.

"I'm feeling you, too," I said.

"You know you my nigga, right?"

"Huh?" I was confused.

"You mine. You belong to me."

"But, we got girls. I got—"

"You got me. I'm yours and you're mines. No other dudes."

"No other dudes?"

"Yeah. We got our girls, but sleeping with another dude is out!" George demanded.

So that school year, George became my secret lover. Nothing changed between us at school. We still spoke, played ball, and hung out after practice. But I couldn't wait until the weekends. That was our time.

We would hook up to play one-on-one at the playground and then go to his house for sex. I wasn't sure what to make of our situation. We weren't boyfriends. We couldn't be, because we both had girls. Besides, I was still uncertain of my feelings for him. When I was away from him I fought my hormones. At odd times my body would instantly become aroused, wanting George.

Science class.

English class.

Practice.

The showers.

My thoughts shifted from thinking about him to hating him, and hoping that this was a dream I would wake up from. It didn't happen.

George and I masturbated together and the sex was mainly oral. We kissed, caressed, and held each other. And man, I loved being in bed with him.

His smell.

His touch.

I held on to every bit of him. But when I would leave his house I hated what I was feeling. George was growing on me. I thought about George while sleeping, eating, watching television, and doing homework. No matter where I was, George was there.

I searched within myself to find out why this was happening to me. *Why did George choose me?* Whatever the reason, it made me excited. My body was screaming, "Hell yes!"

My hormones yearned for George. Every time I was with him or thought of him, my heart thumped like the basketball hitting the gym court. But I was frightened someone would find out our secret. That was my biggest concern—someone discovering what was going on between me and George.

Whenever our boys came around and they playfully joked about someone being gay, I became more afraid.

When I had sex with my girl I fucked her like I was fucking

away my guilt, my preference for men. With each gyrating pump I felt better, but I would close my eyes and see George's face and not my girl's. I would imagine him there. His body and face beneath me. Faster and faster I would go, releasing everything in me, wishing I was with George.

# ELEVEN

The only thing that kept me from thinking about George was my music. It saved me. It became my solace whenever I didn't want to think about what was going on with us.

My dad, Aaron Tremble Sr., was a musician. A vicious saxophone-blowing motherfucker. He played with Motown legends The Temptations and Smokey Robinson. He toured across the country with various jazz bands. I met all of my dad's musician friends and the singers they played for whenever they visited our brownstone in Brooklyn. Our house was filled with laughter, music, and lots of alcohol. They would drink all night and well into the next afternoon.

My dad and his friends taught me real musicianship: how to create music, how to listen for tone, beats, and counts. I would sit with my dad for hours in his study and go through his collection of albums, feeding off the rhythms.

"You got to listen, boy," my dad would say. "Music is in your soul. It's how it makes you feel."

He would groove to the beats, close his eyes, and sway from side to side.

"That's real music," he'd sing. "You can't help but let your body go."

Whatever I needed from my dad, he provided. Talking, sharing, and helping me to grow into a man. I never told him about my desires for other boys, nor did I ever say anything about me and the neighborhood boy poking our dicks at each other. I knew it would have crushed him.

My dad made sure he was around for school events—he didn't want me to miss having him around because he was on the road so much. I'd look out into the crowd and see his big wide smile with the gap in his front teeth and my mother hugged up next to him.

My parents really loved each other. They met on a stormy night in downtown Manhattan. My mother was supposed to meet some friends at a bar. She arrived early, sat at the counter, and waited on her friends.

Waited and waited.

Dad had just finished a set when he noticed my mother. "She was sitting regal and poised," he would often tell me. He edged onto the bar stool next to her, looked in her face, and said he instantly fell in love. "Your mother didn't have to say one word," he would say, smiling, that gap showing prominently. "My heart stopped and for the first time I didn't think about music. I had to have your mother. She put her hands in mine and introduced herself. 'Evelyn Jones. Nice to meet you,' she said. All I heard was sweet melody from a voice more harmonious than my sax," my dad told me, grinning.

Dad refused to leave my mother that night despite her telling him that she was waiting on friends. "They never showed up," my dad would say, doubling over in laughter. "Come to find out your mother went to the wrong bar. Lucky for me. Unfortunate for her friends." Six months later they were married.

I was the result of their love. A beautiful love that a stormy night at a wrong bar in Manhattan had produced.

My father drank, partied, and traveled the road, but he never abused or cursed at my mother. He said he would give her anything, and he did.

His money.

A brownstone in Brooklyn.

The finest of clothes.

Jewelry from around the world.

And his heart.

"Every time I play the sax I just imagine I am holding your mother and sweet music comes out," he told me.

Early one morning when I was thirteen years old, my mother came and sat on the edge of my bed. She had been crying. Her hands were clasped in her lap. She kept twirling her wedding ring on her finger.

"Your father is gone."

I looked at her, perplexed. Of course he was gone. My dad was always on the road. He was never really home.

"It's okay, Mommy," I said. "He will be back this weekend." I hugged and kissed her.

"No, he won't be back this weekend." She was now sobbing. "Your father is dead."

The words stung my ears. I fell back onto the bed. I stared at my mother as the words kept ringing in my head.

"He was killed last night in a car crash." She reached for me. I jumped out of the bed and ran into his study. I wanted to see if he was there, if there was something of him left in the room.

He was everywhere.

I slowly walked over to the record player, where a Miles Davis album was still on the turntable. I turned on the machine, picked up the needle, and placed it on the album. The notes flowed from the speakers and Miles's *Bitches Brew* filled the room. That entire day I sat in the study and devoured music—my dad.

The legacy of music was born in me. I guess you could say music started to become my life my love, that day.

And it did even more so the day George left me.

# TWELVE

I tried to not let my disappointment show when George told me he was leaving. We were lying in his full-size bed. The pale blue flannel bedspread barely covered our naked bodies. Our legs intertwined. His hand was on my stomach, mine on his waist. He leaned in and kissed me softly. My eyes were closed.

Then he said, "I'm leaving at the end of the month. I am going to UCLA in California."

I simply said, "Congratulations. That's good for you."

I wanted to reach out and hold him. Tell him I didn't want him to go, to leave me. George knew and treated me good. I didn't want another man. I wanted to tell George that I loved him, that we could be together in New York.

But at the end of the month he was gone. Out of my life. Moved on like a passing tornado. One moment he was there, and the next he was gone.

Fast and quick.

Just like my dad.

# THIRTEEN

I think a part of me left with George. Well, my heart at least. I couldn't believe he'd really left me.

I cried only once. I had been lying in bed on a Saturday when I suddenly jumped up. It was eleven in the morning. I started rushing around my room. I threw on my black basketball shorts, my crisp white T-shirt, and my black Air Jordans.

Just as I was about to grab my gym bag, I stopped. I froze at my reflection in the mirror. I stared at myself. It had been three weeks since George left and my heart had not come to accept it. *I* had not accepted it.

I was about to run to go meet him at our usual meeting spot at the basketball court, only to realize he would not be there. He was in California.

I realized George was still in me. I sat on my bed and cried. I let it go. All the emotions.

Love.

Joy.

Happiness.

Everything he made me feel, I let it go. I replaced George with sounds, beats, rhythms of another kind. I created music through my loss. I became a music-producing machine. I didn't leave my dad's study. I turned it into my own personal studio.

Every day.

Night.

Hour.

Minute.

Second.

I was channeling Beethoven, Bach, Miles, Coltrane, Marley, Puffy, Dr. Dre, Timberland, and my dad. Anybody with a sense of harmony and music running through his veins was my muse.

I didn't sleep. I couldn't. My body was filled with vibrations only a true producer knows. My life revolved around music. I spoke in a musical tongue.

I continued playing basketball, but my heart wasn't in it. My heart wasn't much into anything else but music. When the scouts from Syracuse came to recruit me, I contemplated it for a minute. They offered me a full-ride scholarship. But music was calling me. It was pulling at my heart. I didn't want to do anything that would remind me of George, like playing ball.

After I graduated from high school I set up shop in the studio I converted from my dad's study. I was serious about music. Hip Hop.

A year later, I met my partner, Kris, a kid from my high school who walked, talked, and breathed music. My musical brethren. A short muscular dude with energy the size of a giant. He understood me. We were kindred spirits, like-minded fools in love with Hip Hop. We were a dynamic duo. I was his left, he was my right, and vice versa. Everyone knew us. We were the Wonder Twins—Powers, Activate!

We began producing for local rappers in our hood. We had dope beats, killer production, and we were hungry as hell to make it in the entertainment business. Neither of us had any connections, but word was spreading. We networked and went to the industry parties. But so was every other kid producing music in New York City.

For three years we were hitting the streets, grinding, sucking up to every nigga in Hip Hop just to get put on.

Nothing happened.

We were frustrated, but determined. The naysayers in the

hood laughed and mocked us for wanting to be "big-time super-stars." We had a lot of hater-juice to keep us going.

"Yo, cancel whatever you got planned for tonight," Kris called to tell me just as I was coming out of the studio one afternoon.

"What's up?" I asked.

"We going to Jersey."

"For what?"

"An invite-only party." He chuckled. "We're going to the mansion of the most powerful motherfucker in the music business."

Silence.

"Nigga, we going to Larry Singleton's spot."

Silence again.

"Nigga, did you hear me?" Kris yelled.

"I'm on my way."

# FOURTEEN

If the music industry was the dope game, then Larry would be noted as a kingpin. He's big, larger than life. Everyone across the world knows Larry Singleton.

He has it all.

Money.

Fame.

Power.

You can't go anywhere in the music business and not see or hear of Larry Singleton, aka "Pop." He's like a father to everyone in the industry.

When Pop got started he was a tall lanky kid from the Marcy Projects in Brooklyn. He was smart, witty, and, some say, "ahead of his time." He got in the entertainment industry straight out of high school.

He helped to leverage and manage artists to superstardom. Pop had insights on what to do to market and promote their styles. He got them gigs at the Roxy, and the Tunnel, and even at high schools, where his groups would be the opening act for their annual talent shows.

The record labels were savvy enough to give him top executive gigs at their companies. Pop had a pulse on the streets and the labels wanted his audience.

He was one of the first black men to become president of a record label. He was a ghetto dream come true. He was the Cinderella man not only for his neighborhood of Brooklyn, but for enterprising black men in all neighborhoods across America.

He shaped the careers of many rappers and singers. Without his guidance and structure many of them would be washed-up has-beens. He led them to their stardom.

Pop is the black Clive Davis.

After twenty years in the industry, Pop retired. No one knew why. He just called it quits. Now he is a consultant to many of today's top celebrities and entertainers. He knows his shit.

"If you got it, you got it," he says. "There are some who can be taught how to be superstars, but there are those who just have that glow."

Going to this party with Kris, I knew movers and shakers would be there. This was my big moment to network and meet some powerful people. I was determined to get my shine on and create an opportunity.

# FIFTEEN

The entire ride to Pop's, I couldn't stop blabbering. My mouth was going and going and going.

"Yo, you know who is going to be there?" I said. "Man, this is it. This is our moment."

Kris just nodded, laughed, and hyped me further.

We arrived at the secluded gated community in Saddle River, New Jersey. There were Bentleys, Benzes, BMWs, and Jaguars parked in the circular driveway.

As we approached the front door of the brick mini-mansion, Kris and I looked at each other and grinned as wide as we could. We were in the right place at the right time. If shit didn't happen it was because we didn't make it happen.

New York's top entertainment moguls were in this house and the players who made it happen were within our grasp.

A man dressed as a butler asked for our invitation. Kris reached into his back pocket and pulled out the invitation he'd received from music's new "it" producer, Clip-O-Matic.

The man took the invitation and welcomed us into the home. As we walked through the foyer I gawked at the marble floors, gold-trimmed moldings, exotic furniture, and exquisite antiques leading to the main living room. Just before we entered the room we both noticed the large portrait of Pop. It was a painting of him sitting behind a large oak desk in a huge black executive leather chair. He was dressed in a navy blue suit with a red tie. His hands were folded on top of the desk and he looked as if he was about to say something profound.

Just then I saw the actual man sauntering toward us, smiling. I could tell he had been living the good life. The tall slim frame he had been known for had become heavier. He was stocky, but solid. There were hints of gray around the edges of his tapered haircut. His signature goatee was trimmed to perfection. He had large hands that swallowed the glass he was holding. On the pinky finger of his left hand was a huge platinum and diamond ring.

"What's up, young fellas?" He extended his hand. "Larry Singleton, but you can call me Pop."

Kris and I reached out our hands at the same time.

Kris grabbed Pop's hand first and shook it vigorously.

"Kris Jackson. It's a pleasure to meet you. Man, you got a phat crib," he exclaimed.

"Thank you," Pop replied in a deep raspy voice. "A pleasure. And you are?" He looked at me inquisitively.

"Aaron Tremble. Thank you for having us at your home."

"Well, thank you for being had at my home," Pop replied, smiling. "Big A.T.," he said, pointing his left pinky finger at me.

"Huh?" I looked at him perplexed.

"Big A.T. That's your name," Pop said. "There's something special about you. You must be a music producer, I bet," he continued, his pinky finger still pointed at me.

"Yeah, I am," I responded.

"Well, who invited you to the party?" Pop asked.

"Clip-O-Matic," replied Kris.

"Aw yes, Clip-O-Matic." Pop nodded his head back and forth. "He's smart and talented. He knows music and he has an eye for good talent. He's going places."

"Well, enjoy yourselves, gentlemen, and we will talk again." Then Pop turned and walked away.

I turned to Kris with a smile. "Big A.T.! He called me Big A.T. That's my name from now on," I said, gleaming.

"Nigga, we 'bout to get our moment," Kris yelled.

Just then, Clip-O-Matic came up behind us, his platinum jewels dripping on his neck and wrist. As the industry's new "it" producer, I found it hard to imagine that this five-foot-three bowlegged man had the entire world dancing to his beats.

"Yo, sup." Clip-O-Matic gave Kris some dap.

"Yo, what up, man," Kris replied.

"Yo, what up, Aaron." Clip-O-Matic looked at me and gave me some dap.

"What up, big money," I replied, looking down at him, "and yo, it's 'Big A.T.' now."

"Oh, aight," Clip-O-Matic said matter-of-factly. "I see y'all niggas made it through. Yo check it, this is some low-low-type gig so don't get funny style and bug out on me here," Clip-O-Matic said. "Only special niggas get invited to this industry-type shit so be easy and get something to drink to loosen up."

"No doubt, no doubt," Kris replied. "We cool, man." He patted Clip-O-Matic on his back.

He took us through the crowd and introduced us. There were entertainment executives, vice presidents, A&R and marketing reps, publicists, and promotions executives. They worked for BET, MTV, Def Jam, Interscope Records, Atlantic Records, and Capitol Records. A few top music producers were there as well.

I was in my element, surrounded by like-minded individuals who loved and lived for music. They were in the game and made it happen. Meeting them and shaking their hands sent vibrations into the universe that my prayers had been answered and things were about to happen. I got it. This is for me. I couldn't stop grinning.

"You aight?" Clip-O-Matic asked.

"Yeah, man. Listen, I have to go to the bathroom. Do you know where it is?" I asked.

"Sure, down the hall to the right."

"Thanks, man, I'll be right back."

"Let's get something to drink," Clip-O-Matic said. He and Kris headed toward the bar. "You want something?" he asked.

"Yeah, get me whatever," I responded.

I made my way to the bathroom, shaking my head. Many thoughts were running around in my mind. I was in a room full of power players. The men who made Hip Hop. I needed to connect and network.

I entered the bathroom and locked the door. Everything was trimmed in gold: the knobs on the faucet, the oval-shaped mirror . . . shit, even the toilet paper holder. Everything. I was afraid to touch things, fearing my sweaty palms might damage them.

For a while I stood over the sink and stared at my reflection in the mirror. I turned the faucet on and lowered my head. The warm running water gushed into my hands. I splashed my face. I grabbed one of the navy blue towels hanging on the rack and wiped my face.

I smoothed out my eyebrows and brushed my mustache with my fingers. I stared again at my reflection and released a sigh. I puffed out my chest and pushed my shoulders back. I checked my clothes.

*Damn!*

I had on Timberland boots, sagging jeans, and a black T-shirt. I sure didn't look like a producer. No platinum on my neck. No bling on my wrist. I looked like any other nigga from the hood. I ran my hand over my fresh Caesar haircut, then flashed my winning smile. Well, at least my face looked good. I unlocked the door and headed back to the living room.

I made a vow I would not leave without setting up a meeting with one of these men. Someone was going to give me something.

# SIXTEEN

I did my thing when I walked back into the room. I parleyed and networked. There was no holding anything back. This was it: my moment, my time. My confidence soared when I met Rex Roger, president of Nu Money Records.

"What's good with you?" Rex asked. His face was smooth as a baby's bottom. His meticulously trimmed mustache barely kissed his upper lip. Rex was a light-skin pretty boy. His face was always plastered in *The Source*, *VIBE*, and *XXL*.

"I'm good," I replied, shaking his hand.

"You a friend of Pop's?" Rex asked.

I thought about it for a moment. I mean I was up in his house as an invited guest, by way of my boy. So, technically I could call myself a friend.

"Yeah."

Rex did a once-over of me, his hazel brown eyes finally resting into mines. A smirk flickered on his face.

"So, you're Pop's friend?"

"Uhm, yeah," I second-guessed myself.

"What's your name?"

"Big A.T."

"What do you do?"

"I'm a producer."

"Oh really?" Rex's eyes beamed. "I'm looking for some new and fresh blood."

Rex reached into his wallet and pulled out his business card.

"You should give me a call and set up a meeting. I want to hear what you got."

I was excited. Here I was talking with Rex Roger, and he'd just invited me to a meeting. This brother actually wanted to hear my music.

"Aight, I will do that."

"Don't wait too long." Rex smiled, his eyes transfixed on mine. "I think you may have something I can use."

Just then I felt an arm drape over my shoulder. I glanced over to the hand dangling near my face and saw the huge diamond on the pinky finger.

"Come take a walk with me, Big A.T." Pop gently pulled at me, his arm still draped around my shoulder.

"It was nice meeting you, Rex," I stammered. Rex's face turned a pinkish red.

Pop and I walked down a corridor, made a left, and entered a secluded room. He strolled over to a large polished oak bureau on the other side of the room. He pulled out two shot glasses and a bottle of Hennessy from a bottom drawer. With both glasses filled, he made a toast: "To Big A.T., music's newest sensation." He raised his glass to his lips and threw the dark liquid into his mouth. I followed and tossed back my drink. I put my glass on the desktop. Pop poured another. I picked it up, looked at it for a few seconds, and then tossed it down my throat.

"What's up with you?" Pop asked. He walked behind the desk and sat in the black leather executive chair.

I sat in the brown leather chair opposite him. I figured this was my opportunity to pitch Pop. He could make my career. He could set me on my way. All those years of struggling, trying to be taken seriously, and here I was sitting opposite the man who'd been in my shoes. I carefully thought about my words and how to phrase them.

"I'm trying to get in this game and have my music heard," I started. "Music is everything to me. I mean, I've studied it with musical greats because of my dad. He introduced me to beats, counts, and workmanship."

Pop's head tilted and he looked at me intently.

"My father." I put my head down. I hadn't spoken of him to anyone. I never spoke of his influence on me and how much I really missed him. The emotions rushed from my soul and into my throat. I fought back the tears.

"You all right?" Pop leaned forward.

"Yeah, I'm good." I quickly wiped a tear away and looked at Pop. "I know I got talent. I know I got skills. I just want to be heard."

Pop stood up and moved away from his desk. He walked behind me and placed his hands on my shoulders. His touch sent an electric surge through my body.

"You know why I called you Big A.T.?" Pop began massaging my shoulders. My heart started racing. I fidgeted with my watch. "Because I know you are going to be a star in this business. Why do you think you are here?" Pop asked.

"I really don't know." My words barely crawled out of my mouth.

"Clip-O-Matic is today's hottest producer. He knows talent when he hears it and he brought you here to introduce you to the family. He believes that if you had the chance and opportunity, you would set the industry on fire."

I turned and looked at Pop, perplexed yet excited. I knew I had talent, but I'd heard on so many occasions from other producers, "Keep your hustle up and maybe someday your music will get some airplay." I heard it so much that when most producers started their sentences, I'd already finished them because they all said the same thing.

"Family knows family." Pop looked down at me, his eyes glossy from the many drinks. "Clip-O-Matic wouldn't have brought you here if that wasn't true. We are all family here. And we look out for one another."

I still wasn't following Pop. What did he mean by "family"? Was I part of the musical family?

"You don't know what I'm talking about?" Pop asked, sensing it from my facial expression. I shook my head.

"Big A.T., listen up. All of us here have to be discreet about our sexuality. We like being with other men. Some of us have wives, others have girlfriends, and some just don't want their business in the streets. We work in a very heterosexual environment and it's an old boys' network. We got to keep our cover so we can maneuver and position ourselves in this business. We are a part of Hip Hop, too." Pop sat on the edge of his bureau in front of me.

I could smell the liquor escaping with each of his words. His eyes were staring deep into mines. I started fidgeting with my watch. My left leg began to bounce.

"Those white motherfuckers running the record labels and the movie companies have double lives, too," Pop continued. "Shit, do you think they will let a gay black man up in there? And the heterosexual black men, they ain't trying to be guilty by association. We work in a very homophobic industry. You try and tell motherfuckers on the job that you and your man are buying a house together, or traveling overseas, or doing anything together, they will look at you crazy, especially the black folks in this business. This business we call entertainment is just that—entertainment—and everyone loves an illusion."

I just looked and listened to Pop. I couldn't believe my ears. This top entertainment mogul was actually letting me in on the secret. He was a gay man and the industry was full of them.

"Don't act like you don't know there are gay brothers in this business?" Pop tilted his head and squinted his eyes and pointed his finger at me. "Let me tell you something: We are all up in the business. Shit, without us half these ignorant celebrity motherfuckers wouldn't be who they are today. How do you think most of them got to where they are? I hope you don't think that it is really all about talent." Pop smirked, then started pacing back and forth across the room.

"I ain't saying all of them fucked or sucked some dick to get to the top, but a lot of them have and continue to do so. Trust me, there is always some new young fresh wide-open rough-neck thug who is willing to do whatever it takes to get a record deal, a movie role, or some press. Some even think they are smarter than the next and that they will get by without having to deal with a gay brother. Like I said, we are everywhere and in all aspects of this industry. Nine times out of ten, we know each other. It only takes a phone call and we can bring you down or help keep you where you are."

I poured myself another drink. I wanted to get drunk and wake up the next morning and believe this was all a dream.

"Tonight you have met and seen the faces of some of the executives who run this business. This is only a small group of us tonight. You should see the holiday parties and other events where we gather."

I was completely dumbfounded.

Pop walked to the center of the room. He stretched out his arms and yelled, "Welcome to my world. Our world."

But I wondered how Clip-O-Matic knew I had sex with men. George and I were very careful when we were together. No one knew. I never told Kris. I was racking my brain trying to figure out how Clip-O-Matic knew my deepest dark secret.

Was it obvious?

Had I done something to give him an indication that I liked being with men?

"Tell me that you've never been with another man, or at least thought about it," Pop said.

I didn't say anything. I knew Pop could see through me.

Pop grabbed the bottle of Hennessy and refreshed his drink. He made his way back behind his huge bureau. It sat in front of a pair of French doors that led to a balcony. He opened them.

"Check this out, Big A.T." Pop waved for me to join him.

"I am the Wizard and the entertainment business is Oz, full of fantasy. You are entering into a world of magical illusions. Anything can happen at any time. I can grant all your wishes and you can have the entire world. You can be a king in this business if you follow my instructions. There are going to be a lot of bumps in the road and you are going to meet a lot of characters, but you got to take heed of my instructions, because I am reigning king."

I understood his analogy. Yes, all of us were in Oz trying to making our dreams come true. At least I was.

I took a sip of my drink and cupped the glass with both of my hands. I wasn't sure what was going on, but I knew I was getting a lesson I would never forget.

He looked out into the night. The moon was full and bright. He turned and reached for me. Reluctantly and nervously, I glided toward Pop. My heart was beating fast. I tried to remain calm and appear at ease.

As I got closer Pop took my hand and pulled me next to him. He put his arm around my shoulder. I set my drink on the bureau and continued to fidget with my watch.

"Relax," Pop said, smiling at me. "Look out there and see how beautiful everything is. Just take it all in."

I could barely pull together a smile. Everything inside me was going haywire. My mind was racing. My heart was in my stomach. I couldn't stop tugging at my watch.

"People are attracted to this industry because of its grandness and the big flashy things," Pop started again. "They like to know who's doing what, when, and where. Many are voyeurs looking in and getting a high from it. Others desire to be a part of it and fancy the idea of being a celebrity themselves. All of us in this, we keep that illusion going." Pop pounded on his chest. He was in his stride. "We let people believe what they want to believe. We never challenge that, because it would bring destruction and chaos to their lives. They need a place to let their minds escape from their mundane lives. *We* are their lives. All I am doing is letting you get a whiff of it. I control this empire and I will not let anything or anyone tear it down. I've worked too hard and too long to get here."

Pop pulled me much closer to him. Our bodies were touching. My body temperature rose. I needed another drink. I needed something to ease my mind, the tension I was feeling in my neck, back, and dick.

"I think you are the next big success in New York." Pop smiled at me. "I can shape you, mold you, and give you all the direction you need to make it in this business. But you've got to have the drive, ambition, and inspiration. I see that in you." Pop looked into my eyes.

"If you want to make it to the top and do what no other has done, I can get you there. It's time for me to give my throne to someone else," Pop said. "It's time for a new king." I glanced at him. He nodded his head at me.

Pop placed his hand on my crotch. I flinched and jumped back without intending to. Things were moving too fast for me. This entire night was not what I thought it would be.

I was shaking. My stomach was hollow. My body was on fire. His touch was rough. I had to fight an erection that was determined to be released. My dick wanted to feel something warm. Something like it had when I was with George.

"Let me get a taste." Pop tugged at my zipper.

He unbuckled my pants and they dropped to my ankles. My dick was hard. It was fighting against the material of my boxers.

This was it.

I was being made an offer. An offer to end all my years of struggling and trying to make it in this business. An opportunity for my big break. It was time for me to eat and eat big. I wanted to hear my music on the radio. And the man sitting with his face sniffing at my crotch was willing to make it happen.

I heard my own voice for the first time in a long time. The words found their way out of my belly, into my throat, and out of my lips. "I don't know. I mean . . . I . . . I . . . I . . ."

"Relax." Pop stroked my erection. "We will work everything out."

"This is between you and me?"

"This is our world, baby." Pop smiled. He licked his lips and then spoke to my dick. "What happens here stays here."

# SEVENTEEN

I learned two things from Kris on our drive back to Brooklyn. One, he knew I got down with guys. Apparently, George had been sexing quite a number of guys in the neighborhood, and Kris was one of them. They had been intimate long before George and I hooked up. Hearing the news from Kris was a blow. It was hard for me to swallow the reality about George.

I hated hearing I wasn't George's first and only. I should have known I wasn't. The way he touched my body and kissed me should have set bells off. He was all too familiar with being with another man, very comfortable with it. I didn't pay it any attention because I was wrapped up in him. He made sure of that.

Two, Kris and Clip-O-Matic had been kicking it. He claimed it wasn't anything serious. "I ain't gay. We just get together every now and then," Kris said. "And we're not fucking!" I wasn't sure if he was trying to reassure me or himself.

"I'm just trying to get ahead and that nigga Clip-O-Matic is talking in my ear telling me what he gon' do for me. I'm looking out for the both of us." He looked at me.

"You're looking out for the both of us or just for yourself?" I said as I turned and looked at him.

"Nigga, we in this together," he responded and reached out his hand for some dap.

I just looked at Kris's hand.

"Nigga, give me some." Kris laughed and punched me in my arm. "You're one of us."

I laughed and gave him some dap. But I started to think, *Am I one of them?*

*Is this something I'm ready to be a part of?*

# EIGHTEEN

I took a long shower when I got home. I scrubbed myself for almost an hour. I tried to erase the touch of Pop's mouth on my dick. I hoped the soap and hot water would wash away the guilt I felt. For some odd reason I felt like I did something wrong, like I was cheating on George, like I was hoping he would come back and things would return to the way they were.

I wasn't ready to start having sex with another man. Technically, George was my first, and I longed for him on many nights, despite what Kris had told me about him.

Besides, I was still trying to figure out this desire I had for men. After all, I still had desires for women. Their bodies.

Smell.

Walk.

Softness.

But I was not having sex with a woman. I didn't even have a girlfriend.

I was thinking more and more about guys. Something tore at my being whenever I saw an attractive man. I thought about being with men sexually, especially George, the bastard, the heartbreaker, the asshole I still longed for.

I had to admit to myself I was gay. But I wasn't ready for that. Not just yet. I hadn't gained entrée into the industry and I knew Hip Hop was not gay-friendly. Pop had verified it for me.

That night I was unable to sleep. My mind was running from thoughts about George, Pop, and Kris and his sex boy,

Clip-O-Matic. I shut my eyes tight and prayed the thoughts would cease. They didn't. Especially the vision of me and Pop.

At Pop's house I let him suck, lick, and taste me. I allowed Pop's mouth on my dick. I tried to fight the feeling but I couldn't. His mouth was warm, wet. And he swallowed every inch and every ounce of my juices.

I wondered what this meant for me. Would Pop follow through with the promise he made? Was Pop going to be a man of his word? Was he going to help me to become a big name in the industry?

It was all a mystery.

I struggled to try and figure it out. The not-knowing was agonizing. The sex scene popped up in my head again. I heard the moaning and groaning. I felt Pop's mouth on my dick. Damn, he knew how to give some good head. My dick began to grow.

To throb.

I was erect. I saw the image of Pop's head bobbing up and down on my dick.

Then the beautiful chocolate hard body of George came rushing into my mind. I felt him lying in the bed next to me. I was feeling the sexual vibe all through my body. I couldn't fight the feeling. I needed to release again. I needed to feel George, badly.

My right hand became that feeling. It was going to have to satisfy me tonight as I pulled and jerked myself to ejaculation.

# NINETEEN

*Ring. Ring. Ring.*

*Who the hell is this calling at eight o'clock in the morning!*
I turned over and grabbed the phone.

"Yeah!" I answered.

"Time to make money," the voice said.

"What? Who is this?" I struggled to come out of my slumber.
Sleep was still in my throat.

"Your dream maker," the raspy voice said.

I sat up and rubbed my eyes. Then it all came to me in an
instant.

"Pop!?"

Two weeks had passed. I thought he forgot about me.

"You need to meet me in the city at Tastemakers Studio
tonight."

"What time?" I asked.

"Ten. Bring some tracks with you. I want K-Luv and Shawty
Mike to hear them."

Kenny "K-Luv" Robinson was the head of Mo' Music. He
had the hottest artist in the game—Shawty Mike, the new
hot rapper out of Atlanta. There was a bidding war involving
every label to get him signed. Shawty Mike had already earned
a reputation in the South for his country slang and lyrical
content.

"Anything else?" I asked.

"Just you."

Click. The phone went dead. I was still holding it to my ear.

Tastemakers Studio is the place many rappers and singers record their albums. It's not impossible to be in one studio session while some other artists are working on their projects across the hall or on another floor in the building. They sometimes take breaks and hit the clubs together or grab something to eat. Others gather together for a weeds-smoking session. They'll have weed from various hoods of different cities, analyzing it to see which hood has the most potent. It provides that extra buzz for their creativity. Late-night sessions are very eventful.

After the call from Pop I leapt out of bed and rushed into my studio. I downloaded my hottest tracks from the computer and put them on a CD. At six o'clock that evening I showered, then double-checked that I had everything, and bounced. I wanted to be early. Real early.

I drove into Manhattan around nine o'clock and parked on Fiftieth Street and Ninth Avenue. I walked over to the studio on Forty-sixth Street and Eighth. I was an hour early so I walked around Times Square. I didn't want to go too far just in case Pop called and said to come early. I ventured over to Bryant Park, at Forty-second and Sixth Avenue. I wanted to distract my mind.

This was it. I was meeting with K-Luv, Shawty Mike, and Pop. Or was it a dream?

Ouch.

I pinched myself.

I kept fidgeting with my watch.

I watched the time slowly go by.

Five minutes past nine.

Nine-ten.

Nine-fifteen.

Okay, it was time to stop looking at my watch.

I decided to walk over to MTV on Forty-fourth Street and

Broadway. I stood in front of the Viacom building, which houses MTV, and glared at the billboard pictures of celebrities who had graced the inside of MTV. I was going to be in there one day. I knew it. I could feel it.

Finally, nine forty-five.

# TWENTY

I hustled my ass over to the studio. When I walked in everyone was there. Pop was on his cell phone. Shawty Mike was in the booth going over his rhymes. K-Luv was sitting on the black leather sofa flipping through the latest issue of *XXL* magazine.

There were three other dudes in the studio room next door. They were huddled around the television playing the latest video game on PS2. They were from Shawty Mike's crew.

The studio engineer was working on the production boards and getting the levels ready for Shawty Mike.

While talking on his cell phone, Pop motioned for me to introduce myself to K-Luv. With my backpack slung over my shoulder, I fingered my watch and walked over to the sofa to introduce myself.

"K-Luv," I began, thinking I should play it cool. "Aaron . . . Aaron Tremble," I said, then corrected myself. "Big A.T."

"Good to meet you, Aaron . . . Big A.T." K-Luv laughed. His massive dark hand shook mine. He tossed the magazine on the table in front of him. "Pop tells me you got some hot shit for my artist."

I looked over at Pop, who was pacing and talking on his cell phone. Pop glanced at me and smiled, then pointed his pinky finger at me.

"Yeah, I got some hot shit for Shawty Mike. My beats are

going to have the streets talking for sure," I said as I continued to fidget with my watch.

"Let's hear this shit!" K-Luv said. He got up from the sofa and walked over to the engineer.

"Where's the tracks?" the engineer asked.

I pulled out three CDs from my bag and handed them to the engineer. My heart was pounding faster. I began to fasten and unfasten my watch. I looked over again at Pop for some support, but he was busy on his call.

The engineer put the first CD into the player and turned up the volume in the studio. I sat next to the engineer and waited for the first track to play.

"How many tracks on each CD?" the engineer asked.

"Ten."

The engineer pressed Play and the beats started with a big boom and startled everyone in the room. I laughed to myself. K-Luv stood behind me and the engineer and let the beats filter through his body.

"Next track," K-Luv said to the engineer. The engineer forwarded the CD.

I looked a little confused, because the first song had not even played a good thirty seconds. Then K-Luv again said, "Next track," and the engineer again forwarded the CD. This went on for the entire CD. K-Luv would listen to about thirty seconds of each track, then ask the engineer to play the next track without looking or saying anything to me.

My watch was off my wrist and now in my hands, where I was fumbling around with it.

By this time Shawty Mike had come out of the booth.

"Yo, who shit is dis?" Shawty Mike asked. He was much shorter than in the pictures I had seen of him in magazines. I mean *short* short. Like five foot two inches. And that's with the Jordans he had on. He was sporting a fresh fade haircut and three platinum chains around his neck, which I figured was why he had three big burly-looking dudes traveling with him.

"This Big A.T.'s shit," K-Luv said, pointing at me.

"What up, playa?" Shawty Mike gave me some dap. "This shit is bangin'. These tracks for me?" he asked.

"I don't know, playa, I'm trying to get on," I replied.

"Put this nigga on," Shawty Mike yelled.

He was definitely an animated little dude. He strutted back and forth with his hand dipping behind his back, his little body bouncing with the beats.

The engineer put in the next CD and K-Luv did the same thing, listening to about thirty seconds of each track.

Shawty Mike was jerking his body and bouncing his head back and forth and smiling from ear to ear during each track. It was obvious to me he liked the music, but I couldn't get a good read on K-Luv. His facial expressions were blank, and he didn't even move to the music.

When the CD ended, Shawty Mike was hyped. He was still bouncing after the music stopped. His hands were frantically moving back and forth. He was mouthing some inaudible words. He asked the engineer to replay a few of the tracks. Shawty Mike started rhyming freestyle over the beats.

K-Luv walked over to the sofa and sat down. He pulled out his cell phone and made a call.

I just sat there looking dumbfounded. I had never played my music for anyone and they not respond. Everyone liked *something* on my CDs, even if they didn't like all the music.

I grabbed my CDs, threw them back into my bag, and stood up. I didn't know what to do next. I didn't know if I should ask K-Luv what he thought or if I should just take my CDs and leave.

I was confused. I put my watch on and slung my backpack over my shoulder.

"Yo, Big A.T.," K-Luv said. "Come sit over here." He pointed to the chair opposite him.

I walked glumly over to the chair and sat down.

"You said you had some hot shit and the streets would be talking," he said, looking at me. "Listen." He put his hand behind his left ear. "I don't hear the streets talking." Then he laughed.

I was pissed.

*What the fuck is he talking about? Ain't nobody in this motherfuckin' studio but us and he is being sarcastic and shit-talking about the streets ain't talking.*

"You're young and fresh," K-Luv said. "The streets ain't talking because we going for the world. The whole world is going to be talking." He sat up. "You see the problem with you young niggas is that you think locally. You got to think bigger than the block, bigger than the hood. You got to think the world," he said.

My face lit up.

*Damn, I was thinking small.*

Smiling, K-Luv said, "You got some fire with you. I'm going to give you a production deal with Mo' Music Records."

My eyes grew wide. My hands stopped fidgeting with my watch.

K-Luv continued, "Tracks three, four, and eight off the first CD is what I want for Shawty Mike. The rest I'm going to use for other artists on the label."

I was so excited I leapt from the chair. I reached over and gave K-Luv some dap. I ran over to Pop and knocked him down. I lifted him off the ground and hugged him.

This was it. I got it. I did it.

"Welcome to the *family.*" Pop grinned. I looked at Pop and then over at K-Luv, who was talking with the engineer and Shawty Mike.

"Yes, he's one of us," Pop said, pointing his pinky finger at K-Luv.

I couldn't believe it.

K-Luv was dating top celebrity actress Karina Blue. She

was in damn near every movie, starring opposite Hollywood's biggest names. I never thought or ever heard of anything gay related to K-Luv.

I pondered over the words Pop told me about gay and down-low brothers in the entertainment industry who are part of the family.

"We are everywhere."

# TWENTY-ONE

Over the next few months my career went into full speed. I was in the studio every day, spending late nights and working full-time with K-Luv and Mo' Music Records.

My new production deal with the label had me working with some of the hottest artists in the industry—Shawty Mike, Miss Missy, Hot Gunners, and Black Boyz.

I didn't complain. Fuck naw. This was what I wanted.

I already knew what to expect from this life. My dad prepared me. I was determined. Nothing was going to get in the way of me making music, my first love. Besides, working with K-Luv was a job within itself. He was controlling, demanding, and a workaholic. I was on his schedule.

K-Luv wanted me close just in case he got some inspiration. He put me up in one of the three condos he owned on Twenty-eighth Street and Park Avenue. He'd bought them for the artists and other producers under the Mo' Music label. When I moved in, I had the entire bi-level condo to myself. Pop would visit me occasionally.

Famed celebrity interior designer Courtney Sloane furnished and styled the condo for K-Luv. They were good friends and she knew his taste. She designed the home in a modern style, with lots of European flair.

I hated walking on the cherry hardwood floors. They were immaculately polished and I didn't want to scuff them, so

I would take off my shoes before I entered. And the living room . . . simply bananas.

There was a butter-soft black leather sofa with sky blue, blood red, and bright orange suede pillows. A large circular glass tabletop with K-Luv's initials inscribed in the middle of it.

The plasma television and stereo system were built into the wall. With one touch of the remote the entire system was enabled and a computer voice said, *Good Day, K-Luv.*

The two bedrooms had their own bathrooms and walk-in closets. The master bedroom had a king-size bed with a platinum stainless-steel bed frame. The headboard extended from the floor to the ceiling. At the end of the bed was a sitting stool the length of the bed. There was also a large-screen plasma television in the room.

I loved the space; however, I spent most of my time working in the studio. If I wasn't there I was meeting with artists at other labels, going to industry parties, or getting together with other gay and down-low brothers at Pop's parties. On some nights Pop would stop by for a rendezvous. It was oral sex mainly, with Pop servicing me. I still couldn't manage to return the favor. Besides, George was a constant reminder. Every time, George crept into my mind. Then I wondered if anyone could tell if I had sex with men. It seemed like everyone was watching me or they knew.

I began to take more of a notice in other men. I wanted to know if they held the same secret as me. I watched their walk, talk, dress, mannerisms. I tried to drown out the thoughts by staying late in the studio and working on my beats. I wouldn't let anything keep me from my music.

One night after Pop left, I called Kris. I needed someone to talk to. I wanted to know if this was something I was ready to do and have as part of my life.

"Look, man, I totally understand what you are going through," Kris said. "I've been there and I still struggle with it. I ain't saying it's going to be easy, but you got to figure this out on your own. You got to ask yourself the questions and look to yourself for the answers."

"I know, man," I replied. "I just need to know I am not the only crazy person having these feelings and experiences."

"Trust me, you're not."

"How come I am so conflicted? Why am I struggling with myself?"

"Because you are afraid to be yourself and explore what you've probably been denying for a long time."

I went into the kitchen and grabbed a Heineken from the refrigerator.

"But why am I struggling with this shit?" I asked. I walked back into the living room and plopped on the sofa.

"Because you want to struggle," Kris answered. "Stop struggling and it will get easier."

Silence.

"Look," Kris started, "me and Clip-O-Matic are going strong now. We have become serious."

"What?!?" I practically spit out my beer.

"Yeah, I know. It was nothing I had planned on happening. I didn't think it was for him either. We both struggle with it, but we are doing it together. We are taking it one day at a time. It ain't easy because we have strong feelings for one another and we can't be out in the streets like that. You know what I mean?"

"Yeah, so how are y'all doing it? I mean, how are you handling it with your family and working in the studio?" I asked.

"Like I said, it ain't easy. We are constantly sneaking around. He got his girl he got to maintain and keep happy. He has his image of being in the public. It's hard as hell, but I ain't stressing it. I know how I feel about him and I know how he feels about me. We know what this situation is about and we ain't trying to complicate it."

"So, what about you and your image?" I asked.

"Man, I still got a few girls here and there. Nobody ain't

said nothing to me about some gay shit and I know they ain't. I don't carry myself like a flamboyant sissy, so I ain't worried about it."

"What about his boys and his crew?"

"Man, most of them get down too." Kris laughed. "Trust me, it's a lot of us in this game."

"Damn," I said. "I've seen some of that happening at the studio but I don't say anything. I just stay focused on work. It's crazy."

"Yeah, it is," Kris said. "Look, man, just stop thinking so hard about it. I know it's difficult, but trust me it will definitely get easier when you find the right nigga."

"I don't know." I sighed. "This shit is crazy."

"You'll be all right."

"Thanks, man. It feels good to talk to somebody about this."

"No doubt," Kris said. "Man, I'm your boy and I got your back. I'm here for you."

"I know, I know."

"I gotta run," Kris said. "Me and Clip are getting together after he gets out of the studio. I need to download some music before he gets here."

"Aight, man. It's good to hear about you and Clip," I said.

"Thanks. You'll find that nigga. But I'll hit you later."

I sat wondering if what Kris said was true. Will I really be all right? Will this all pass?

I turned on the stereo and put on Mary J. Blige's *My Life* CD. She was somebody I definitely wanted to work with. No: I *was* going to work with. I laid my head back on the sofa. Took a big sip of my beer and let the words of the CD filter into my mind as I longed for a love of my own.

# TWENTY-TWO

When I wasn't in the studio I was going to lunch or dinner with a brother from the network of gay and down-low men. Pop kept bragging about me as his new protégé. So, the brothers wanted to meet the new entertainment sensation. Yeah. Lots of pressure. I had to show these brothers who I was. What I was about. And what I could do.

I met with executives from J Records, Warner Music Group, Atlantic Records, Def Jam, Sony, MTV, and BET. Each was a leader and player. Bigwigs. They made the business.

A few dinners happened at Pop's home. That's when I learned some of them kept separate apartments away from their wives and girlfriends. It was their way to escape for a secret rendezvous with their lovers.

One evening K-Luv asked if I could meet him at the Mo' Music offices. When I arrived we went into the conference room.

"Yo, Big A.T., I'm proud of you," K-Luv said. He walked to the head of the large conference table and sat down. K-Luv pointed for me to sit in the chair to his left.

"Thanks, K-Luv. It's all because of you and Pop," I replied.

"Well, I needed to talk with you about something very important," K-Luv said, looking serious.

I braced myself.

*What's he talking about "very important"? I've been working hard as hell with this nigga. He better not be pulling some shit on me and trying to pass me off.*

I looked at K-Luv, just as serious.

"Better yet." K-Luv stood up and walked over to the huge stereo system behind him. "I'm going to let you listen." He pushed the Play button on the system.

I fell back into the chair. My eyes and mouth grew wide. Shawty Mike's Southern drawl rhymed over my track.

"Congratulations. I couldn't have made this album without you."

"Hell yeah! Hell yeah!" I pounded on the table, screaming.

K-Luv picked up the phone. "I need everyone to come into the conference room now."

Everyone entered, congratulating me. They started dancing and grooving to the music. Then I saw Shawty Mike bopping with two bottles of champagne. Behind him was an entourage of waitstaff pushing in carts of champagne and cake.

"It's party time!" he screamed.

A tear fell from my eye. I was on top of the world. I was in the Mo' Music offices listening to my music on a top rapper's album that was about to be released.

I did it. I put my head down and thanked God. Then I said, "Dad, I know you are proud of me."

"K-Luv, did you tell that nigga yet?" Shawty Mike yelled.

I looked up, confused.

K-Luv looked at me and smiled. " 'Street Dreams' is going to be the first single released."

I put my hand over my mouth. The first single off the Shawty Mike album was going to be my music. My beats. My sound. My hard work.

Shawty Mike walked over to me with a glass of champagne in hand. "Congratulations, nigga," Shawty Mike said. He put his arm on my shoulder.

"Thanks, man." I smiled and raised my glass of champagne. Everyone in the room followed suit, picking up their glasses for a much-deserved toast.

# TWENTY-THREE

"Street Dreams" was the summer's biggest hit. It debuted at number one on *Billboard*. The entire country was pumping the song. My phone wouldn't stop ringing. I was the hot new kid on the block. Every major recording artist wanted me on their projects.

My schedule went into overdrive. I traveled to Los Angeles. Miami. Atlanta.

I was making more money than ever. Several record labels offered me deals to start my own label. They wanted me to nurture and produce other artists. I had that touch. That sound. That ear. And everyone wanted a piece of the action.

Pop was right there helping to shape my career and giving me industry tips. The sex between us wore off. Pop took interest in another hot young artist.

Thank God.

"I still got love for you," Pop said one day when he stopped by the condo.

"Yeah." I was smiling on the inside. "I got love for you, too."

"I'm still taking you to the top. I am not going to let you fail." Pop hugged me.

"Thanks, man. I really appreciate all you've done."

"But it is time for you to take up one of those offers from the labels."

"I'm not sure if I'm ready to make that step, Pop."

"Why not? This is huge. You know how many producers would love to be in your shoes right now?"

"Yeah, but I'm not trying to run a business and create artists. I just want to make music."

"That is why you hire those who are smart and talented to work for you," Pop said. "Besides, all you have to do is build one artist at a time. It's your empire. Remember?"

"Yeah. I know." I smiled.

When Pop left I thought about what he told me. I could take the next step. Run a label. Produce other artists. Yeah, I could see it. Me on top. But it had to be the right artist. And I knew the right guy. He was from Fort Greene, Brooklyn.

Jerome "Tickman" Taylor.

We worked together for a minute before I got set up with Pop. Tickman was very talented, smart, and had "the gift of gab," as most people around the way said. His storytelling was so believable you would think you were actually there when it took place.

Tickman was always listening to the radio or messing around with his brother's keyboard. He would emulate what he heard on the radio and play it back on the keyboard. That skill won him every school and local talent show.

He rapped about people he knew and their experiences, while adding a little flavor to the story. Tickman even made a rap about the girls in his little black book, which were many. He rapped about his sexual conquest of each girl and the games he played to get them in bed.

Tickman had a gift and everyone knew it. They would tell him that he was going to be a "big star." Hustlers in the hood wanted to get involved and invest in him. Everyone wanted a piece of Tickman. Finally, a group of friends got him in the studio and helped him create a demo tape.

The next day I called Pop to let him know I had the perfect first artist to sign.

"Good," Pop said. "What are you waiting for?"

"I'm on it now."

"You decide which label you're going with?" he asked.

"Yeah, Warner Music Group. They offered the most money and kickbacks."

"Very good. Now you're thinking like a CEO." Pop laughed.

# TWENTY-FOUR

I had my lawyer start the negotiations with Warner Music Group. They were ecstatic when they heard I agreed to work with them. Now, I had to find Tickman.

I called Kris and had him track Tickman down. An hour later he was on the phone.

"What up, Big A.T.?" He laughed. "Mr. Super-Duper Producer. Congrats on everything."

"Thanks, man," I said. "Listen, you still doing your thing?"

"I'm eating. What's up?"

"Can you meet me at Junior's Restaurant in midtown?"

"What time?"

"Now."

"I'm on my way."

Things were working out perfectly. Life was good. So was I.

I was proud of myself. I was about to sign my first artist to my label. I decided to call it Change Up Records. Yup. I was changing the game. And Tickman was about to set it off.

I arrived at Junior's Restaurant forty minutes later. When I walked in, the aroma of their notorious cheesecake hit me. Damn. I missed that smell. I knew that smell as a kid. As soon as you cross the Brooklyn Bridge your senses kick in and it tickles your nose.

Junior's was crowded for lunch. I spotted Tickman sitting in a booth not too far from the entrance. I stepped around a waiter who was hoisting a tray over his head.

"What's up, my dude?" Tickman stood and hugged me.

"What's up?" I smiled.

"Man, I'm trying to get where you at." Tickman laughed.

We sat in the booth. I motioned for the waitress and ordered a Coke.

"You want something?" I asked Tickman.

"Let me get an orange soda for now."

The waitress tilted her head and smiled at me. Then she turned and walked away, shaking her head.

"Thanks for meeting with me," I started. "So, tell me what you been up to?"

"Man, I'm doing my thing. A couple of shows here and there. Still trying to get a deal. But I'm good."

"Aight."

"How's your mom?" Tickman asked.

"She's good. You know how moms can be." I chuckled.

"Yeah, man. I want to really take care of my mom." Tickman laughed. "She's been very supportive. I know she's ready for me to get out of her house."

We both laughed.

"Well, that's why I asked you to meet me." The waitress brought our drinks to the table, then she stood around with her hands on her hips. Again, she tilted her head from left to right. Then she turned and walked away, shaking her head.

"I'm starting my own label and I am looking to sign my first artist." I took a sip of my Coke. "I've been knowing you for a minute. I love your flow. And basically I want you as my artist."

"Hell naw! You shitting me." Tickman lay on the seat in the booth.

"I'm for real. I want you. I need you to jump-start this label with me."

"Come on, dude. You fuckin' with me."

"I'm serious."

Tickman stared at me with a smirk on his face. He was in

shock. Unable to register what I was saying to him. Then his eyes started to water.

"Man, I can't believe you doing this." Tickman reached over and gave me a hug and some dap.

"We got to help each other. I believe in you. So, let's make this money together."

"Let's get it!" Tickman yelled.

"Come on. Let's go celebrate."

# TWENTY-FIVE

Man, did we celebrate.

To success.

Our success.

We hit up bars in SoHo, the Village, and Times Square. There wasn't a spot we didn't visit and a drink we didn't partake of. Hennessy. Bacardi. Courvoisier. We were doing it like real moneymaking brothers.

By one in the morning, we made it back to my bi-level condo on Twenty-eighth and Park. I purchased it right after "Street Dreams" became a platinum-selling single.

Tickman and I were very drunk. Falling over each other and singing, "We're in the money." We stumbled into the living room and collapsed on the beige plush carpet. I was lying spread-eagle and facedown. Tickman was beside me on his back with his long muscular arms stretched out to his sides.

I tried to kick off my sneakers but couldn't get them off my feet. After several failed attempts I finally rolled over, sat up, and untied them. They fell off and I collapsed back on the floor.

"Hey, man, check it. We are about to bloooowwww uuuupppp!" Tickman slurred.

I didn't respond. I just lay there with my eyes closed. I did not want to open them. Each time I did it felt as if the condo was spiraling over Park Avenue. So I shut my eyes tight. Very tight.

"Yo! Big A.T.! Man, you hear me? You okay?" Tickman

asked. He was shaking my shoulder. I tried to speak but nothing came out of my mouth.

In my mind I was responding, but the words just wouldn't come out of my mouth. Tickman got up and his solid muscular body stood over me. He was wobbling from side to side. He swung at my legs and missed. He swung again and this time he hit them.

"Man, why you hitting me?" I asked, straining to look in his eyes.

"Yo, I'm just trying to make sure you still living."

"Hell yeah I'm living. Aren't you in this same room that's fucking spinning?"

"The room ain't spinning, it's your head." Tickman doubled over laughing.

He couldn't maintain his balance and fell on top of me. His body was warm. We were face-to-face. I noticed his perfectly trimmed goatee. I smelled his breath. All the alcohol.

"Oops, sorry, man," Tickman said.

He tried to get up but kept falling down, so he just rolled over next to me.

"You know, man," Tickman started. He turned and faced me. "It's all because of you all this shit is happening. Man, I really owe you."

"Man, we helping each other," I said.

"True that, but you got talent and skills," Tickman said. "You would have made it regardless."

"Don't knock yourself, you got the same abilities."

Tickman just stared at me. He looked deep into my eyes. I glared back at Tickman. My heart began racing. His eyes were soft and inviting. The room stopped spinning. And, Tickman leaned over and kissed me on the mouth. My heart started beating faster and faster. We fondled each other's mouth with our tongues. The kiss became more passionate with each second.

It seemed like an eternity had passed when we stopped kissing. I lay there thinking, *What just happened?* It was wrong.

Yet it was right.

Good.

His lips were juicy.

Soft.

It was a wonderful feeling and I enjoyed every minute of it. Tickman appeared cool and calm. I didn't know what to do next. I never initiated anything with a dude. George and Pop approached *me.*

I wanted to turn and look at Tickman but I was afraid. Afraid he might get up and leave, and I would lose my new artist.

Tickman turned again toward me. He put his hand on my face. It was delicate and gentle. I shivered from his touch and turned toward him.

We lay facing each other. Our bodies practically touching. I could feel his breath as he inhaled and exhaled. Tickman's dark chocolate thick frame tensed as he moved closer to me.

"I shouldn't be doing this," Tickman said.

"Naw, it's cool. It felt good," I said.

Tickman looked at me and then pressed forward to kiss me again. Without hesitation, I leaned in and kissed him back. Before long, we'd both removed our clothes. We lay naked in each other's arms.

Tickman felt good.

I caressed his broad chest with my fingers, playing with his erect nipples. I nibbled on his earlobe and neck. Tickman closed his eyes and moaned.

I swept my hand across his rippling stomach. His abs shivered with my touch. I felt his body gyrate and I slowly moved my hand to his thick erect dick. It pulsated in my hand. I stroked him slowly. I played with the tip. It was big and fat. I felt the veins protruding from his dick. He moaned louder as I cupped his balls.

Then, I inched my head toward his massive hardness and, for the first time, placed another man's dick in my mouth.

I wanted to taste Tickman. I wanted to know him. I licked his pre-cum. He was sweet, tasted like a thick syrupy peach. I felt his dick jump as I sucked the head and then his balls. I slurped and swallowed as much of him as I could. He was massive.

With each suction of my lips his body jerked. I continued licking Tickman all over his body. His broad back. His thick thighs. His firm stomach. His fat fingers.

Tickman moaned and gyrated his body with each of my kisses. He became louder in his moans as I played with his neck, nibbled on his ears and shoulder blades. Tickman grabbed my ass and squeezed it each time I made contact with one of his erogenous zones.

Then Tickman flipped me on my back. He played with my dick in his mouth. He licked and sucked on the tip of the head, then the shaft. He stuffed my balls in his mouth. He gently licked and sucked on them, taking each one in his mouth and sucking on them like a sweet piece of Jolly Rancher candy.

I grabbed Tickman's head and glided it up and down my hard dick. My body jerked and flinched each time Tickman swallowed me whole. I moaned in ecstasy.

It was good.

Excellent.

Amazing.

After what seemed like hours of foreplay, Tickman said to me, "I want to feel you inside me."

I got condoms and lubrication from my room. I lay back on the floor. I greased my dick and slid on the condom. Tickman wiped my hand with his and put some lube in his ass. He straddled on top of me and guided my dick toward his entrance. Tickman flinched each time I pushed my dick inside of him.

With each thrust Tickman let out a grunt. He kept winding his ass on my dick. The passion and excitement allowed Tickman to become more comfortable and relaxed. He finally opened up and I was able to put my entire dick inside him.

Tickman moaned loudly as I held him tightly by his waist. He began to grind slowly. He reached down and kissed me. I thrust my dick deeper inside of Tickman each time he came down on me.

Our bodies moved erotically together. We moved faster and faster. Tickman wound his body in a circular motion. We called out each other's names. I began stroking Tickman's thick long erection. "Faster, faster," he moaned.

At the height of sexual enjoyment, we climaxed together. For the first time I'd fucked a man. Damn, it felt amazing. My heard was swirling.

I wanted more.

Tickman let my dick stay in him. He began winding again. His body jerking and flexing. My erection grew stiffer. I pumped hard. Harder. And harder.

Tickman was enjoying it. "That's it. That's it, Big A.T."

He stroked his dick. I felt his body quiver.

Deeper.

Deeper.

I pushed my dick deeper. Tickman stroked himself faster and faster. He was coming again. Both of our bodies shook with intense pleasure.

He fell on top of me. We wrapped our arms around each other. Smiling and kissing. Our naked bodies glistened with sweat and musk. It was magical and exactly what I wanted and needed. Someone to feel comfort with. Someone to let myself go with.

# TWENTY-SIX

The next few weeks me and Tickman continued to make love every chance we could. I was really feeling Tickman. His style. Talk. Walk. Mind. Everything about him. I found someone I could trust. My soul was relieved. Tickman made me feel good. I was smiling and laughing more. Something was happening to me and I liked it.

But, we knew we had to take precautions. We needed to keep our cover. I was the CEO of a record label, and his producer. It needed to look professional. We needed to maintain a distance. And it was difficult.

My heart continually tugged for Tickman. I yearned for his touch. His lips.

Dick.

Ass.

Heart.

Tickman shared with me that he'd had sexual relations with men in his past. "I messed around with a few dudes. It was nothing serious, though. Not like how I feel about you," he told me. "I used to fight and struggle with myself, but once I became comfortable with me, things got easier."

"That's what I'm dealing with now," I told Tickman. "I feel and know this is who I am, but it's so hard to accept."

"I just learned how to appreciate and accept who I am," Tickman shared. "I got tired of fighting the feelings. I got tired of crying at night. I had no one to talk to."

"When did you start? I mean, how did you know you were attracted to dudes?" I asked.

"It was always in me and I didn't understand why I had these feelings. I thought it was a phase or maybe just some ill hormone shit. I got with a lot of girls to fight the way I was feeling. But it didn't work. The more I kept trying to suppress it the more I craved a dude."

I reached over and kissed Tickman. I tried to kiss away the pain. The hurt he felt. I kissed Tickman to let him know that I had his back. I was in his corner.

We were two men sharing our hearts, learning to love not only ourselves, but each other. We decided Tickman would move in with me. I was producing his first album and needed him close to the studio. To me.

I knew the long nights in the studio would get tiresome. The drive back and forth from Brooklyn to Manhattan would be taxing. Besides, it was not unlikely for an artist to live at the home of his manager or record label head. I figured no one would ever suspect a thing. And no one did.

Everything was working according to plan. Tickman was busy in the studio most nights and would sleep a lot during the day. I handled business during the day and stopped by the studio at night for the recording sessions. We were making sweet music together.

# TWENTY-SEVEN

We did everything to keep our secret. Tickman maintained a few ladies, and I was the busy executive focused on music. The only thing out of the ordinary was that we lived together. We were together often. And many of the brothers in the business knew about my sexuality, but I did not tell them about Tickman. Not yet.

I wanted more time. At least to make sure it was real. But I didn't want to make the announcement because, uhm, well, I was concerned. I was worried about the other gay and down-low brothers in the industry who would try or make an attempt to sleep with Tickman. I heard the stories of how some of them would try to sleep with another brother's man. Even though we were a close-knit family, many didn't always play by the rules. And Pop made it a point to tell me about the rules.

"Rule number one, never fuck with another man's man," Pop said. "Rule number two, never fuck an employee. Rule number three, refer back to rule number one." Pop also filled me in on the different groups of brothers who catered to our family.

"There are the *Celebrity and Executive Fuckers*." Pop laughed. "They are an exclusive group of brothers who only have sex with celebrities and executives in this business. Generally, these men are not in the business themselves. They are from the hood, or average blue-collar workers. They don't require much, and usually are only used for sex. Good sex. They are good-looking attractive brothers who are probably married or have girlfriends.

"Then there are the *Opportunists*," Pop continued. "These brothers are always looking for an opportunity. They generally hang out at the industry parties, preying on executives and celebrities they suspect are gay or on the down low. Once they sleep with an executive, they start asking for invites to parties, or to meet certain celebrities, and to get CDs, movie passes, concert tickets, or anything free. They generally don't make it far once one of us catches on and lets the rest of the crew know.

"Finally, there are the *Never Gonna Make It* brothers." Pop chuckled. "These guys are usually struggling rappers, singers or actors who can't get their careers started. Most are attractive and have some talent, but no smarts. They are presented with many possibilities and opportunities but they just can't seem to make it work for themselves. Unfortunately, they are taken advantage of by brothers in this business that have no qualms feeding on them. Brothers promise to help them jump-start their careers. However, they just become trophy pieces and boy toys. After a while, they get passed over, and passed on to some other brother who makes the same empty promises."

I refused to let Tickman fall into any of those categories. I really wanted to make Tickman a superstar. I believed in Tickman. He was someone from the hood who just needed a chance. Besides, I didn't initiate the sex. Tickman started it. And now it had grown into something I hadn't planned on. A relationship.

# TWENTY-EIGHT

"Come on, Big A.T., I already know about you and Tickman," Pop said, laughing.

"But how?" I asked. We were having lunch at one of Pop's favorite restaurants, the Palm on Fiftieth Street.

"I've been in this game far too long to not know when folks are sleeping together. Especially something that is happening right under my nose."

I laughed. "I wanted to tell you."

"I know, but you are in love."

"Huh?"

"I can see it in your eyes. Your walk. I hear it in the music you're doing with him. It's all over you."

"What do you mean? I am not in love," I said, dismissing the idea.

"Okay. But I know you are."

Pop was right. I had fallen in love with Tickman. I couldn't stop thinking about him. I wondered what he was doing when we were not together. I wondered if he was thinking of me. And he was. He would call at that moment.

"But this can get really tricky, because he is still seeing women and you are not," Pop said, pointing his pinky finger at me.

"Is it that obvious?" I asked.

"You are spending all your time with him and your label. No women in sight. People are going to start talking. You've got to protect your image. And to prevent that, I feel it's time you start dating a few women."

"It has been a minute since I've been with a female."

"I know. So now is the perfect time. But don't get too serious with one girl. Date a few women and keep it moving."

"All right, Pop."

I knew I wouldn't have a problem getting the ladies, it just hadn't crossed my mind. Between producing other artists, traveling across the country, managing my own label, and shaping and sleeping with Tickman, I had not even considered having a girl.

I was content in my relationship with Tickman. But Pop was right. I had to protect my livelihood. I needed to be seen with women. Nothing serious. Just some dates. No emotional attachments. No physical contact. Just hanging out. A few girls here and there wouldn't be a problem.

# TWENTY-NINE

When I first saw her my dick jumped. The blood rushed through the veins and to the tip of the head. I almost forgot what it felt like to be aroused by a woman. I still had some feelings for women . . . well, sexual feelings.

DAMN! She was that chick.

That one.

But I knew she would just be a cover-up girl. Someone to hang out with and pass off to the press and fans that I was, uhm, straight.

We were at Tickman's video shoot. She was standing across the way with the video dancers. I watched her from the distance. I wanted to see what she was about. Was she some type of groupie or industry ho? I wanted to make sure she wasn't a hanger-on and trying to get in the game by who she fucked.

I was chilling and checking my BlackBerry by Tickman's trailer waiting for the director to set up the next scene. Tickman was inside smoking weed with some of his boys.

The video was being shot in the Fort Greene Projects in Brooklyn. It's the housing projects where Tickman grew up. He wanted to let the streets know he didn't forget where he came from and wanted to keep it real.

I kept my eyes on the shapely beauty as she interacted with the video dancers. She was dressed like she stepped out of the pages of *Essence* or *Vogue* magazine. She had on a pair of dark skinny jeans, a pair of three-inch black pumps, and a bright white T-shirt logoed with "I Luv Black People" in bright yellow. The T-shirt was rolled up to her full breasts. It was tied in a knot in the back, revealing her smooth and flat stomach. Her skin looked as if it was dipped in caramel. She had on a few bracelets and some large faux emerald and ruby rings on her fingers. She carried a large Christian Dior bag—the gold "CD" was dangling on the side.

She looked hood fly, yet she was demure. Her long black silky hair cascaded down her back and she had on just a hint of makeup. Her body was tight, with a juicy-apple bottom. She was definitely my type of girl. Pretty and thick.

I made my way over to the group of women and introduced myself. "What's up, ladies? I'm Big A.T."

"Hello," they replied in unison.

"Are all of you dancers?" I asked.

"Well, I'm not a dancer," the woman I'd been eyeing responded. "I'm just here to support my girl Kim."

"Girl, please," Kim said, "you here looking for a man just like the rest of us." She laughed, and all the women in the group laughed and gave each other high fives.

"Well, can I steal you away for a minute or will your girl be okay without her bodyguard?" I asked.

"I think she'll be okay—it doesn't look too dangerous on this set." Kim smiled.

We walked away from the group and sat on two chairs placed off the video set.

"You are definitely a pretty woman. What's your name?" I smiled, extending my hand.

"Thank you," she replied. "Jasmine . . . Jasmine Bourdeaux." She shook my hand delicately.

"You have very soft hands and you smell nice," I said. Jasmine smiled. "So how come you don't have a man?"

"What makes you think I don't?" she said.

"Because no man would let someone as fine as you leave the house." I smiled. "I'd keep you locked up."

She smiled. Her glossy lips were beautiful and full. "So where is your girl?" she asked.

"I think I just found her." I winked and smiled at her. "What you got planned this weekend?"

"Well, let's see," she said as she pulled out a daily calendar from her bag. Glancing through it, she said, "Oh, I'm booked," and closed it.

"Give me that." I reached for her calendar.

Jasmine screamed and laughed as she pulled her bag away from me.

"I know you're joking. You don't have any plans," I said, laughing.

"I do. I'm busy." She laughed. It was soft and innocent.

"Aight, I'm going to pick you up Saturday evening and we're going to dinner at Mr. Chow," I said.

"Well, in that case I can switch some things around." She smiled.

"I figured that would get you." I said with a laugh.

"Please, Mamma ain't raise no fool." She laughed.

"I like that—a woman who's real and has a sense of humor." I smiled and nodded.

# THIRTY

When I went to pick up Jasmine that Saturday evening, she looked even more beautiful than when I met her. She had on a tight-fitted strapless black Donna Karan dress with black Donna Karan high heels. The dress was hugging every curve of her body.

Clinging.

Her breasts and ass were sitting perfectly round.

Plump.

Ready to be picked.

Her hair was flowing down her back. Jasmine was sexy.

I smiled as she made her way out of her building. I opened the passenger door of my silver Mercedes-Benz SLK. Jasmine slid in. Her perfume danced around me. She smelled like passion and wildflowers. Her long brown legs shimmered in the night glow. I was turned on. I felt my dick rising.

At Mr. Chow we laughed and talked about our experiences growing up. We shared stories of playing kid games like "Tag," "Hide 'n Go Get 'Em," and "Spin the Bottle."

"I grew up in Westchester," Jasmine said in between bites of her tilapia. "I guess you can say I come from an upper-middle-class family. I am the youngest of three girls. I attended private schools all my life."

When she spoke her eyes sparkled. They were full of life and love. I was mesmerized. I loved hearing about her and her family.

"My mother is a piece of work." Jasmine laughed. "She is actively involved with her sorority, Alpha Kappa Alpha. She is the president of the local chapter in Westchester. She's also involved with Jack and Jill, where my sisters and I participated."

Jasmine picked at the brown rice. Smeared it over her plate.

"After I high school I went to Spelman, where I got my degree in Comparative Women Studies," Jasmine said.

"Oh, so you one of those pro-black, down-for-the-cause, feminist sisters." I laughed.

Jasmine sucked her teeth. "There you go. And, yes, I'm proud of my heritage and sisterhood."

She took a sip of her wine and delicately removed the hair that had fallen onto her face. "Anyway, my mother has always told me and my sisters the values of marrying for money, because you can fall in love later. My two sisters married doctors. I guess you can say I bucked and wanted to be independent. I don't think like my mother."

"Oh really?" I stated. "You would marry a broke man and live in the projects with ten kids on welfare?"

Jasmine laughed. "No, I'm just saying love isn't about money. It's what you feel in here." She placed her hand over my heart. It skipped a beat. Her hand was like an electrical surge as it rested on my chest.

"I want to be in love. I want to love a man and have his heart," Jasmine said. She smiled at me with a sweet innocence.

We had a good time together. I mean she was dope. Addictive. She lured me in and captured something. But I kept thinking of Tickman. He was my heart. My love. My joy.

But Jasmine was doing a hoodoo on me. The evening was going so well I didn't even notice we drank nearly three bottles of wine. After dinner I suggested we go back to my condo. Jasmine agreed. Neither of us wanted the night to end. I was feeling her. She was feeling me. Oh, what a feeling!

When Jasmine walked into the condo, she smiled warmly.

"You want something to drink?" I asked.

"If you have some wine, yes," Jasmine answered as she sat on the sofa. She crossed her long brown legs. Her dress riding up her thighs. I smelled the musk of pussy.

Warm.

Sweet.

I walked into the kitchen and tugged at my dick. It was erect, standing at full attention. I had to calm myself down. I didn't want to walk back into the room and greet her with a massive erection. I waited . . . waited . . . and waited.

Five minutes later I came back into the living room with a bottle of Pinot, two wineglasses, and a semi-erect dick. Jasmine had taken off her shoes. Her manicured feet looked like edible bits of juicy red candy. The kind of candy you suck and let savor in your mouth.

I poured her glass first, then mines. In my mind I knew I was going to fuck her. My body was yearning for her. My dick wanted to enter her wetness. My heart was saying, *Hell no! What about Tickman?!!?*

I put on Sade's greatest-hits CD. Jasmine excused herself and went to the bathroom. A few minutes later she returned and stood in front of me. I was lounging on the sofa. Totally relaxed. Jasmine turned. Her round fat ass sitting in my face.

"Unzip me, please," she said. Her voice was low and sweet.

I immediately got an erection. My dick was bulging in my sleek black pants. Jasmine slipped out of the dress and was wearing a Natori black satin bra-and-panties set. I stood and cupped her breasts, kissing her passionately. She responded. Her tongue played with mines. I slid my hand in her panties. She was moist.

Wet.

Slippery.

I found her clit and played with it. Her body began to shake. She gently moaned. I picked her up, carried her into the bedroom, and laid her on the bed. I gently pulled off her panties. She moaned and raised her legs, revealing her shaved pussy.

I unbuckled my belt and pants and pulled them off. I climbed in between Jasmine's legs and continued kissing her. We were panting and grinding on each other.

I flipped her over to let her sit on top of me while I unfastened her bra. Her big brown breasts were like melons. I couldn't resist her nipples. They were thick and erect. I pulled on them. She leaned forward and I sucked them. Then my tongue flickered around the tips.

She reached down and massaged my hard dick. She licked, caressed, and teased me. She wanted me. I wanted her.

She grabbed my dick and guided it inside her pussy. She slowly eased down, inch by inch, allowing all of my erection to go inside her. She let out a moan as I stroked inside her. Her body trembled when I would thrust inside her. She bounced up and down on my dick. I worked with her body's rhythm. I pumped my dick inside her each time she came down on me. I knew I was hitting her spot.

"Yes! Yes! Yes!" she cried out.

She moaned and threw her head back. Her breasts bounced with each thrust. Our bodies were burning with sexual lust.

Jasmine released her juices on my dick. She became wetter. Her juices flowed onto my dick, down my shaft, between my legs.

"You like that dick?"

"Yes. I love that dick," she panted.

I could tell she had not been fucked like this in a long time. She was enjoying it. No, she was loving it. Her body started to shake.

Each climax she reached, she shrieked. She didn't want me to stop. "Please, please, please give me more!" I worked harder and faster.

I pulled my dick out of her and put her on her knees. Her body was still shaking from the multiple climactic orgasms.

I smiled.

I knew I was working her over. She wanted more and I had

more to give. I climbed behind her and guided my dick inside her. She worked her body with mine. She swayed her hips back and forth and each time she moved I pumped and stroked her with force.

I wanted to feel all of her.

Jasmine's knees started to shake. She was reaching her orgasmic climax again.

"Your . . . dick . . . is . . . so . . . good!" she yelled.

"I . . . love . . . your . . . pussy!" I yelled.

She worked her pussy so I could put my entire dick inside her. I worked with vigor.

Determination.

Force.

I reached and grabbed her hair, forcing her to arch her back. Jasmine rocked her hips and moved back and forth in rhythm with my body. Her sweet juices oozed from her and onto my dick. She was wet and slippery.

Our bodies slapped against each other's. I pounded her hard. She loved it. She wanted more. The gyration caused my body to jerk. I was ready to release. I pumped and grabbed her waist. "Oh shit!" I yelled. "I'm getting ready to come!" Feeling my dick pulsating inside her pussy, Jasmine completely let herself go. When I climaxed inside her, she climaxed with me. The timing was perfect.

That night we fucked three times.

# THIRTY-ONE

JASMINE

The next day Big A.T. drove me home. I was so giddy and filled with excitement, I thought I would burst. I held my composure in the car. I didn't want to let on I was really into Big A.T. This was something I wanted to last forever.

When he pulled up in front of my building, I didn't want to go. I could tell he didn't either. We were holding hands the entire drive and he kept kissing my fingers.

He got out of the car and came to my side and opened my door. He was such a gentleman.

When I stepped out of the car he pulled me close to him and whispered in my ear, "You are so beautiful. I'm never going to let you go." I started to cream all over again.

He leaned in and kissed me, gently and passionately. My gosh, I wanted him to come up to my apartment and make love to me all day long. But he had to go to the office and the studio.

"I will come back later," he said.

"Okay," I said.

We reluctantly let each other go from our embrace. I watched him pull off and jumped up and down in the lobby of my building. I was so excited.

When I got into the house I called my friend Kim. I had to tell somebody about my night. It was magical and definitely one of the most beautiful nights I've had in a long time. Besides, I wanted to share the news; I found a man. A man I felt I could settle down and be serious with.

"Hey, girl," I said.

"Girl, what's up?" Kim yelled into the phone. "Hooker, I have been calling you all night. I know your trifling ass is not just getting home? I want all the details."

I laughed.

"Girl, you crazy," I said.

"Come on, start talking, girl."

"Hold on, Kim." Then ten seconds later I said, "I needed to have a moment of silence because, girl, he put it down!"

We laughed together.

"He put it down?" Kim asked.

"Girl, he put it down."

"What happened?"

I told Kim all the details of my night with Big A.T.

I was on a high. The sex was perfect.

There was a connection between us. It was something that felt so right, and I knew it was definitely for me.

Big A.T. was a celebrity and I was going to be a part of that. Mom would be proud of me.

# THIRTY-TWO

Things moved fast. I kept telling myself Jasmine was just someone to keep the press and media off me and any rumors about my sexuality. She was nothing serious. Nothing at all.

But we started seeing each other regularly. You can say she was my main girl. I didn't switch up and see various women. I knew I was supposed to, but I was caught up and before I knew it we had been together for a year.

Jasmine was everything a man could ask for. She was smart, funny, beautiful, and very attentive. I liked what Jasmine was about. She always made sure I was okay.

It confused me at times, because my heart belonged to Tickman. I loved being with him. He was everything to me. I knew I was gay, but I wasn't ready to admit it to myself.

Besides, my heart wasn't really with Jasmine. It was more mental. She was more of a challenge. A game. Every time I wanted to end it with her, I couldn't find myself, or the time to do it. Trying to juggle her, Tickman, my label, and my own life became hectic. Pop warned me to keep her at arm's length and not get caught up. "I told you to date several women, not make her your main woman," Pop said. "What are you thinking?"

"I know, Pop. I am going to break it off. I'm just busy with so many other things. My head is spinning."

"I'm warning you," Pop said. He pointed his pinky finger at me. "That girl is going to be more trouble the longer you wait."

Every time I made up in my mind to end it with Jasmine,

she made it harder to resist her. One time she showed up at the office in the dead of winter wearing a full-length mink coat and nothing underneath. She dropped the coat.

Her silky smooth soft body, perky titties, and shaved pussy were right in front of me. I couldn't resist. I fucked her all over my office. Jasmine knew how to seduce my mind. She was very methodical. Everything Jasmine did was over the top. She kept me on my toes and I loved the suspense.

I managed to juggle my time between Jasmine and Tickman because he was in the studio working on his album or other projects. While Tickman was working I was with Jasmine. And vice versa.

Tickman was not fond of the relationship. "Man, you always with her," he would say.

"But you got your girls, too," I said. "You know you're my heart. My relationship with Jasmine is for the press. The media. The fans."

"I know you got to do what you got to do, but I don't like her games. I think she's up to something else," Tickman said.

"I think you got her wrong. She's cool people."

"Man, I know these women. Especially someone like you who got a name and fame. She's plotting something."

"You and Pop with your suspicions," I said. "Jasmine is not like the other girls. She's different. You just got to get to know her."

"No thanks," Tickman said.

With Tickman's dislike and distrust of Jasmine, my life became complicated. I loved him. I always valued his opinion. I trusted his insights, just as I did Pop's, but I followed my own head. I just wanted everyone to get along.

I continued to play the happy man with a girlfriend, but then Jasmine started asking questions I wasn't ready to answer. "You're always away from me," she said. "What do you think of me? What do you think about us?"

Then she wanted to move into the condo with me. She'd

already started staying some nights and weekends. Yeah, Tickman was still living with me. I don't know what I was thinking, but I wasn't.

Jasmine started arguments with Tickman about him coming into the house late and not cleaning behind himself in the kitchen. He left marijuana and beer bottles all over the place. They just bickered all the time. Tickman had had enough.

"I don't want anything to come between us," Tickman said. "I love you, but this is too much for me. I got to move."

That weekend Tickman and all his things were gone. He moved uptown in Harlem. I didn't think he was serious. I thought he would stick it out. I figured he would stay by my side and just work around it. I knew Tickman wanted me to get rid of Jasmine, but I knew he wouldn't ask me to. I probably would have considered it if he'd asked me. Maybe even followed through. But I needed Jasmine. Plain and simple.

My career was important. I'd worked too hard to get here. I'd parlayed and played the game. I was not going to give it up. Besides, Tickman's and my reputations and livelihoods were in the same boat. Neither of us was going to sink it.

I tried to smooth things out between them. I had them sit down and talk, but it didn't work. They could not be in the same room together. I just kept them separated. As much as I wanted to let Jasmine go, I couldn't.

One night I'd just gotten home from a long studio session with Tickman. I was tired. I was not in the mood for anything and wanted to relax. I heard Jasmine crying in the bedroom. I walked in and found her on the bed rocking back and forth. She was disheveled.

I sat next to her and put my arm around her. She laid her head on my shoulder.

"What's the matter?" I asked. She had a box in her hand.

"I'm pregnant," she kept crying.

"Pregnant?" I asked. "You sure?"

"Yeah I'm sure," she said. She thrust the Early-Pregnancy

Test box into my hands. "I wanted you to see for yourself, so you wouldn't think I was lying."

We did the test again. Together. The two of us in the bathroom, sitting, watching the stick. Yes, Jasmine was pregnant. She was going to have my baby.

I wasn't sure if I should've been ecstatic or angry. I was more like confused. I thought about Tickman and how I would tell him. I thought about my career. I thought about me being gay—hell, I was sleeping with my main artist.

But I was in too deep now. I couldn't go back. I had come too far with Jasmine.

I thought about us having a baby out of wedlock. Did I want to deal with baby mama drama? I thought about child support if I decided to leave Jasmine. Even the thought of marrying Jasmine crossed my mind.

My mind was flooded with so much to think about. I put my head in my hands. Jasmine started crying again. "I'm so sorry," she said.

"Shhh, it's all right," I said. I held her close to me, trying to comfort her. "It's going to be all right."

"You sure?" she asked. "I mean . . . do you want to be a father, because—"

"Yes, I want to be a father," I cut her off. I didn't even want her to finish the statement. "Everything is cool."

"We're pregnant," Jasmine smiled. Her tears stopped flowing. She beamed with excitement.

I smiled. *A child*, I thought. *Me, a dad.*

# THIRTY-THREE

JASMINE

I was on cloud nine. My life was complete. I'd found the perfect man. I was pregnant. What could my mother say? I mean, he was a Hip Hop executive and not a doctor or lawyer. That would be her complaint. It didn't matter to me. I was happy.

But when I told Big A.T. about my pregnancy, I should have known something was wrong. He wasn't as excited as I was.

I didn't set out to get pregnant, either. I wasn't trying to trap him. But something inside me made me feel that is what he thought. I had an unnerving and unsettling feeling in my stomach. I dismissed it because I didn't want to start stressing and make something out of nothing. But I made a mental note.

And if he really wanted to I would have gotten rid of the baby, but he kept telling me he wanted a child.

I loved him. I really loved him. He was so sweet. Big A.T. was everything I dreamed of in a man and I was happy to be having his baby. I just wanted him to be just as excited.

# THIRTY-FOUR

Fuck.

Fuck.

Fuck.

Fuck.

I was not ready for this. What the hell was I thinking? Why didn't I just keep Jasmine as a jump-off? A girl I simply saw from time to time.

I had no choice but to man up and deal with it. I made the bed and now I had to buy new sheets for it. I definitely had the ultimate cover-up—a girl who's pregnant.

Reluctantly, I called Pop. No one knew of the news. I kept stalling Jasmine because she was ready to blab it all over the place. She was ready to make a public announcement.

"We got to do this right," I said. "We will get Tracey to write up a press release and send it to the media. Don't you say anything."

Jasmine beamed. "I'm not going to say anything. When will we make the announcement?" She kissed me on the lips.

"Give me a month. I need to make sure everything is in place. I want to do this big."

"I love you," Jasmine said. She looked me in my eyes. I smiled. I never responded when she said those words. I knew I didn't love her. I loved Tickman.

Jasmine took my hand and placed it on her stomach. "This is our creation, our love. Don't you love me?" she asked. Her head tilted. Her eyes pleading for a response.

"Come on now. Why you asking a question like that?" I moved away from her. Avoiding her eyes. I didn't want her to read my mind, to see I didn't love her. My love was someplace else.

"Because every time I say it you never respond. You just smile." She followed behind me.

I sat at the dining room table. I looked at the crystal vase with the red and white roses lying one over another. They were from Tickman. I'd never received flowers from a guy before. He sent them because I'd just gotten him an endorsement deal with a vodka company. He was going to have his own line of wine coolers.

Jasmine stood behind me rubbing my head. I started fidgeting with my watch. This was the moment. The time to tell Jasmine the truth. But how could I explain my feelings without her being upset? How could I explain the fact that I really liked her, but I was in love with a man. I didn't want her to abort my child. I wanted to be what she needed. But could she handle it? I'd really fucked up.

"Well, we got a baby on the way," I said. "So you don't need to be stressing. I got you."

Jasmine threw her arms around me and kissed me on my ear. I laughed and pulled her off me again. "I thought you were going shopping?" I asked.

"I am. I was just getting myself together to meet up with Kim." She walked over to the end of the table and picked up her Gucci bag. Her bright yellow sundress was flowing as she crossed over toward the living room.

"Don't forget, not a word to anybody!"

"Boy, you stop stressing." She waved her hand and walked out the door.

When the door closed, my gaze went back to the vase. I stared at the flowers. Delicate and effortless as they sat in the water. That's what I wanted for my life: delicate and effortless. No stress, strain, or worries.

I called Pop. I hesitated in telling him about Jasmine's pregnancy. I knew he wouldn't be happy. He kept telling me to not get serious with her. He wanted me to date around. But I got caught up. I didn't take his advice.

I also had to tell Tickman. Yes, I was stalling. For what? I don't know. Maybe to wake up and realize it was a dream. I wanted it to be just right, but there would be no perfect moment. It didn't help he wasn't really around. I preferred to tell him face-to-face, not over the phone. He deserved better. I loved him more than anything. He was everything to me and, yes, I fucked up.

Real bad.

I felt I'd let down the two people I loved the most, Pop and Tickman. They both warned me. But I let my dick take control. What was I trying to prove? I was so caught up in trying to protect my image I failed to protect my heart, and the heart of the man I loved.

I was hoping Pop wouldn't answer his phone when I called. On the second ring he picked up. "What up, Big A.T.?" Pop asked.

"I'm good. What you up to?" I asked.

"I'm getting ready for a meeting in an hour."

I started fidgeting with my watch. I felt my underarms perspiring. "Well, I just wanted to tell you that me and Jasmine are having a baby."

Silence.

"Hello?" I said.

"Wow! Congratulations," Pop said.

"Yeah, she is three months pregnant. We just found out."

"Hmm," Pop said.

"What does that mean?" I asked.

"I thought I told you not to get caught up with her? I said for you to date several women and keep it moving."

"Yeah, Pop. But everything happened so fast."

"I see. So what are you going to do?"

"Well, we are going to send out a press release to the public to let the media and the fans know. And then—"

"No, I'm talking about Tickman," Pop cut me off.

"I am going to see him tonight. I am going to tell him then. He can handle it."

"You sure?"

"Come on, Pop. Tickman got his girls, too."

"How many of them are pregnant?"

Silence.

"Well, I am happy for you and Jasmine," Pop said.

"We want you to be the godfather."

"Of course I will. We have to celebrate. But you know this puts us in a very sticky situation."

"I know." I sighed. "I've been thinking about telling Jasmine about me." I knew Pop was concerned about my sexuality, but to bring a woman and child into the mix was another set of issues. My life was seriously complicated.

"You can't tell her."

"I know. But I feel like I need to."

"What will that solve?"

"Well, for one, I will be relieved and I think she can handle it. I mean there is a way out of this."

"Oh really!?!" Pop said.

"I've got to do the right thing. Trying to juggle her and Tickman and now a child coming into the world, yeah, I need to tell her. The sooner the better. Don't you think?"

"I told you what to do from the beginning. This is your mess now."

Silence again.

"When you figure out what to do, I'll be here. Until then I'll call the crew," Pop said. "We're going to celebrate. This is big news."

"Thanks, Pop."

I understood Pop's concern. Tickman was my love, my heart. Two things could happen: Either this would crush him and put a strain between us, or it would make us stronger. I prayed for the latter.

I called Tickman and told him to meet me at his house. "There is something I need to talk with you about," I said.

"Aight, no doubt. Meet me at nine."

# THIRTY-FIVE

I decided to take the scenic route to Tickman's new condo in Harlem. I love driving up Broadway. There's so much activity happening on the streets. People hustling and bustling from the underground of the train stations to their homes. You can definitely see the transition of color from the Upper West Side to Harlem. Once you cross over 123rd Street the shades of white and pink skin transform to shades of browns and black.

The music blares in Harlem, speaking in tongues called Hip Hop. Poetic licenses are handed out to urban scribes who studied street phonics from great iconic figures like Rakim, Notorious B.I.G., Tupac, Jay-Z, and the Wu-Tang Clan. Young men strutting around in the streets with their dicks in their hands, each step bopping and dipping.

Young women cluster together watching and listening. Their hair, nails, and clothes reflect the sprinkling colors of the rainbow. Their asses and tits are too big for their ages.

I turned onto 125th Street and cruised the culture. I passed M&G's Soul Food, where greasy heart attacks and fried strokes are served on a platter with a smile.

On the next block, packed as always, is Popeye's Fried Chicken. The line of single mothers, little kids, homeboys, and homegirls is almost out the door. Panhandlers are waiting outside: "You got some spare change?"

One-two-five, the Times Square of Harlem. Bright lights.

Tourists. Traffic. Street vendors. Urban hustlers. Tables filled with whatever you need. Yes, they got it.

"Yo, my man, check out these T-shirts with Malcolm, Martin, and Ali!"

"Get your oils, incense, and black soap," they yell.

The five-percenters are dressed in all-black garb like Arab sheiks, yelling, "The Black Man is God!" They have a captive audience as they preach their gospel.

The stores. Jimmy Jazz. Mart 125. Champs. Foot Locker. Soul food and fast-food restaurants are nestled in between. Shop, eat, and spend your money. Men and women crowd the concrete walkway, bags in hand, with fresh new kicks.

"Money-makin' Manhattan!"

The Apollo—where legends play. Get your shot. Rub the tree of hope. "I'll be there one day soon," they say.

I get to Adam Clayton Powell Boulevard and turn left. I make my way to 139th Street, Strivers' Row.

Streets 137, 138, and 139 make up the section that the black upper-middle-class calls home. A few blocks filled with trees that shade the neighborhood from intruders who don't belong. Steps are secluded away from the urban terrain and b-boy corner jockeying nuisances that otherwise infest Harlem.

The brownstones are beautifully renovated. Bricks look fresh and clean, as if they just came from the masonry. Untainted from colored graffiti.

Fancy cars.

Yes. The elite.

Tickman's condo was here. The top floor of a brownstone.

I looked at the clock illuminating on the dashboard. It was nine twenty-two. I took my time, not really ready for the conversation. I was dreading it actually, but it had to be done. When I came through the door Tickman grabbed me and gave me a big hug. It felt good to be in his arms.

Strong.

Holding me close.

Pulling me into him.

Perfectly.

We fit.

I was his and he was mines.

I inhaled, taking in his aroma. His smell—a mix of street, hard work, and Gucci cologne—triggered my memory. Yes, I loved him. No, I didn't ever want to forget his scent.

"What's up?" I said. Reluctantly, I pulled away from his grip.

"Yo, baby, what's good with you?" Tickman said. He looked me over and licked his lips. I wanted to have sex with him right there. His wife beater fitted snuggly on his broad chest and his bulging biceps were on display. I followed him to the living room. His pants sagging, falling off his ass.

I looked around. It was practically empty. Only a sofa and a stereo. No remnants of anyone really living there—possibly a squatter. It was perfect for Tickman. Yet he didn't belong in this neighborhood. It wasn't him. He wasn't from a prep school or a two-family home, nor was he Ivy League pedigree. Tickman didn't attend college. He was born in the streets and lived for the streets. He was Brooklyn, the Fort Greene projects, definitely not Strivers' Row.

"Man, this album is fire—niggas not gon' be ready for this," he said. His voice echoed off the vacant, hollow condo walls. I just smiled.

"Baby, yo, when we doing the album cover shoot?" he asked.

"Uhm, in two weeks," I said.

"Aight, cool. Yo, who the stylist doing it? I want my shit to be fly, naw mean?"

"Pamela from Fly Gyrls," I said. I crossed over toward him. Fidgeting with my watch. "Listen, I got something to tell you."

"Aight, no doubt, what's up?" Tickman sat on the sofa.

Seconds went by. Silence. It seemed like a lifetime. I paced the floor. Then, I finally blurted, "Jasmine is pregnant." The words regurgitated from my mouth.

"Pregnant!?!" His head dropped. His body fell back onto the sofa. His chest heaved up and down. The blow was a shot. Fired from a cannon. Loaded and loud. "Wow. Wow," he repeated.

"Yeah, three months," I said. I sat next to him. I put my hand on his shoulder.

"Wow," Tickman said again. "Congratulations!" He sat up and smiled. He reached over and gave me a hug. But it wasn't genuine. It was halfhearted. It felt forced.

"You not upset?" I asked.

"Upset about what?" Tickman said.

He feigned a smile. His eyes widened. He tried to appear as if he was unbothered. "Please, man, y'all were fucking and shit. It was bound to happen. Baby, you know I love you," Tickman said. "You got a seed coming into the world. Nigga, you should be happy."

I could sense Tickman was pretending. He hugged me again with the same half-ass embrace.

"Pop also said I should be happy." I put my hand inside Tickman's. His large dark fingers intertwined with mine. I felt his rough calluses. "But I think I am going to tell her the truth. It's eating me up inside."

"So you're going to tell her about us? You and me?" He snatched his hand away. His face was distorted. Confused.

"No, no, no," I said. "I am just going to tell her about me."

"I don't think that's a good idea." He shook his head.

"Why not?"

"You're going to ruin your life. She's going to tell everybody."

"I don't think Jasmine will do that."

"Oh really? How are you going to convince her to not say anything?"

"We will talk about it. She will listen to me."

Tickman sucked his teeth. "Good luck with that."

"She's not like other women. She's more mature than that."

"You're very hopeful for someone who hasn't really accepted himself."

"What you mean?"

"Come on, Big A.T. You're going to sit here and tell me that you're okay with your sexuality? All the sneaking around we do. Nobody outside of the crew knows about you. And now you're ready to tell the world."

Silence.

Tickman was right. I'd not been honest with myself. I had to learn how to accept me before I could ask Jasmine to. And was I really ready to come out to the world?

"Things just really got out of control. I didn't plan this."

"Nobody plans life. It just happens. But I'm here for you." Tickman leaned in and kissed me on the mouth.

"Thanks, baby," I said. "Pop wants the crew to get together at his house for a party."

"Now that's what I'm talking about," Tickman said. "Look, baby, she can give you something I can't, and ain't nothing wrong with that. But two things I know she ain't got," he added, moving closer to me. "She ain't got your heart and this dick—that shit is mine." Tickman laughed and grabbed my crotch. I laughed and moved in closer to him.

"I want you to have the best and to be the best," Tickman said. "I love you for you."

"Damn, baby, I love you, too." I smiled. "We in this shit together. Just be patient with me." I hugged him. "We will get through this. I know we will," I said.

# THIRTY-SIX

That weekend part of the crew met at Pop's house to celebrate me becoming a father. Just the boys—the family. Chris Cherryman, vice president of programming at MTV. Eric Billings, vice president of urban music at J Records. Big Mike, the head of A&R, and Brian Wright, the vice president of marketing and promotions, from Def Jam. James Miller, the head of A&R at Warner Bros. Records. And, Mark Hartman, the head of programming for BET.

We gathered in Pop's huge living room for a toast. The very place where I'd gotten my start some few years ago. Now here I was, standing as a member of the family.

"To my son, my boy," Pop said. "You're going take this bigger than you know, and now you are bringing your legacy into the world to live and have a good life. I know you and Tickman got y'all thing, and it's all good—well, from what you tell me," Pop said. He tilted his head behind Tickman's back and nodded toward his ass. Everyone laughed.

"To success and a healthy baby," Pop said. He raised his glass, and everyone followed suit. We all took sips of our drinks.

"It's my turn to say something," Chris said. His deep baritone voice seemed odd coming from his short tiny muscular body. He pushed through us and stood in the center. His light skin started to fluster.

Chris was a cool brother. He was all about business in the office, but he let loose when he was around the family.

"To the Diva," he said. He pointed his glass toward me. I laughed. "You're fierce and you got a cute man. I give you that. Now you've knocked up Ms. Jasmine and she's going to wear you out!" Again, everyone laughed and raised their glasses.

"And for the rest of us who came without a man. I've arranged for some dick and ass tonight," Big Mike said. The men erupted in cheers.

"Damn, we got some dick and ass coming," James said. "I knew I should have brought the toys." Everyone laughed.

Big Mike and James, the party animals of the crew. They liked to have a good time.

Both were funny and smart, and they were always together. Those two stayed in trouble. Sex was not inhibited for them. They were into it all—threesomes, foursomes—and the guys they got down with were certified freaks from the elite roster they put together based on looks, background, and credibility. They could not be openly gay, and they had to have a girl.

Despite their positions in the industry, they were good-looking guys who didn't have a problem getting the guys. Big Mike was tall and slim. He had an oval-shaped bald head and wore wire-rim glasses. James was average height and thick, with a beautiful smile. He lit up a room with his toothpaste-commercial white teeth. I always poked fun at him, telling him he should do a commercial spot advertising Colgate or Crest.

While the fellas were mingling and laughing, I pulled Tickman into the kitchen. We stood by the double sink. I wanted to know how he was really handling the news of Jasmine's pregnancy.

"I just want to make sure you're okay, you know, with Jasmine and me."

"I'm cool," Tickman said. "Man, I told you it's all good. Stop stressing."

"Aight, no doubt. I've just been sensing a little tension from you since I told you."

"Man, it's just you projecting onto me. You're the one with the tension." Tickman hugged and kissed me. "Yo, baby, everything is cool. Just relax and let's enjoy tonight." Tickman gave me another kiss. I smiled as we walked back into the other room. Hand in hand.

The music was blaring and everyone was laughing and talking, enjoying themselves.

Chris and Mark walked over to me and Tickman.

"Congratulations, Tickman." Chris shook his hand. "You are about to become a big star. We at MTV are gearing up for you. So, Big A.T., I need for you to come by the office this week so we can talk about the particulars of having Tickman doing an exclusive interview. Get him to perform and all the other good stuff."

Tickman's eyes grew big. A huge smile showcased all his teeth. He looked over at me. I just smiled and tipped my glass of champagne to him.

"Yeah, man, we would like to follow you for a day, and do 'A Day in the Life of a Rising Artist' over at BET," Mark said. "Big A.T., I want to talk with you about the network having a special promotion for fans to win a trip to the set of Tickman's next video."

Tickman was gleaming. He gripped and hugged me, knocking my glass out of my hand, spilling the champagne on the floor. Then he hugged Chris and Mark.

"Man, thank y'all. This is dope!" Tickman said. "I can't believe all this is about to really happen."

"Well, believe it," Mark said, "because your life is going into overdrive right now."

"Yeah, so get ready for the interviews, long hours on the road, and nights without Big A.T.," Chris said. He smiled at me.

"He'll be ready," I said. "Besides, he got the cover of

*Billboard* next month, *VIBE* following, and then *XXL* and *The Source. Complex, Details,* and *Fader* want to get interviews with him too."

Tickman shook his head in disbelief. We, the family, were working together and everyone was helping to make it happen.

# THIRTY-SEVEN

After the fun-filled weekend at Pop's, it was back to the grind. Back to building my empire. I was on top of the world. I had it all—my man, a girl, a baby on the way, and my music. My phone was ringing off the hook for collaborations. Everyone wanted a piece of me—my sound, my touch.

I was going over some new music for Tickman when Kenya buzzed me. "Big Mike is on the phone for you."

"Okay. Thanks, Kenya."

Me and Big Mike had become very close. We'd started hanging out more. He was someone I could talk to about anything. He was a good listener and crazy as hell. I met his many girlfriends . . . and boyfriends, plus his moms and his brothers and sisters. Big Mike was a family man, and definitely a mama's boy. He spent a lot of time with his mother, and talked with her damn near every day.

Although Big Mike had his share of women, he also had his share of fun with men. He was a straight-up freak. Let him tell it, it was his Scorpio nature. He and James were always looking to freak with some new undiscovered talent waiting to get in the industry.

"Yo, what up, playboy?" he said.

"What up, Big Mike?"

"I'm still recovering from this weekend."

"I heard you and James got into something, or should I say some *bodies,* after me and Tickman left Pop's."

"You know me," Big Mike said. "Man, these three kats James had come through were some straight-up freaks. The three of them was sucking and licking on me—man, I almost lost it in the first few minutes."

"Nigga, you know you a two-minute brotha," I said.

"Shit, nigga, I got stamina fo' yo' ass. Them niggas wanted me to do some shit I ain't never done before." He laughed. "I was fucking one of them and the other nigga got behind me and started sucking on my nuts and eating my ass. That was fucking wild! Then the other dude opens the closet doors and pulls me in there with him. He bends over and spreads his cheeks. I fucked the shit out of him."

"There you go," I said. "You better slow your ass down, nigga, before you get something from one of these niggas. You don't who and what those niggas be doing with other men."

"Nigga, I ain't worried about that," Big Mike said. "I always use protection. Shit. I'm still looking to get me a wifey and have some seeds like *your* ass."

"Yeah, I know, don't remind me."

"But anyway, playa, check it. I referred this fine-ass nigga to you. This nigga got mad skills. He is talented as shit. Nigga can freestyle and battle-rhyme. He got the look—nice body, fat juicy booty, and a big-ass dick."

"So what you refer him to me for?" I asked.

"Because I can't do anything with him. James already fucked him. Then sent him over to Eric, who fucked him, and Eric sent him to me. Shit, the nigga came through the door practically coming out of his clothes. He knew what was up. You know me—I ain't turning down a good head job and some nice ass."

"Damn, you niggas always running game on somebody," I said. "I'm so glad that Pop didn't let you niggas get to me."

"Anyway, nigga. James found this dude up in Harlem rhyming freestyle at the barbershop last year," Big Mike said. "The nigga was fresh from North Carolina. You know, being head of A&R at Warner Bros., James will take these young kats and flaunt them around. They get all excited because they think he can help them in their career." Big Mike paused. Then he continued, "Shit, James was letting this nigga live up in his spot and fucking him for a good six months before he decided to pass the kid off to Eric."

"What the fuck!" I said. "How the fuck you take a nigga from bum-fuck nowhere and let him live in your spot. Just for some ass? Shit, how the fuck you come from bum-fuck nowhere and stay at some nigga's spot you don't know and let him run up in you and run game on you?"

"You know everybody trying to get in the game," Big Mike said. "Niggas will sell they mama's ass if they could to get in this game. You know how many niggas are trying to get a deal? You know how many demos I get a day? You know how many niggas run up on me on a daily basis asking if I can listen to them sing or freestyle?"

"Man, you ain't telling me anything I don't already know," I said. "I get the same shit too."

"Aight, nigga, so don't act brand-new on me. Anyway, I sent the kid to you. Maybe you can freak him or tell him to hang in there and hopefully someday he'll make it in this business. You know, give him your Jesse Jackson 'Keep Hope Alive' and Martin Luther King 'I Have a Dream' speech." We both laughed.

"I'm not interested in freaking some other dude. Tickman is it for me. Besides, he will kill me if I freak another dude. I hope you didn't tell that country nigga to come over here without calling first?"

"Oh shit, my bad," Big Mike said. "Listen, I got to run—my diva artist Cyn is calling. She got rid of her old producers and now wants to work with these new kats."

"Aight, Big Mike, I'll talk with you." I hung up the phone.

I leaned back in my large black executive chair and stared out into the New York City skyline. I started thinking about the baby and Jasmine. How was I going to handle the relationship with her? I needed to tell her the truth about me.

I thought about Tickman and our relationship. Tickman was about to become a major figure in the rap game. I had to make sure everything was lined up properly for him.

I was still producing other big-name artists who were calling and requesting my services.

I had to run a record label. And I'd been approached about investing in real estate throughout the city. My life was moving fast. Full speed ahead. I was making a lot of money. Big money. The type people dream about. Things were going too good, and they say that when things are going too good, something bad is on the way.

# THIRTY-EIGHT

Kenya knocked on my office door. By now she'd become my right hand. She was smart, witty, no-nonsense. She had a street edge to her, yet she was book-smart. When she came to work for me she was in her senior year studying business at New York University. She graduated with honors.

"Come in," I said. Kenya walked in with some folders.

"I have some contracts for you to look over and sign," she said. I leaned forward and let out a sigh.

"What's wrong?" Kenya was good at sensing when I wasn't really focused and something was bothering me.

"I'm cool," I said.

"You look like you got a lot on your mind," she said.

"Just the same ole shit, you know."

"Yeah, I know. Your girl Jasmine has been running around preparing for the baby shower. Everybody knows she's carrying your baby. She won't let anyone forget it's your baby." She laughed.

"I told her to chill with that, but you know how females can be," I said.

"Naw, I don't know how females can be." She put her hands on her hips.

"See what I mean, all sensitive," I said. I tried to do my best mimic of a female voice in a high pitch. Kenya laughed at me.

"Anyhow, I brought in the schedule the promotions and marketing team worked on for Tickman. He is leaving for his promo tour next month. The video will start running next week and he has an exclusive interview with *Rolling Stone.*"

"Damn, time sure does fly," I said.

"Yeah it does, and you got to start thinking about that property on the Upper East Side, because they're planning on breaking ground next year."

"Shit, get the developer on the phone. I want to talk with him and see what he's offering."

Kenya started walking for the door and then turned quickly toward me.

"I almost forgot. There is this fine country boy from North Carolina in the lobby. He said Big Mike sent him over to you. Do you want to see him?"

"How long has he been in the lobby?"

"About an hour," she said. "I tried to get rid of him, but he started rhyming and singing about how beautiful I was. He's good. I like him."

"All right, send him in," I said. "And don't forget to get the developer on the phone for me."

I really wasn't interested in signing any new acts. I had a lot on my plate just dealing with Tickman. But my curiosity got the best of me. I wanted to know if this kid from North Carolina really was as fine as everyone was saying, if this country boy really had any talent.

When he walked through the door of my office my mouth nearly fell open. *Damn, he is gorgeous!* He walked in with a gleaming smile on his face. He was wearing dark navy jeans, a black hoodie, and a pair of Jordans. They were scuffed on the sides. The laces were darker than they should have been.

He glided toward my desk. He looked about six foot two inches. Built like a basketball player. His skin was the color of butterscotch. He looked delicious. He had short curly hair and just a hint of a mustache. His face was smooth, clear, innocent. His eyes were seductive and sleek. They didn't look real. They were as brown as his skin. He looked like a star.

"How you doing, sir? Mah name is Antwan Smith, but folks call me Southern Gent," he said. He extended his large hand. His Southern drawl drew me in instantly. Warm. Sweet.

He smiled when he shook my hand.

"I'm good. How about yourself?" I asked.

"I'm good, sir. It's truly a pleashure to meet you. I've read everythang 'bout you and listened to awl the music you produced," he said.

"Thank you, thank you."

Then without warning, Southern Gent pulled down his pants and boxers. He lifted his hoodie over his head.

"What the fuck are you doing!?!" I yelled.

"Well, Big Mike tole me to come see you and—"

"Man, pull up your pants and put your hoodie back on," I said.

I was pissed. Disgusted. Saddened.

*But damn that country nigga got a big-ass dick,* I thought.

"Yo, don't do that again. You hear me?!" Southern Gent nodded his head.

"How old are you?" I asked.

"I'm nineteen, sir."

"Don't ever let me hear about you doing some shit like that in this business." *I ain't got time for this shit. Another young dumb-ass nigga thinking he got to sell his ass for a deal. I don't have time to be schooling these motherfuckers,* I said to myself.

"I'm sorry, sir, I didn't mean no harm." Southern Gent held his head down. His eyes avoided mine.

"I know, man, you just don't know any better. Look, man, sit down." Southern Gent sat in the chair facing me.

"This is the entertainment business, not a sex video audition. You got to stop letting niggas take advantage of you," I said. "I hear you got some mad skills and that you can freestyle and battle-rhyme. Use your skills and not your looks or body to get a deal." Southern Gent's head sunk farther.

I knew I sounded like a parent or teacher scolding a child for something they did wrong. But Southern Gent was young. He didn't know any better. I hated seeing young kats being taken advantage of. I think it's because of how I got in the game. I refused to do it to someone else. I wouldn't use my position in the game to make eager dudes sleep their way in.

"Let me hear you spit something," I said. Southern Gent's face lit up. This was his moment, his chance to shine.

He stood up and started flowing effortlessly. When he moved and glided across the floor it was like watching a whole other person. He personified and looked larger than life. I was definitely impressed.

"Yo, hold up, Southern Gent." I rose from my chair and walked over to the entertainment center. I put on some beats for him to rhyme to.

"Let me hear you rhyme to this," I said.

Without skipping a beat he started freestyling again. The music made him even more energetic and animated. He was definitely on fire. I smiled as I watched him. He had it—that glow, that gift. Southern Gent was it.

"Aight, aight, you got skills and you can flow," I said. I stopped the music.

Southern Gent's body was still moving back and forth. He continued rhyming even after the music stopped. It was like he was still hearing the music in his head and couldn't stop.

"Slow down, my man, slow down," I said.

"Music is my life. Rhymin' is who I am," Southern Gent said. "I live fo' dis!"

I smiled. "You're from North Carolina. Where you staying in the city?"

Southern Gent sat back down. He looked nervously at his hands where they fidgeted on his lap.

"I've been ridin' the subway at night from da Bronx to Coney Island and den sometimes to Jamaica, Queens—depends on da night," he said.

"So you don't have any family here?" I asked.

"Naw. I told 'em I was comin' to New York City to be a rap star. But nobody believed me. I met dis guy from Brooklyn down in Wilmington, North Carolina, where I'm from. He was visitin' his folks and he was talkin' 'bout how big he was and he was 'bout to get signed and all dis hype. He told me I was dope and I needed to be in New York if I wanted to make it. So I asked 'im if I could come and stay with 'im. He said yeah. So I saved some money from my job and came up to Brooklyn. He let me stay at his place for a monf, but he got evicted and he went to his girl's place. I just roamed da streets and started ridin' the subway."

"So when did you meet up with James?" I asked.

"I was in da barbershop in Harlem battle-rhymin' dis kid. James was dere and after we finished battlin' he came over to me and tole me who he was and what he could do fo' me. He let me stay at his spot for a while, but he never really made any-thang happen fo' me. I kept askin' 'im if I could go in da studio and work on somethin'. I just needed an opportunity. Dat's all I needed. But it jus' didn't work out. He kept tellin' me next time or dis was not da right time. Den he would take me out to eat at fancy restaurants and den back home to fuck him."

"Ohhh, a never-gonna-make-it brother," I mumbled.

"Huh?" Southern Gent said.

"Nothing, man."

"Well, anyway, I guess after I kept askin' 'im all da time 'bout gettin' put on, he got tired of me and sent me to Eric."

"And the rest is history," I said. "Look, Southern Gent, you are a good-looking brother and you got some skills. This in-dustry is hard and it's not always favorable. You've got to learn how to work it and not let it work you."

I reached into my pocket and pulled out five one-hundred-dollar bills.

"Consider this an investment. Get you something to eat. Clean yourself up and get a hotel room for the night. Also get

some new gear; you're in New York City, not North Carolina."

"Aw, man, thank you, sir, thank you," Southern Gent said.

"And stop calling me 'sir.' Call me Big A.T."

"Aight, Big A.T." He smiled.

"Meet me back here tomorrow morning at nine o'clock. I'll
give you some work around the office. You can help Kenya out.
And, starting tomorrow, you can crash at the label's apartment.
I just need to get it cleaned."

Tears came to Southern Gent's eyes. I could tell it was the
first time during his experience in the industry someone was
being nice to him without asking for something in return.

"You've got to work hard if you want to get in this business,"
I said. "Niggas are not just going to let you get in. They want to
make sure you can hold your own. That money is part of an investment in you, and I want a huge return on my investment."

"I'm gon' do it and be the biggest rapper in the industry.
Believe dat," Southern Gent said. He stood up smiling and
pounding his chest.

"Just be here tomorrow at nine o'clock."

"I'll be here by eight-thirty." Southern Gent ran out of my
office beaming.

*Damn, that nigga had a big-ass dick,* I thought again,
laughing to myself.

# THIRTY-NINE

The next morning at eight-thirty when I stepped off the elevator, Southern Gent was sitting in the lobby. Impressive.

"Good mornin', Big A.T.," Southern Gent said. He stood up. "What you think?" He held open his arms, showing off his crisp new jeans, new Jordan sneakers, and a white button-down shirt.

Fresh new gear. Definitely impressive.

"Now you look like a New Yorker." I smiled.

I set him up with Kenya to help her around the office. I wanted to see if he really wanted this. Was he willing to do the grunt work? She immediately put him to work faxing, copying, and making calls.

I smiled and walked into my office. The night before I'd made up my mind I was going to sign Southern Gent. My second artist. I was going to do it right after Tickman's album release. I planned to feature him on Tickman's next album.

Southern Gent could be just as big as Tickman. He was young, fresh, and naïve. He could be molded and worked into a star. I didn't have to worry about the diva attitude of someone already thinking they know the business better than me. I was willing to make the investment in Southern Gent. The ladies would love him because he was good-looking and charming. The men would like his Southern flow, and some would find him handsome as well. He was a total package. Something hard to find.

"Yo, what up, baby?" I said. I'd called Tickman to tell him about Southern Gent.

"Chillin'," Tickman said. "I'm at this fitting for my appearance on BET's *Video Countdown*. What's going on?"

"I just wanted to holla at you right quick. Big Mike sent over this young nigga from North Carolina who got some crazy skills. He freestyled for me yesterday in the office and was off the chain. He definitely got the rhyme skills and he knows how to work the beat. I'm going to sign him, but right now I got him working in the office to see how dedicated he is."

"Aight, no doubt," Tickman said.

"I want you to introduce him to the world on your next album. He is going to be just as big as you're going to get," I said.

"Yo, anything you touch is golden. I'll put him on. Shit, let's all make this money."

"Aight, so I'll hit you later. I got a lot to get done before I sign off on that property on the Upper East Side."

"Aight, get back."

I then called Pop. I wanted to tell him about my newest discovery. New York was about to explode. My career was going through the roof.

But there was also one other thing I wanted to take care of. Kenya had been working her ass off and doing a great job of handling all my businesses. As much as I wanted to keep her as my personal assistant, it was time for her to grow, to become a success in this business. I knew of the challenges and difficulties women faced in becoming executives in this industry. I was not going to hold her back.

"Hey, Kenya, could you come into my office?" I spoke into the phone's intercom.

Kenya walked in with pen and pad ready. She always came ready to take notes. I trained her to always write down what people say because then you can refer back to it later if there are any discrepancies.

"Hey, what's up?" she said. She sat in the chair opposite my desk.

"Look, I am going to cut to the chase," I said.

She looked suspiciously back at me.

"Effective immediately your new job title is Vice President of A&R. You will oversee the department and make all decisions regarding artists signed to Change Up Records. I've thought about it and I know you can do the job. You have consistently proven to me that you are more than capable of handling anything I throw at you."

Kenya's mouth dropped open. She was shocked.

"I know this is probably overwhelming right now." I laughed. "But, baby girl, you know your shit. I need to make sure you are happy. I want to keep you around here before somebody else try to scoop you up from me." I smiled.

"Oh my gosh," she said. "Wow, this is huge. I don't know what to say."

"Say yes. Say you will take the job. Say you will stay here with me."

She smiled widely. Then she said, "Yes, yes, I will take the job."

"You're moving up now and you have a lot of responsibility," I said. "I need some hot new acts. I need for your eyes and ears to be to the streets. You got to let me know who and what the next hot thing out there is doing."

"I got you," she said. "You know I am not going to let you down."

"I know you won't," I said and stood up. I extended my hand. She rose and came around the desk and gave me a hug.

"Congratulations, Kenya," I said.

"Thank you, and thank you for believing in me." She smiled.

I immediately sent an announcement to all the trade magazines informing industry insiders of Kenya's new role with the label. Everyone responded. Kenya received congratu-latory notes, bouquets of flowers, and spa gift certificates. She was welcomed with open arms. She was now officially on the playing field, alongside some of the top names in the business.

# FORTY

JASMINE

Things were moving too slow for me. I couldn't understand why every time I wanted to talk with Big A.T. about our relationship and where we were going he "always had something to do," or "the timing was not good."

What was the holdup? I wanted to get married. I wanted something stable. I wanted a commitment, a ring. I was carrying his child.

Something had to be going on. I figured he was probably seeing another woman. Maybe he was seeing many women.

I was so busy with doctors' appointments, the baby shower, and shopping for myself and the baby that I never thought Big A.T. could be cheating. But it had to be the reason he wouldn't marry me. It had to be the reason why he kept putting me off.

I decided to confront Big A.T. to know for sure if he was cheating on me with another woman. And if he was, I would forgive him. I knew the industry had many up-and-coming girls who would try to take your man if you weren't paying attention, especially a man like Big A.T. He had his own record label, a lot of money and fame, and he was powerful. I would forgive him and tell him we could work through it. I would explain to him I understood and although I didn't agree with it, if he had to have his women he could, so long as he didn't flaunt or showcase any of the women in public. I wouldn't allow any of them to call the house. This was my domain. I was the queen of this nest and I wasn't going to have any chicken-heads calling our house interrupting what I was building with my man.

Besides, I was having the biggest baby shower New York had seen in a decade. It was being held at the Waldorf-Astoria Hotel. Nothing was too good for me and my baby. I was expecting over two hundred guests. Lots of celebrities and industry people. Many were the wives and girlfriends of Big A.T.'s friends. Chris's fiancée Christine was coming, along with Eric's girlfriend Monica. I sent an invitation to Big Mike for one of his many girlfriends, Penelope. And, James's girl of the month, Erica, along with Mark's wife, April, was attending.

There was so much to be done my mother and good friend Kim helped me put it all together. There were the gift bags to prepare. We got MAC and L'Oreal to sponsor with giveaways. I had to prepare the menu, the games, and of course the seating arrangements.

As I was poring over the last-minute details, Big A.T. walked in.

"Hey, baby," I said.

"Hey." He plopped on the sofa next to me. He leaned over and kissed me on the cheek. "What you up to?"

"Just going over these last-minute details for the baby shower." I was working on the seating chart. "I'll be glad when this is all over."

"Well, it will all be over this weekend." Big A.T. stretched his arms and yawned. "Man, I'm tired."

"Long day?" I asked.

"Yeah, Tickman's album is slated to debut at number one on *Billboard* next week, so the phones are ringing off the hook and the meetings are nonstop."

"Hmm, I see." I crossed names out and rearranged people on the seating chart.

"I'm about to sign this young new rapper from North Carolina named Southern Gent," he said.

"I like that name."

"Yeah, he's off the chain with his rhymes. He's a little green, but I can shape him. Besides, he's got the look."

"That's good, baby." I was diligently working on the seating chart. I wanted to make sure the right people were sitting in the right places.

"I also made Kenya the vice president of A&R," he said.

"Wow, that is great. We need more sisters in power."

"You women got all the power *now*." He laughed. "Look at you and all the money you are costing me."

"It's not about money." I looked up at him. "It's about having decision-making abilities and the power to make change."

"Well damn. I guess beauty and brains do mix."

I grabbed the pillow I was sitting on and threw it at him.

"What?" He laughed. "Man, I am hungry, what about you?"

"No, I ate something earlier."

"You mean to tell me my little one in there isn't craving anything tonight?" He put his head to my stomach.

"She's been good tonight." I caught myself and put my hand over my mouth. I hadn't told Big. A.T. the baby's sex. I wanted to surprise him.

"'She'?"

"Damn it, I didn't want to tell you."

"You knew it was going to be a girl and you didn't tell me?" He smiled.

"I wanted it to be a surprise." I kissed him gently on the lips.

"Wow, a baby girl."

"Yes, you're going to be the father of a precious little girl."

Big A.T. just sat and smiled. He was happy. He really wanted a girl. Although most men would want to have a boy, Big A.T. always wanted a girl. He told me while growing up as an only child he always wished he had a sister. Everyone in the neighborhood had brothers, but not too many had sisters. Ever since then he always wanted to have a little girl.

"I guess I got to call my moms and let her know," he said

as he got off the sofa. He picked up his cell phone from the hall table.

"She already knows."

"What the fuck! Everybody knows except me?"

"Let's see: Kenya knows, Pop knows, Tickman knows, uhm, Kim knows." I laughed.

"Oh, that's really fucked up. How the hell they all kept it a secret from me?"

"Baby, don't be mad. We all wanted it to be a surprise for you. We all know how much you wanted a baby girl." I got up and hugged him.

"I guess. But damn, my girl and my boy didn't even leak it to me. That's fucked up." He kissed me, then let me go and began walking upstairs. "I'm going to take a shower and go to bed. I have a lot to do tomorrow."

"Baby, let me ask you a question," I said. I was a little hesitant. Not sure if this was the right time. But if I wanted answers I had to ask questions.

"What's up?"

"Is there another woman or women you're seeing?" I looked at him seriously.

"What!?!" Big A.T. stopped midway up the stairs. He turned toward me.

"I mean if there is, I just want to know. I don't want to find out from reading the magazines or seeing the pictures of you with another woman at some event or party," I said. "We can work through this, because I know how these trifling young girls can be and I know it's not your fault. You're rich, powerful, and a celebrity. Many women will throw themselves at you. I know this comes with the territory."

"What the hell are you talking about!?! I don't even have time for myself. How the hell I'm going to be out there fucking some other woman? Damn, you women are always thinking a nigga *doing* something when he busy. But you know what? I'm going to let it slide. It's probably the pregnancy that's got you thinking some shit like that. I'm going to bed. You can sit down here and talk by yourself." He continued up the stairs, mumbling to himself.

"Well, I guess that's a no!" I yelled as he disappeared up the stairs.

I sat down and continued working on the seating chart for my baby shower.

# FORTY-ONE

BIG A.T.

I couldn't sleep that night. Jasmine's questioning kept me awake. This was my opportunity, my moment to tell her. I thought about it. Really I did. I tossed the idea around my head. How would I tell her? I would just be blunt. I wouldn't beat around the bush. Sit her down and tell her what the deal was. No more lying, hiding, or playing this house shit.

This was the perfect time. Right now. But I couldn't. I thought about what Tickman said. He was right: I hadn't really accepted myself. I sure as hell knew the world wouldn't be ready. And was I ready to throw my career away over it? Truthfully, I wasn't. I'd tasted success. I'd gotten used to my name being on records. Rappers and singers wanted me to produce their records. I was a name in this business.

*Soon, I'll tell Jasmine,* I promised myself. She deserved to know.

The next morning I had an eleven o'clock meeting at MTV to meet with Chris and his staff. We were going to discuss the details of Tickman's appearance. New York was buzzing about Tickman's album. All day long Hot 97 and Power 105 were pumping his single "What You Gonna Do?" Funkmaster Flex, DJ Clue, and DJ Envy couldn't get enough. We released the single early because it was leaked to the radio stations and had become the number-one-requested song.

I entered MTV's offices on Forty-fourth Street and Broadway. Just a few years ago I was standing outside dreaming of being in this building. Now, here I was on my way inside for a meeting with the head of programming, Chris, my boy, my family member.

Chris's assistant greeted me when I got to the twenty-fifth floor. She escorted me to the conference room. The room had a television monitor, stereo system, large projection screen, and a huge conference table that could seat at least thirty people. The table had a display of fresh fruit, orange juice, bagels, croissants, and sweet rolls. The conference room was decorated with images of Tickman and Change Up Records logos. There were posters and a life-size cardboard cutout of Tickman. I smiled to myself.

"What's up, Big A.T.," Chris said as he entered the conference room. We gave each other a pound.

"What's up, Dapper Dan," I said. "You are looking sharp and pimped out."

"What?" Chris smiled. "This ain't nothing, man." He did a turn on his heels in front of me. Chris was wearing a blue seersucker suit with a blue oxford shirt and an ivory Joseph Abboud tie. His dark, tusk-colored Salvatore Ferragamo shoes sparkled and shined. He looked more like the network's president than VP of programming.

"Hey, before everyone gets in here, just to let you know, I've got the whole network working and getting geared up for you and Tickman. I'm happy and proud of you. You're doing your thing and you know you have my support and the network's as well." Chris gave me another pound.

"Thanks, man," I said. "I really appreciate it. It definitely makes my job a lot easier knowing I can count on family to make things happen. Shit, I can imagine what somebody on the outside has got to go through." We smiled at each other.

"Hey, how's Jasmine and everything?" he asked as we took our seats at the conference table.

"She's good. The baby is due in three months, so she's taking it easy. Well, she's still shopping, but other than that, everything's cool. I'm just taking it one day at a time. You know what I mean?"

"Yeah, man, I know," Chris said.

"So when are you and Christine going to tie the knot?" I asked.

"Man, I'm trying to delay it as long as possible. And, well, I met this dude and we have been kicking it strong."

"What?" I was shocked. Chris didn't seem the like the type of dude to be strung out on a guy. "Who is he? You haven't told me or anybody in the crew. What's up with that?"

"You know me, man. I haven't been looking to settle with no one man, but this dude, he's cool." Chris leaned back his chair. Then he said, "It's Scott Jaredson."

"Word! The entertainment news broadcaster with *City Access*? Yeah, he is cool people. Every time he interviews me or sees me at an event he speaks. I didn't know he was family."

"Me either, man." Chris sat up in his chair. "One day I ran into him with his girl in SoHo, and he gave me his number and told me to give him a call. They were going to the Hamptons for the weekend and asked if Christine and I wanted to join them. I told him sure. When I called he told me his girlfriend wasn't able to go, but if I still wanted to come down with Christine it would be fine. Well, Christine was studying that weekend because she was getting ready to take the bar exam. I told him I was still interested in coming because I had not been in a while. To make a long story short, it was just Scott, me, some Hennessy, weed, and Ecstasy. That was the freakiest weekend I ever had with a man. Ever since we have been kicking it, and it's been working."

"Wow," I said.

Just then someone knocked on the door. It was one of Chris's staff. They were starting to arrive for the meeting. "We'll talk later," Chris said.

As everyone piled into the room they each acknowledged me and told me how much they enjoyed my music and were looking forward to working with me and Tickman. Chris started the meeting once everyone was in the room. "I want to thank you all for being committed to the Tickman project," Chris said. "We have the man behind it all, Big A.T. Please join me in giving him a big round of applause."

If I could have blushed, I would have. Here I was being acknowledged at MTV for my work, my music. The network had been supportive of my career from the beginning, when I'd worked with Shawty Mike and the other artists I produced.

"So, let's talk about the show *Breakout*," Chris said. "What are the plans for Tickman?"

A young blond girl stood up. "Well, we are planning on doing an exclusive interview with him in his Brooklyn neighborhood," she said. "We have been talking with his publicist, Tracey Chambers, and we agreed on this. We'll follow him to different places in his neighborhood, and then we'll do the interview in the home where he grew up."

"Sounds good," Chris said. He looked over at me.

"I like it, but make sure that posters of him, the album cover, as well as Change Up Records are in the background shots during the interview," I said.

"Got it," the young blond girl said and sat down.

"Okay, what about the video rotation?" Chris asked the director of programming.

A tall, skinny white guy with glasses and dirty blond hair stood up and in a collegiate voice said, "We are already running the video and we are planning to keep it in heavy rotation. Today it will be number one on *The Countdown*. And the video will run immediately following the *Breakout* interview."

"Good, good," Chris said. "Also make sure that it's played during the *Morning Mix*. I didn't see it this morning."

"I'll check on that, but it should have been in there," the white guy said.

I smiled and nodded my head. I liked the attention they were giving me and Tickman.

"Can someone dim the lights?" Chris asked. "I want to show Big A.T. the graphics of the Tickman promotion."

The young blond girl leapt from her seat and dashed over to the lights. When the lights dimmed a graphic image of Tickman's face appeared on the screen and then a microphone flashed onto the screen dancing to the beat of his single "What You Gonna Do?" The voice-over announcer said that a hundred lucky viewers could call in to a special 800 number and win a free autographed CD and free concert tickets. Callers had to watch throughout the day for special clues and the time to call in. They had to provide the correct clues in order to win. Then a spray paint can appeared on the screen and wrote out Tickman's name in graffiti letters.

"Wow! I like it a lot," I said. "How many times during the day will this run?"

"Currently it's slated to run seven times throughout the day. It will run once in the morning, twice in the afternoon, twice in the evening, and twice at night," the director of promotions said.

"Make it ten times," Chris said.

"All right, good," I said.

"We also have Tickman coming on *The Countdown* next weekend to talk about the album. And he's scheduled to perform that day," the producer of *The Countdown* mentioned.

"I'll come with him," I said.

"Oh, cool." The producer smiled.

"Does anyone else have anything to add or mention?" Chris asked. No one said anything. "Okay, this meeting is over, and thank you all again for your commitment to Tickman and Big A.T." Everyone exited the room except me and Chris.

"Man, I really appreciate all you're doing for us," I said.

"It's no problem—we family, man. I got your back and you got mine," Chris said. We gave each other a pound.

"Next time dinner is on me—just name the spot and date," I said.

"I'll keep it in mind," Chris said. "I got another meeting to get to. It's for Big Mike's diva singer, Cyn, and then on to another meeting for our annual awards show."

"Yeah, I got to run too. I'm meeting with Mark over at BET in an hour to see what they are going to do as well."

"Now, you know we got first priority," Chris said.

"I know, I know." I smiled. "But if they make a better offer, you know I got to do business."

"Nigga, you fuck up if you want to," Chris said, laughing, as we walked out of the conference room and to the elevator bank.

"You still got to fill me in on your man Scott Jaredson," I said, imitating Scott's broadcaster voice.

"See, there you go. That's why I didn't want to tell y'all." Chris laughed. Just then the elevator doors opened.

"Aight, man, I'll talk with you," I said, stepping into the elevator.

"Tell Mark I said what up, and let me know if you want Tickman to be on Scott's show. I can make it happen." The elevator doors closed as Chris continued laughing.

# FORTY-TWO

I stepped outside of MTV's offices and hopped into the back-seat of the black Mercedes sedan that MTV and BET had got for me. Soon as I got inside my cell phone rang.

"Yo, what up, fam? What's good with you?"

"What's up, Big Mike," I said. "I'm good, man. I just got out of this meeting with Chris and now I am going over to meet with Mark to talk about Tickman."

"Oh, aight, no doubt."

"Oh yeah, that kid from North Carolina, Southern Gent? I'm going to sign him," I said.

"Oh word?" Big Mike yelled.

"Yeah, he's nice and he can flow. I like his style. I know I can develop him and make him into a superstar."

"Nigga, you must have seen the dick or fucked him."

"See, there you go. I haven't fucked that kid. You know I'm straight on that with Tickman. But the kid is really nice and he's got the look. Plus he has tenacity and ambition."

"I've seen his tenacity and ambition." Big Mike laughed.

"You niggas always fucking over somebody in this industry. One day that shit is going to come back and bite you in the ass."

"Yeah, yeah, nigga, long as the nigga biting can suck some dick."

"And yeah, I did see the dick." I laughed. "That young boy got a big-ass country dick."

"I knew you seen it, nigga. Why you over there buggin'?"

"But I schooled him real quick. I'm not looking to sign somebody who everybody in the industry has already fucked."

"Anyway, nigga," Big Mike said. "Yo, man, remember when I told you the other day Cyn was looking to work with some new producers?"

"Yeah."

"Yo, she's looking to work with that nigga Odyssey."

The words stung my ears. My breathing increased. I began fidgeting with my watch. My face scowled. I hated hearing his name.

Odyssey.

He was the one man in the industry I did not get along with. He was the one man I knew was my enemy. Everybody has someone in life they do not like or get along with. For me it was Odyssey.

"Get the fuck out of here," I said, disgusted. "He doesn't do any original beats. He steals from everybody."

"Man, I've been trying to convince her to not work with him. I've given her other names to check out. There are some new producers I know out in Queens. But she's being a diva. She thinks Odyssey can do something for her like he did for that singer Rachel Blue."

"Watch your back," I said. "He is shady. Remember when he was running around telling everybody I stole beats from him?"

"You ain't got to tell me. I know, man," Big Mike said. "I just know once he hears you already got two cuts on the record he's going to try and pull some shit. Anyway, nigga, I just wanted to hit you up and tell about the drama I got going on."

"Aight, good-looking, and it's all good. I know you can handle it."

"You know me," Big Mike said.

The tension between me and Odyssey was well known in the industry. Odyssey always had a beef with somebody in the business. He felt like he never got his just due for being an underground rap legend. He gained a lot of street credibility because he was grimy and hard-core with his lyrics. There's always an audience who love those types of rappers. They feel they keep it real and gutter for them. They can relate to the experience of those who are out there hustling and grinding every day to keep food on the table and money in their pockets.

Early on when I started producing some local acts in the neighborhood, I met Odyssey. He wanted me to do some beats for him. Odyssey was already rapping in local clubs throughout Philly, D.C., New Jersey, and New York. We worked together for a couple of months. Then Odyssey tried to get the original tapes from me. I'd heard of him strong-arming other not-too-popular producers with his goons. Odyssey would tell them he was about to be signed to J Records, Def Jam, or Capitol Records. He always claimed the labels were in a bidding war over him. He offered the producers a couple of hundred dollars up front for their original tapes with the promise that once he got signed he would put them on and help launch their careers. If they didn't agree he brought his goons with him to rough them up and steal their music. Others believed him because they were desperate for money and needed to get put on. So, they sold their original tapes to him.

He tried strong-arming me but it didn't work. I told him I wasn't interested and kept my original tapes. I told Odyssey if he was still interested after he got signed, then we could continue working together. But I would never give up my original music to anyone. My father had taught me that important lesson—the real money came from producing, songwriting, and publishing, not being an artist.

Odyssey tried to confront and muscle me into giving up my tapes, but I wasn't intimidated. I had a few of my boys waiting for him when he showed up. Odyssey left without incident, but threatened he would get back at me.

Odyssey never signed with a major label. Instead he got

some up-front capital from some street hustlers he knew. With their investment he created his own label, Dreams. He was able to release his own albums, mainly from the original tapes he extorted, and created his own empire. He garnered a lot of fans and then the labels offered to sign him. He did a distribution deal with Warner Bros. Records and he just kept putting out his own albums, making lots of money.

Odyssey convinced some artists to leave their label and sign with him. Those that left made a lot of money, but soon found his business practices to be unscrupulous. Eventually, they'd leave Dreams.

Odyssey approached Tickman when he found out I signed him to Change Up Records. Odyssey and Tickman knew each other on the underground circuit. They often performed at the same club and on the same bill. Sometimes they would battle-rhyme against each other. Tickman told me about Odyssey trying to sign him and I went ballistic.

One night me and Odyssey had a brief altercation in a restaurant over the dirty dealings he was trying to do with Tickman. Members of both our entourages broke up the potential fight. After that, we avoided each other in public because there was already enough media-attention-diverting beefs among other artists and producers.

The black Mercedes sedan pulled in front of BET. It was an obscure structure and unnoticeable compared with MTV, where billboards of artists and the network's logo blared for attention in Times Square. BET had no pomp. Nor circumstance. They'd recently moved into this new location because they had outgrown their other location and had been purchased by MTV.

I noticed the movers bringing in various desks, chairs, and cabinets as I walked in. The receptionist immediately called Mark's office when she saw me step out of the elevator.

"Mr. Hartman will be right with you."

"Thank you," I said. I stood near the television monitors in the lobby. Shawty Mike's video was playing. I smiled. Shawty Mike was now one of the top rappers in the industry. *That's where it all started,* I thought.

"Big A.T.," Mark said as he came through the smoked double-glass doors.

"Mr. Hartman." I smiled and shook his hand.

"Thank you for coming over." Mark guided me through the doors to his office. "We are really excited about the things we have coming up for Change Up Records and Tickman."

"Well, I'm looking forward to hearing what you all have planned."

Once we were inside Mark's office he closed the door and we laughed. We gave each other some dap and a hug. When we were in public we didn't want to appear too familiar. You never knew who was watching. It was business and we wanted to keep it professional.

"Man, what's up with you?" Mark asked.

"No complaints. I'm good. Things are going very well for me actually," I said. Mark crossed behind his desk and I sat opposite him. "I got this new artist I'm about to sign, Southern Gent. This kid is hot. He's going to take the industry by storm. I'm excited about the baby, and Jasmine's going crazy with the baby shower."

"Yeah, I know. April got the invitation and RSVP'd, so we'll be seeing you this weekend. She's very excited. She got the baby something from Tiffany's." Mark smiled.

"Thanks, man. This baby shower is going to be out of control, but I'm excited."

"So who's this new artist you got, Southern Gent?" Mark asked.

"He was sent over by Big Mike, so you know he and James already ran game on him. But I set him straight about how I roll and what I am expecting from him. He's from North Carolina and he's got the look and the style. He's young, motivated, and fresh, something a lot of artists are missing."

"That's really good to hear," Mark said. "With Tickman opening up the doors to something fresh, and with what you're doing, the industry is changing and going in a new direction."

"What's going on over here, boss man?" I asked.

"Man, I'm just trying to make this operation work with our own new direction. We are getting a new lineup of shows, a whole new look for the network, and some fresh new faces. It's time we started doing things that make us competitive and edgy," Mark said.

"Now that's what I'm talking about."

"Well, what we got for Tickman is something new and different. We are planning on giving him the camera and letting him document his own travels and do his own interviews with other artists in the industry. This way the audience gets to see the point of view from the artist's eyes. Along with this, we are going to let him guest-host one of our new shows, *One Hour Power*. This show is going to let Tickman and other future guest artists talk about the power and motivation of their music."

"Now that's what I'm talking about." I smiled. "I like it."

"We're getting larger in our audience demographics. We need to start thinking of them and how to create programming to keep them returning to us."

"Man, I know what you're talking about. As I'm sitting here, I am thinking how I could create a show for the network. It could be a win-win situation for all of us."

"Do it!" Mark said. "You're right, it would be a win-win situation for all of us. This could be a tremendous boost in our ratings and advertising dollars, so I suggest you give it serious consideration. I'll even give you access to one of our executive producers to help you develop the show idea."

"That's what's up. I really appreciate it." I smiled. "Pop keeps telling me to expand and continue building the empire."

"He's right, and you know the family got your back." Mark winked and smiled.

"So with Tickman, I'll make sure he is available for you. We're going to the top with this, and he's going to be big."

"Hey, we're right here with you."

And the family was. They were there for everything I needed. With Pop's guidance, I was ready to build an empire in the business like no other. I was going to supersede Pop.

# FORTY-THREE

The baby shower was a whirlwind. It came. It conquered. It was everything Jasmine anticipated: hundreds of guests, celebrities, fun, and gifts.

A month after it was over, people were still talking about the baby shower. The media couldn't get enough of me. Our pictures were plastered throughout *People, Sister 2 Sister, Entertainment Weekly,* and *Us* magazines. *Essence* did an exclusive coverage of the event and a huge photo spread in the magazine.

Yes, I had turned into a media sensation. I found it odd and disturbing how people wanted to know where I was eating. Who I was working with. What I was wearing. Who I was partying with. My life had completely changed. I went from nobody to A-list celebrity.

I became so large it was impossible for me to go anywhere without being mobbed by fans wanting to touch me or get my autograph. My music was being played all over the country. On the radio there were at least three of my songs being played in heavy rotation at any given time. I was the "it" producer and was riding the wave.

With all the promotion, marketing, and publicity help from the family, Tickman's album, *This Is My Story,* debuted at number one on *Billboard.* It topped the charts for ten weeks. The album sold over four hundred thousand copies in the first week. His single "What You Gonna Do?" had gone platinum before the album dropped.

Tickman's career was on fire. He was traveling everywhere promoting the album. He was on MTV nearly every day and was the guest host on BET's *Video Countdown*. Then we got the announcement: Tickman had been nominated for four MTV awards. Yes, four. Best video, best new artist, best single, and best album. Needless to say I was elated beyond my wildest dreams. My dreams were unfolding right before my eyes.

We left for Los Angeles for the MTV Video Music Awards being held at the Kodak Theatre. It's the second-biggest night for music, second only to the Grammys.

The family went into overdrive working the machine and keeping the buzz going for Tickman. He was my greatest achievement to date and quite possibly the most successful act ever endorsed by the family. Pop was very happy and proud of me. He'd helped one of his own create an empire.

Thanks to the family, it was easy to gain access to magazines, newspapers, television, and radio entities. We worked together because we all wanted to see someone like us make it. We looked out for one another. Family took care of family. It was an unwritten code we had. Besides, there were other brothers in the industry who were up-and-coming. They were being mentored and trained by the seasoned brothers who had worked their way to the top.

The network was deep. So deep, in fact, many of us didn't really know who was a part of it. The network extended from assistants to CEOs. Who could keep count? Even those who were part of the family and didn't work in the entertainment industry seemed to want to make it happen for the one who got through. It was a bragging right. It made it possible for others to dream big and know they too could rise to the top.

Along with Tickman, I brought Kenya and Southern Gent with me to Los Angeles. Jasmine was unable to fly because the baby was due any day. Pop flew out earlier that week. He met up with us once we arrived.

After we arrived that morning, the limousine took us to the

Four Seasons Hotel in Beverly Hills. Tickman and I had separate rooms to keep our cover, but we had our own suite in the hotel on another floor under Kenya's name.

Tickman checked in and got the key to his room. I then checked in and got the key to my room. Once the bellman dropped off my bags I phoned Kenya and she brought me the key to the suite that was for me and Tickman.

I went upstairs to the suite and ordered a bottle of champagne. I wanted to celebrate with Tickman's nominations.

His day.

His rise.

His fame.

When he arrived at the suite the champagne had already been delivered.

"Oh, you looking to get the party started early," he said.

I laughed and popped open the bottle.

"Close your eyes," I said.

Tickman looked at me, confused. His eyes lowered and his brow furrowed. "What's up? What you up to?"

"Just close your eyes."

Once he closed his eyes I pulled out a black plush jewelry case from my Louis Vuitton duffel bag. "Okay, you can open them now." I handed him the case.

Tickman's eyes grew wide when he saw the diamond-encrusted bracelet and platinum chain inside. He immediately put them on and profiled in the bathroom mirror. He took off his shirt and stared at the diamonds glistening against his firm chest.

He turned and grabbed me. He kissed me deep.

Hard.

Long.

Passionate.

I became aroused.

"Thank you, baby," Tickman said. "This shit is sick!" He smiled.

"You deserve it. I want you to have the best."

"WOW!" He looked in the mirror again. "I'm rocking this shit tonight at the show."

"Well, you need to start getting ready," I said. "You got to pick up your date for the show. And you know how Cyn can be. The diva!" We laughed.

"Yeah. But she cool people around me. She don't pull that shit with me. I'm like, I know you got seven multi-platinum albums, and everybody caters to you, but I will put my foot in your ass."

"That's *all* you better be putting in her ass."

It was Tracey's brainstorm to have Tickman and Cyn hook up. She knew their relationship would draw a lot of press, thus catapulting their careers, as well as preventing any speculations of Tickman's sexuality from ever arising.

Cyn was totally down with the idea. She had been romantically linked to other singers, but never a rapper. She was enthusiastic to be on the arm of a "bad boy."

And Cyn knew about me and Tickman. "Uhm, I'm no fool," she told us when we met to devise the plan. "I've been in this industry since I was a child. I have met many men like you and Tickman. I have even dated a few down-low and gay artists. Honey, it's impossible to get around it in this business."

Now they are the hottest couple in the game. The media and their fans can't get enough of them.

But I know he's all mine. He's my man. My love.

Tickman walked toward me again. He kissed me. His tongue danced in my mouth.

Succulent.

Juicy.

Wet.

"Nobody got me but you," Tickman said.

"I know, but let's make sure the public keeps thinking you're with Cyn for now."

"But why Tracey had to put it out there that Cyn is some

good girl from a good background, and I got to be the thugged-out bad boy who is turning her out?"

"Don't take it personal. It just raises your profile. Think of all the interviews and interest you've gotten. Everybody wants to know how the two of you hooked up. How long you've been dating, and if it'll last. It's publicity, baby!"

"I guess. I just don't like it."

"It's only temporary," I said. "Well, I'm getting out of here. I got to make sure Pop, Kenya, and Southern Gent are ready. They are riding with me to the Kodak for the show."

"Aight. I'll see you there."

I'd decided to bring Southern Gent because I wanted him to see, hear, and feel the excitement and the electricity in the air. I wanted Southern Gent to want it so bad he could taste it. I knew after this experience Southern Gent would be hungrier than ever to have his career take off. I also decided against taking Southern Gent to any of the down-low parties happening after the show.

Yes, the family had a lot of parties lined up. A party was happening for us each night in private homes, clubs, and hotels throughout L.A. Taking Southern Gent was not a good idea. He would get eaten alive. He had not learned how to handle his good looks, nor had he learned when people were making passes at him. No matter where he went, either a woman or a man would flirt with him. Being from the South, he figured most people were being friendly. In New York, though, it was always a blatant attempt to pick him up.

So instead, I arranged for Kenya to take him to some of the after-parties being given by other record labels, magazines, and celebrities. Several singers and rappers had parties planned at local clubs. This was a great way for Southern Gent to be seen.

When we arrived at the Kodak Theatre there was a huge mob scene, lots of security, and paparazzi snapping photos and yelling, "Turn around. Over here." There were screaming fans reaching, stretching their hands toward us to be touched. And, of course, there were celebrities.

Southern Gent was mesmerized by everything. I saw a glaze in his eyes. When the fans saw me they went crazy. Girls contorted their bodies toward me, screaming. The cameras flashed nonstop. It seemed like everyone was yelling my name at the same time. I smiled and waved my hand and then I yelled, "What's up, L.A.!" The crowd went into a frenzy.

I laughed and walked down the red carpet, stopping occasionally to have pictures taken and talk to reporters. Pop, Kenya, and Southern Gent followed behind me. Pop received his fair share of attention too. He was a well-known figure in the industry. A legend. He smiled and waved to fans. Some photographers asked me and Pop to take a picture together. "Let's get the old school with the new school," they yelled.

Not too far behind me was Odyssey. He was always at an award show, event, or premiere. Anyplace that had cameras, Odyssey was there. This night one of his artists had been nominated for an award. Controversy followed Odyssey to these events. He'd do anything for attention: running up and down the red carpet, showing up with half-naked women, riding circus animals. Odyssey caused a ruckus everywhere he went. The paparazzi loved him because he was always stirring up something. Odyssey commented on everything regarding the industry as well as celebrities and their personal lives. He loved to go after me. He hated that I was more famous than him.

We glanced at each other on the red carpet. I knew something was going to happen. It was Odyssey. The cameras were rolling. People were watching. He had to do something. I felt the tension in my neck. I tensed and started fidgeting with my watch. Uncontrollably.

Out of the corner of my eye I saw Odyssey making his way toward me. Then I felt a few bodies behind me. When I turned I saw it was a few members of the family. The look on their faces was not happy. They were ready, waiting for something to go down. Fists were balled. Chests puffed.

Odyssey sidled up next to me. "Yo, what up, playboy," he said.

"It's a good day today," I said. "Let's keep it that way."

"It's all good," Odyssey said. "I see you came with your weak rhyming-ass artist."

"I see you came with yours as well." I smiled. The cameras snapped our pictures.

"Get closer!" the paparazzi screamed at us. They wanted to get pictures of us together because they knew how much we did not like each other. These pictures would sell for a nice bundle to the gossip magazines.

"Look, playa, when you're ready to be a real producer and stop being a fake-ass nigga, holla at me. I need a flunky to collect my shit." Odyssey smirked.

"Fuck you and your crew," I said. "You fake broke bitch-ass nigga."

"Look at the fucking faggot. He got balls now," Odyssey said and blew a kiss at me.

Odyssey then turned and shoved me, forcing me to stumble backwards. I regained my balance and threw a right uppercut at Odyssey's chin, followed by a left jab to his nose.

Crunch!

Pow!

I hit Odyssey so hard he fell to the ground. A loud collective gasp filled the air. Security rushed between us and pulled me away before anything further could happen. The paparazzi cameras fluttered nonstop.

Security rushed me, Pop, Kenya, and Southern Gent inside the Kodak Theatre. I turned around and saw Odyssey's crew helping him off the ground. Other guards rushed over and escorted them from the red carpet. Odyssey's white suit was red, soaked with blood. His nose busted. He pushed the guards' arms away. "Get the fuck off me!" he yelled. "I'm all right. Where the fuck that nigga at?" He pulled a handkerchief from his jacket and held it to his nose. His boys tried to bum-rush the building, but the police stopped them at the door.

"Man, we are glad you cold-cocked him," one police officer said to me. "He's been causing trouble since he got here. I wish it would have been me." He laughed. "Don't worry about anything. We got you." The police stayed close as we took our seats.

Me, Tickman, and his date, Cyn, were seated in the front row. Pop was six rows behind us. Kenya and Southern Gent were ten rows behind Pop.

The awards show started promptly at eight o'clock. Tickman's left leg started to bounce, knocking into me. I nudged him. "Everything's going to be all right," I said.

"I know. I just want to get it over with," he said.

As the night moved along, I noticed Tickman's nervousness returning. His palms were sweating. His forehead started to perspire. We were all anxious for him. We wanted him to win. It would be a big victory for all of us.

I kept reassuring him that no matter what, we were there to have fun. It was just an honor to be nominated. Tickman decided not to write an acceptance speech. He said he was going to wing it.

It was time to announce the nominees in the category of best video. Tickman was nominated along with Shawty Mike, Ms. Freeda, and Sunny D. As their names were announced, the camera displayed their smiling faces on the big screen. Fans screamed for each of them, but went crazy when they heard Shawty Mike's name. Then the presenter announced Shawty Mike's name for best video. Tickman smiled, but I could sense his disappointment in not hearing his name. I leaned over to him. "Everything is going to go well. We got three more categories."

After a few other categories it was time for best new artist. Again, as the presenter mentioned the names of the nominees, the fans went crazy. But this time they screamed loudest for Tickman.

Then the presenter ripped opened the envelope. "Tickman!" she screamed.

Tickman leapt from his seat. He leaned over and kissed Cyn on the cheek. I stood up and we embraced. It was an exciting moment. Then Tickman grabbed my arm and pulled me along with him onto the stage.

"Yo, what up, L.A.!" Tickman started. He had a huge smile on his face. He hoisted the award in the air. "Man, this is crazy. First and foremost, I got to give thanks to God for me being here. I want to thank my boy, boss, manager, Big A.T., and my label home, Change Up Records. Thanks for making this possible. Thanks to my moms and family back in Brooklyn. Yo! What up, BK! We did it!" he screamed. "Thank you to MTV for playing my video. Thanks to Chris Cherryman, Pop, Kenya, my publicist Tracey Chambers, and my beautiful date Cyn. To radio and DJs across the country who played my single. And, yo! I definitely want to give love to all the fans," he said as he pointed to the balcony. The audience screamed loudly. "This definitely couldn't have been possible without you, the fans."

Backstage, we embraced again. "I love you and I am proud of you," I whispered in his ear. The media coordinator came over and led us into the pressroom for interviews.

Tickman won twice that evening. He won for best new artist and for single of the year. He was thrilled to be on the stage again. It was a major accomplishment for a new artist to win such a big category. He was virtually a nobody a year ago, and now he was one of the biggest rappers in the game. He was riding high with his awards.

After the show ended, me, Tickman, Kenya, Pop, Southern Gent, and Cyn all went to MTV's after-party in the hangar of an airport in Santa Monica.

Once we made it to the party, everyone clamored to congratulate Tickman. He was the man of the hour. We partied and took lots of pictures for the magazines, newspapers, and online websites. We drank and celebrated all night long.

Free food and drinks were everywhere. Champagne, wine, beer, and every type of liquor were available. There were ample amounts of food at every table in the huge hangar. There was shrimp, lobster, crab, chicken, and fish, all prepared in various ways.

As the night began to fade, I noticed Southern Gent getting drunk. "Hey, Kenya, make sure Southern Gent makes it back to the hotel, alone and okay," I said. "I don't want to have any scandals or unexplained disappearances from an up-and-coming artist."

I had to protect Southern Gent. I kept a watchful eye over him. I didn't want his reputation to get tainted early, and I didn't want any questionable rumors or gossip floating around about him.

We split up. Kenya took Southern Gent back to the hotel. Pop, Tickman, and I had to go to the family gatherings. We had to make an appearance and thank our family members person-ally for all their help.

# FORTY-FOUR

I rode in the limousine with Tickman and Cyn back to the hotel. The plan was to drop off Cyn before we headed to the family party. When we arrived there were some paparazzi milling outside. It was perfect timing for Tickman. Pictures of him and Cyn arriving at the hotel together would look good for his image.

I instructed the limo driver to pull around to the back of the hotel as they exited the car. There was a back door where Tickman would exit once he took Cyn to her room. The front entrance of the hotel was shot, because the paparazzi would be suspicious of him taking Cyn inside, then leaving without her.

Fifteen minutes later Tickman burst through the hotel's back door and got back into the limo. I instructed the driver to take us to the parking garage. Once we were in the clear we climbed out of the limo and into our rented black Yukon SUV with tinted windows.

We hopped into the SUV and kissed like long-lost lovers. It was our first time alone since the awards show.

I started the SUV and pulled out of the parking garage. The paparazzi were still standing in front of the hotel. I turned in the opposite direction and headed toward the Hollywood Hills for the family gathering.

We touched, fondled, and kissed the entire ride. We couldn't keep our hands off each other. He rubbed the back of my head, sending chills down my spine. His fingers grazed my ear and the nape of my neck. Our fingers intertwined as I steered anxiously, wanting to get out of the car and ravish Tickman in the streets.

We both wanted to stay in the room, but we had to show our faces at the party. We were on the West Coast and the brothers wanted to congratulate us on our successes. Besides, we could catch up with our L.A. brothers, since we didn't make it here often.

I pulled the SUV into the long semicircular driveway of the Hollywood Hills home. We looked into each other's eyes. We were savoring the moment before we got out of the car. "I love you, man," Tickman said.

*Ring.*

*Ring.*

*Ring.*

I answered my BlackBerry.

"What's up?" I asked.

"It's time!" Jasmine said, breathing heavily into the phone. "It's time!"

"You sure? I mean is this it?" I moved away from Tickman.

"Yeah, this is it!" she panted. "Oh my gosh, this is it!"

"I'm on my way." I hung up the phone. I gripped the steering wheel. Staring straight into the darkness.

Tickman looked at me with concern. He placed his hand on my leg. "Is everything okay?" he asked.

"It's Jasmine." I started the engine and sped out of the driveway. "The baby's coming. I got to get back to New York."

# FORTY-FIVE

I didn't think I was going to make it back in time to witness the birth of my daughter as I rode the red-eye flight back to New York. When I arrived at the hospital the nurses rushed me into the delivery room. I was thrilled I made it on time. I didn't want to miss this moment. I had to be there.

This was my first child. Having a daughter was exactly what I wanted. After all the pushing, yelling, and screaming, Tiffany entered the world. Tiffany Nicole Tremble was born in New York City at Columbia Presbyterian Hospital. She weighed seven pounds and eight ounces. Jasmine was in labor for fourteen long, intense hours.

When I laid eyes on her, I cried. I was proud and happy to be a father. I held my little angel in my arms. She was the perfect gift from Heaven. Her golden brown skin was so pure and smooth. She was innocent and untainted, a bundle of love. I felt joy and happiness. I smiled and kissed my baby girl. She was my daughter.

After a few days in the hospital, we brought our baby girl home. Jasmine created a nursery for Tiffany next to our bedroom. Jasmine had moved in permanently. We lived together. Living as husband and wife.

Everything was ready for my daughter's arrival. Her room was painted in a soft pink pastel color. White cloud puffs were painted on the ceilings, with dark angel babies sitting on the clouds. Jasmine filled the closet with baby clothes. Nothing was too good for our daughter. The room was filled with stuffed animals, toys, bottles, and diapers. Everything needed for a baby, we had.

The dresser, crib, and diaper-changing station were specially designed by furniture designer Tres Mark. He designed many specialty items for celebrities and their children.

Each piece of furniture had Tiffany's initials engraved on them. The knobs on the dresser were solid brass. The hand-crafted crib had a specially designed bed with cashmere throws and pillows. We were ready. Prepared for Tiffany.

Having a baby in the house changed me. I was lighter, happier, and more patient. Nothing seemed pressing or important.

Music was my life, but having a hit song on the radio didn't matter as much to me as my little girl Tiffany did. I found joy and peace in the small things. Working hard meant something new to me. I worked to create a legacy for my daughter. I wanted her to never have to worry about anything. That's what mattered to me.

Time seemed to pass faster having a child. But six months after Tiffany came home there was something else important I needed to take care of.

# FORTY-SIX

## JASMINE

Oh my gosh! When Tiffany was born my life changed. Holding your own child in your arms is an out-of-body experience. She was so beautiful. And she looked just like Big A.T.

We were a family. The three of us. I was so happy.

I knew once Tiffany came Big A.T. would ask me to marry him.

He became a different man. He was so much happier. Easier to talk to. I saw love in his eyes.

I just waited for the day he would come home with a ring and get down on his knees. It was going to come. I felt it.

# FORTY-SEVEN

"Hey, man, I need you to meet me at Mr. Chow at seven for dinner," I said to Southern Gent. We often met at the restaurant to talk about Southern Gent's career and future.

It was crowded when we arrived. The maître d' immediately sat us. Tables were always available when celebrities arrived. We ordered a few appetizers and a bottle of champagne.

"So, how is everything?" I asked Southern Gent.

"I'm good," Southern Gent said. "I can't complain. Jus' workin' hard and goin' into da studio, learnin' as much as I can. I've been writin' and gettin' my rhymes tight."

"Good, good." I smiled. "The reason I asked you to dinner tonight is because I want to sign you to the label." I pulled a pen and contract from inside my blazer pocket. "I've been wanting to do this for a while now, but things got busy. I knew I wanted to sign you when I first heard you rhyme in the office, but I had to finish Tickman's album. That took off and then we started working hard to build him. Then the baby came. So, it's just been a busy time. I believe in you, Southern Gent, and I know I can help make you a superstar. You got that 'it' factor."

Southern Gent had a huge smile on his face. His eyes grew bright.

"Aw, man, dis is tight right here." He reached over to shake my hand. "Man, I get to be part of da label. Dis is unreal." Southern Gent picked up the pen and signed the contract. He was now an official recording artist for Change Up Records.

I filled our glasses. "To the next big artist to hit the industry," I said.

"Fo' sho'!" Southern Gent gulped down his champagne.

After making Southern Gent part of Change Up Records, I arranged for him to go home to North Carolina and celebrate with his family and friends. I gave him a two-week vacation, because when he returned he was going to be working hard in the studio on his first album.

# FORTY-EIGHT

When Southern Gent returned to New York he was hyped, excited, and ready. I arranged for Shawty Mike, Ms. Freeda, and Big Bad Mamma to do guest spots on his album. Tickman was going to introduce him to the world on a collaborated song. We planned to release a single to the public, then use the fanfare to bring out Southern Gent.

He was determined to work day and night on his album. He wanted to be a superstar. The fire in him was burning. I kept him amped. "Yeah! You're the number-one rapper now. Claim your spot. Take your spot. This is all you, baby!"

The first day in the studio was crazy. Southern Gent had so much energy we kept the music running. He rhymed nonstop. I didn't want to interrupt his flow. I wanted to capture the moment. We recorded everything he said just in case he may have forgotten something or there was something we could use later as a hook for a song.

Southern Gent's energy had the entire studio rocking. He was going to be bigger than I'd thought.

Tickman was scheduled to drop by the studio to lay down a few rhymes with Southern Gent, but first he had an all-important live interview on *The Wendy Williams Show* with the television vixen herself.

Wendy was a fan of Tickman's. Before the interview, she teased her audience every chance she got. "He's tall, dark, chocolate, and a sexy rapper," she cooed. "And he's coming to my show!"

Tracey worked overtime to get Tickman ready. He knew he could handle Wendy, but she was a barracuda. She asked off-the-wall questions that intimidated many celebrities. Some were afraid to go on her show. She would ask questions about their drug use, and even if they had prison or criminal offenses. She wanted to know who they slept with in the industry, or about any infidelities. Her most infamous questions were about a celebrity's sexual orientation. If she suspected someone were gay, bisexual, or on the down low she would say in a brassy feminine tone, "How you doin'?" It was her way of letting her audience know she suspected that person of hiding their sexuality.

Tickman wasn't worried about her probing into his sexual orientation. He did everything to cover up his relationship with me. Besides, he was linked to R&B diva Cyn. The media had printed the pictures of them hugging and kissing as they entered the hotel when they were in Los Angeles for MTV's Video Music Awards.

Before he went on Wendy's show Tickman sent a bouquet of flowers and a certificate for a full-body massage treatment, facial, manicure, and pedicure courtesy, of Bliss Day Spa. He also sent large Louis Vuitton and Gucci bags filled with shoes from Jimmy Choo and Christian Louboutin. Wendy loved shoes and handbags, especially one-of-a-kinds. These gestures were to soften her for the interview.

Once Tickman made it to the studio he sent me a text saying, "Damn, baby, I wish you were here."

"I am with you," I responded. "And, stop bouncing your leg."

"You know me all too well. Tune in. They are introducing me now."

I went into the studio's office and clicked on the television. There he was, sitting next to Wendy on the sofa. He had on a navy blue button-up sweater over a white T-shirt. Dark denim jeans and fresh blue and gray sneakers. He looked good.

Damn good.

"Thank you for being on my show," Wendy began. "I know you're very busy with so much happening for you right now. You really are a cutie," she said.

"Thank you." He smiled. "Yeah, I've been busy, but I made time to come see the Queen of Television." He laughed.

"Well, I got to say thank you for the lovely gifts you sent over. I love the bags and shoes. They are not even out in stores yet—how did you get your hands on them?" she asked.

"You're welcome. I had some help from a very beautiful woman. She helped me with picking out the bags and shoes. She figured you would love them."

"So may I assume this beautiful woman is Ms. Diva Cyn?"

"Yeah, you got it."

"Well, Cyn, girl, you've outdone yourself," Wendy said, pointing at the camera. "The shoes are fierce. I am loving the gifts. Thank you for helping your man pick them out. But Tickman, let me ask you, is she really the grand diva she is reported to be? Like, does she need specific flowers in her dressing room, specially made drinks for her tour, and have stores shut down just for her to shop?"

"Naw. See, you can't read everything and take it as truth," he said. "Cyn is mad cool. She's like a homegirl. She's down-to-earth and likes to have fun. People make her out to be the bad guy because she's a celebrity. She's not a diva at all."

"Oh, I see, so it's all just negative stuff that we should ignore?"

"I'm sure your audience is much smarter than that." The camera panned and showed the audience clapping to his response. "But it's hard not to believe something, because people read it in the papers and magazines. Like I said, she's my girl and I know she ain't like that."

"So you two are a couple?" she asked.

"We just hanging out and enjoying each other's company."

"So what are you saying? You guys are having sex or you're hanging out like friends and homies?"

Tickman laughed. "We cool. We like being with each other."

"I see," Wendy said. "I'll let my audience read between the lines. So do you think you two will get married?"

"Well, I don't think neither of us is thinking about marriage. We got a lot going on and so right now ain't really the time. I still got things I want to do so I'm not really focused on getting married yet."

"What about kids? Is she baby mama material for you?" Wendy asked.

"There you go." He laughed. "I ain't looking to have any kids right now either. Me and Cyn are just chilling. That's it, nothing more."

"You heard it here on *The Wendy Williams Show*," she said. "So, congratulations on your MTV awards. Were you surprised? Did you think you would win?"

"Thank you, thank you," he said. "Naw, I didn't think I was going to win. I mean I'm a new artist so I was just happy to be nominated and to be there. It was crazy that night. When they called my name I was shocked like everybody else."

"Yeah, I know because when the camera was on you I noticed the reaction on your face."

"Yeah, no doubt. I was like, Oh word! I didn't prepare anything because I really didn't think I was going to win. It was bananas."

"Well, it must be something nice to have. How are you handling all the success and everyone pulling at you, because you're from Brooklyn, the hood no less?"

"Yeah, it's crazy. I'm from Brooklyn. Yo, what up, BK," he said as he looked into the camera and smiled. "But yeah, things are happening fast. You don't get prepared for this. I just took off. Everyone kept telling me it would take a few years and not to expect much from the first album."

"Yeah, but you've gone platinum five times and when your album dropped it went straight to number one," she said. The audience clapped and cheered.

"I know, it's bugged. Like I said, I wasn't expecting for it to take off. I didn't think things were going to happen and move so fast. I've been on the road for the past year and a half. I ain't really had a chance to sit and enjoy it. I got to get back into the studio soon and start work on the next album."

"You're hot right now. They are saying you are the next big thing in Hip Hop."

"I'm just doing me," he said. "I just want to make music and give the fans something they can enjoy, naw mean?"

"I hear you," she said. "Now you are signed with Change Up Records with Big A.T. and he produced your album. What's it like working with him? I've heard he can be a slave driver in the studio," Wendy said.

"He's cool people. That's my man. He came back to BK and got me. He remembered me and was like, Yo, I want to sign you. That's love for real. A lot of kats forget about you, naw mean? Working with Big A.T. is the best experience any artist can have. He has a good work ethic, and a lot of producers really don't have that. He likes to be in the studio and he's about business. As an artist you got to be about making music, but also about your business. He teaches that in the studio, but you learn it by watching him. Besides, every producer got their own style of how they work, so you got to learn how to adapt to different personalities in this business."

"Now, what's up with the beef between him and Odyssey? Reportedly he knocked him out at the awards show. Does that affect you at all, since you are on his label? I mean do you have extra bodyguards with you?" Wendy asked.

"Yo, Wendy, I only got bodyguards at the shows because kats always going to try you. No matter who you are, some kats are just jealous and want what you got. I ain't got no beef with Odyssey, but dude stepped at Big A.T. and you see the end result. Big A.T. handled his. I don't know the details, but you know you got to be careful because people think you soft and you got to let 'em know. I know they are just two kats who don't necessarily get along. Everybody got somebody they don't get along with. We are all adults in this business. We got to learn to let some stuff stay in the streets and keep business in the office. It's crazy how kats be trying to act gangsta in this business. It's music and we all can make money in it, naw mean? And I ain't worried about no kat. I'm very well protected." He laughed.

"Now, what's the laugh for?" she asked. "Are you carrying something on you or is someone with you carrying something?"

"I'll just leave it at I'm protected." He smirked.

"Have you ever been arrested for hurting someone or on any drug charges?"

"I was in the system for a minute when I was younger. I was hustling . . . making money, you know, doing my thang. Got busted and did three years. I was real young."

"Wow, so you been in the joint! Is that what changed you?" she asked.

"I guess you can say that, but I was always rhyming. I just had time to sit down and write out a lot of my rhymes when I was locked up," he said.

"I'm sure you had lots of time," she joked. "With all the time you had you probably got a few albums written while you were there."

"Yeah, I got a few albums from being in there. That's a good thing, naw mean? I got a lot done so it's all good. I just hope the fans like it. This is for them."

"Well, unfortunately, we're almost out of time, but I have a few more questions before Tickman leaves," she said.

"I do have to get to the studio," he said. "I got to get to work." He laughed.

"We understand," she said. "But I have a pressing question for you." Tickman's leg began to bounce up and down. I knew he was nervous. I wondered if this was it. Was Wendy going to ask him if he had sex with another man?

"You are an attractive man and I am sure you get lots of people telling you that," she said. *Uh-oh, here it comes. She's about to ask him about having sex with men.*

"Tell us what women celebrities you've slept with or you want to sleep with," she said. "I am sure the Hollywood starlets are lining up for you. You're young, sexy, and good-looking. I am sure there are lots of women coming on to you."

"Naw, now you know I can't kiss and tell. Besides, growing up, females would go after my boys because they were light-skinned. I'm dark so I ain't get too much play, but, you know, it's all good now." He smiled.

"I'm sure it is all good now." She laughed. "Are you a boxers or briefs man?"

"Straight boxers—got to let it breathe." He laughed.

"And I'm sure it's hanging," she replied.

"There you go, Wendy," he said, still laughing.

"Well, ladies, he's young and virile but he's taken. Thank you so much, Tickman, for coming on my show," she said. "We'll be right back after the commercial break. And don't you dare move, because I got some juicy gossip for our hot topics discussion."

# FORTY-NINE

When Tickman arrived at the studio, I congratulated him on the interview. "You did really well."

"Could you tell I was nervous?"

"Of course." I laughed. "I saw your leg bouncing when she asked you the last question. You thought she was about to expose you." I laughed and punched him in the arm.

"Naw. I wasn't thinking about that." He laughed.

"The look on your face was classic! I thought you were about to pass out."

"Anyway. So where's your boy?" Tickman asked as he shoved past me. I was doubled over laughing.

"He's in the studio. Come on, we were waiting on you for the collabo."

Tickman and Southern Gent greeted each other with daps. Then they sat and listened to a few tracks. Their heads bobbed back and forth to the bass line beats. They started jotting down their lyrics. After thirty minutes they were ready.

"Come on!" Tickman yelled. "Let's do it. This is fire right here." Southern Gent smiled and ran into the booth. It was good to see them make a connection.

When they got into the booth they started flowing and vibing off each other. It was like they could finish each other's thought, read each other's mind. Their energy was infectious. Before we knew it we had been in the studio all night working. It felt good having them work together. I didn't want the night to end. I could feel we were making history together. Tickman was the newest sensation. Southern Gent was being prepped to be a mega-superstar as well. Change Up Records was the hottest label in town and I was riding high. Everything was happening and moving in a positive direction. Life was good. It was very good.

## FIFTY

Tickman was getting a lot of good press. The fans loved him. He was being courted by Hollywood for movies. General Motors even called me to pitch an "All-Rap Tour" with Tickman. They felt that sponsoring this tour would help them with a new audience of car buyers. They also wanted to show the world they were supporters of Hip Hop and wanted to promote its positive aspects.

I decided Tickman would go on tour with Shawty Mike, Ms. Freeda, and Big Bad Mamma. I also thought it would be a great idea for Southern Gent to go out for spot dates. He would be an opening act in some of the cities on the tour. This would help introduce him to the public and create a buzz on the street. He had already got a mention on MTV courtesy of Chris. The network featured Southern Gent on a segment about up-and-coming artists to look out for. They did a ten-minute interview with him.

The All-Rap Tour was being billed as one of the biggest and hottest concerts ever. There had not been a rap tour of this magnitude in a long time. The last big rap tour received negative press because of the many fights and arrests amongst concertgoers. This was not going to happen again. Not on my watch. I had a good name and good standing in the industry. None of my artists were gangsters or thugs.

All of the artists on the tour were interviewing with the media, announcing to everyone that this tour was going to be about unity and positivity. Part of the proceeds from ticket sales were being donated to youth organizations in the various cities of the tour. General Motors planned to do a car giveaway in each city, too.

Tickman was excited. He was headlining his first tour. Tickets were sold out in every city. Fans couldn't wait. Tickman, Shawty Mike, Ms. Freeda, and Big Bad Mamma were going to show the world just how powerful Hip Hop was.

We prepared for the tour for the next several months. I worked nonstop on Southern Gent's album. We dropped a single, "Da Hotness," featuring Tickman. Radio and nightclub DJs couldn't get enough of it. It was in constant rotation on the radio. "Da Hotness" introduced Southern Gent to the world. He had the most anticipated album since Tickman's.

Southern Gent was an enormous bundle of excitement. He bugged me constantly to hurry and get the album done because he wanted to do his promotional tour. He was eager to meet the world and let them know he was ready to be on top. Tracey prepped him for the interviews, television appearances, and magazine shoots.

Southern Gent now had a following. Bloggers were talking about him. AllHipHop.com. Gyant Unplugged. Straight From The A. YBF. Hello Beautiful. What's The T. Sandra Rose. Myra Panache. Media Outrage.

He loved when people noticed him on the street and asked for his autograph. Fans let him know they liked his slow country drawl. He was smitten with attention.

I spent a lot of time with Tickman before he left on tour. He'd recently purchased a home in a gated community in Saddle River, New Jersey, not too far from Pop. Too many people had discovered where he lived in Harlem. People started dropping by unannounced. Extended-family members began calling and asking for money. He wanted and needed his privacy.

The night before the tour we were lying in each other's arms of his California King–size bed. We made love twice that day.

I wanted to savor the moment, because Tickman would be on the road for eight months. I planned on visiting him on the road for a few of the dates.

"This is it, baby," I said. "You ready for this?"

"Baby, you know I was born for this." Tickman smiled.

"I know, but I just want you to make sure, and keep your crew in check. We can't afford any negative publicity for the label, and to your career," I said.

"I got them niggas under check. They know not to bring anything on my bus. I got it covered," Tickman said.

"Aight, I know you do. This is a major tour with some heavy hitters. Just do your thing and be mindful of things going on around you."

"I hear you, but don't worry about me. I'll be cool. This tour is going to be fire." Tickman leaned over and kissed me.

"Just stay out of trouble and keep the groupies back," I said.

"Now you bugging." Tickman laughed. "With all your boys out there with their eyes on me, I can't take a shit without them rushing back to tell you something. Besides, I don't need anybody else. I got you." Tickman reached for my dick and began massaging me.

That was all I needed. Touches from Tickman always stirred my body.

Whenever I saw Tickman or was near him, I became sexually aroused. The way he looked at me with those dark brown eyes made me feel good inside. And that night we made love again. And again.

And again.

## FIFTY-ONE

The General Motors All-Rap Tour began as a major success. By the fifth month there were no negative incidents or bad reports. Plus the money we donated to the charities in each city helped to maintain the tour's positive image. The press ate it up. They loved that the artists were in the neighborhoods, visiting communities hit hard by the recession. Tickman and Southern Gent visited schools and youth groups. It was all love. Good energy. A phenomenal tour. So far, an amazing event.

I decided to meet Tickman when the tour got to North Carolina. I brought Southern Gent along as a surprise opening act. I knew the fans in his home state would love the special treat. Unfortunately, a radio station leaked the news and it didn't stay a secret. Fans went crazy when they heard one of their own was part of the tour. North Carolina had produced a few rap celebrities, but none like Southern Gent. He was a rising superstar.

When Southern Gent hit the stage that night, the stadium erupted. Girls were screaming and crying, stretching their bodies toward the stage. Southern Gent tore off his T-shirt, showing his worked-out body, and the girls went wild, jumping up and down yelling his name.

For twenty minutes, Southern Gent rocked the house. When he exited the stage the audience chanted, *Southern Gent, Southern Gent, Southern Gent.*

Backstage it was hard to contain his energy. He jumped around, whooping and hollering. "You hear dat! Dey love me!" Southern Gent screamed.

"Yes, they do." I smiled. "Now, keep this energy up for the rest of the tour."

"You don't have to worry about dat. I'm ready!" Southern Gent wiped his lean muscular body with a white towel.

"All right. Well, enjoy it. We leave in the morning for New York to finish your album."

"Fo' sho'!" Southern Gent ran into the dressing room and put on another T-shirt. He came out with the biggest grin on his face.

Pure perfection.

So innocent.

So ready.

# FIFTY-TWO

Southern Gent's energy magnified when we got back to New York. In the studio, I saw his hunger. He rhymed with fire, his wordplay matching the beats I produced.

"I got mad skills/I get big bills/My flow so ill/Like Jesus Christ I lay hands to heal."

Yes, he had it. My newest sensation.

Pop was thrilled with him. "You've done well. That boy is going to be a superstar," he said, pointing his pinky finger at Southern Gent.

Yes. I'd done well.

"Let's grab something to eat at Tamarind," Pop said.

"Sure. Let me tell Southern Gent we'll be back." I pushed the Talk button on the sound board. "Yo, Southern Gent!" Startled, he turned and looked out from the booth. "Pop and I will be right back. We're going to grab something to eat. I'll bring you something back."

Southern Gent gave me the thumbs-up and turned back to his notepad. Pop and I left the studio, headed to one of my favorite Indian restaurants, Tamarind. This spot was it for me. Opulent décor. Upscale for an Indian restaurant. Chandelier lighting. Plush seating. Gold plate service. The food matched the setting.

Tasty.

Warm.

Kind to the mouth.

Once we were seated, the waiter took our orders. Drinks first. Pop got a glass of red wine. I ordered a Thai iced tea.

"So how is Tickman doing on his tour?" Pop asked.

"Good, good," I said. "He is having the time of his life."

"Wonderful. How are Jasmine and my goddaughter Tiffany?"

"Awww man, Pop, Tiffany is growing so fast. I love that little girl. She is my heart." I smiled. "Jasmine is doing well." I looked down. I put my hand on my watch. "I am going to tell her everything, Pop. I am going to do it after Tickman comes off tour."

"Why? Why are you going to tell her anything?" Pop looked agitated.

"I'm tired, Pop. Tired of lying. Deceiving her. We don't have sex anymore. I avoid going home at night because I can't do it anymore."

"Then just end it. Don't tell her anything."

"I got to be honest with her, Pop. I can deal with the consequences. Whatever they are."

"Your career? Us?"

I looked over at Pop and shook my head.

"Pop, this—" I tilted my head, looking past Pop. I saw Kenya and Southern Gent running into the restaurant. As they got closer to the table, I jumped from my chair. Kenya was crying hysterically. I rushed toward her. I grabbed her by the arms and looked into her eyes.

"What's wrong, Kenya!?!" She hugged me and tried to speak, but the only thing that came out was a loud shriek. The maître d' walked over. "Is everything okay?" he asked.

"No! Is there someplace we can be alone?" I asked.

He escorted us to a small room in the back of the restaurant, then brought napkins for Kenya and a glass of water.

"What's wrong, Kenya? Tell me what's wrong!?!" I yelled.

"Tickman was shot!" Kenya cried.

"Shot?! What? Where? When??!" I stammered, looking at her confused.

"He was shot and killed after his concert in Indiana."

My face dropped. My knees grew weak. I couldn't speak. The words hit me like a head-on collision. I couldn't believe what I'd heard. Finally I mustered the strength and asked, "Kenya, was Tickman killed or just shot?"

"He was killed. That's what he said."

"Who is 'he'!?!" I yelled.

"Shawty Mike. He was there with him when he was shot," Kenya said.

I refused to move. Tears fell from my eyes. I put my arm around Kenya. She leaned her head into my chest, crying hysterically. Pop sat stunned. Southern Gent paced back and forth, shaking his head in disbelief.

We immediately left the restaurant and piled into Pop's Range Rover. We drove to my house, which was not too far from the restaurant. On the way I called Shawty Mike.

"Man, I'm so sorry," Shawty Mike said. "I can't believe this shit."

"What happened?" I asked.

"Tickman was killed instantly. He was shot three times in the chest. At the end of the concert Tickman was leaving the stage with Cyn and the bodyguards. Backstage there were people all over the place—groupies, photographers, press people. There were some contestants who won backstage passes from the radio station. It was just too many people backstage. It was hard to tell who was with who. The police were trying to get everybody to clear out but it was too chaotic. There were some girls screaming and reaching for Tickman, trying to get his autograph. Then these three dudes came running through the crowd in black army fatigues. One of the bodyguards saw them and tried to shield Tickman. The dudes pulled out their pistols and just started shooting. People scattered and started running in all directions, trying to get out of the way. Tickman was trying to get Cyn out of the way. While he was running with Cyn one of the dudes just ran up on him and opened fire. He collapsed on the ground. Two police officers rushed the dude who shot Tickman and tackled him to the ground. The body-guards tried to resuscitate Tickman, but it was too late."

Shawty Mike also told me four other people had been killed. The police had arrested all three men and had them in custody. But none of them was talking.

# FIFTY-THREE

Once we got to the house, I immediately started making arrangements to get to Indianapolis. I was going to fly with Tickman's mother to identify the body. She called as we were driving. Hearing her cry stung my chest. My heart ached. The pit of my stomach was filled with her pain. I needed to regurgitate, but nothing came out.

Jasmine rushed through the door with Tiffany. "I heard the news while driving home," she said. "Is it true?"

"Yes. It's true," I said.

Jasmine threw her arms around me. I removed myself from her grip, reached over to my daughter, and kissed her on the forehead. "Take her upstairs to bed," I said to Jasmine. "I don't want her to see or hear what's happening."

Kenya turned on the television. All the networks were covering Tickman's death. Reporters were live at the scene asking concertgoers to recall the evening's events. When Jasmine returned from putting Tiffany to bed, she sat next to Kenya on the sofa, comforting her. Kenya could not stop crying. Neither could I. On the inside I screamed, wanting to be held by my love . . . my man.

Southern Gent was still in shock. He didn't say anything at the restaurant, in the car, or now, at the house. Pop called the crew. Chris, Big Mike, and James made their way to the house.

I spoke with the travel agent and we were able to get the last flight to Indianapolis. I asked Jasmine to stay home with

Tiffany and take care of things in my home office for me. Pop drove Southern Gent to the condo. The crew told me that whatever I needed, they were there for me.

Kenya and I took a car service to the airport. I arranged for a car to pick up Tickman's mother and take her to the airport to meet us.

I called Tracey and told her to create a press release for me and send it to the media: *I am in deep shock at this moment. Words cannot express the pain I am feeling. Tickman was more than an artist with Change Up Records. He was a friend, a brother. This untimely and devastating turn of events has truly affected all of us who knew and loved him.*

There wasn't much conversation on the plane. Kenya slept the majority of the time. She needed the rest. She hadn't stopped crying since the restaurant. Tickman's mother held on to her Bible. The look in her eyes was distant. She seemed transfixed, unable to comprehend what was going on. I stared out the window into the sky, crying silently, sporadically.

I could not believe I was on my way to see my love for the last time. I had never seen a dead body, let alone identify one. I knew it would be gut-wrenching to look at my lover lying underneath a sheet in a morgue. I thought of all the good times we shared together. I thought about the vacations and the surprise visits I made while Tickman was on tour.

I laughed to myself thinking about the food fight at the W Hotel in Miami. Tickman accidentally squirted some ketchup on my cream-colored shirt. Shocked, I threw some mustard on his face. We began throwing food at each other. There was ice cream, pastries, shrimp, mashed potatoes, steak, and all types of vegetables. We made a total mess of the room.

The plane descended into Indianapolis. I awakened Kenya. She gently grabbed my hand and held on to it. When we arrived at the police station the detectives and prosecutor assured us they would prosecute the men to the fullest extent of the law. They planned to charge the men with first-degree aggravated murder. It carried a mandatory life sentence in prison with no possibility of parole.

The police discovered that the men were retaliating for an altercation that occurred the night before. Shawty Mike and his crew were hanging out at one of the local clubs. One of Shawty Mike's boys approached the girlfriend of one of the men. He was flirting with her and trying to get her to come back to the hotel with him. Her boyfriend saw what was happening and confronted him. There was a brief hurling of insults and throwing of fists. The bouncers broke up the fight and threw the men out, but let Shawty Mike and his crew stay. The next day, the men were able to get backstage by using fake press credentials they'd received from a female associate at the radio station.

Tickman's mother leaned on me during the conversation with the detectives. I felt her grief rising out of her heart. I fought back the tears. I needed to be strong. For her. For me. For Tickman.

"I will be here in court every day if I need to be," Tickman's mother said. "I am going to make my presence known."

"Don't worry about a thing." I held her close. "I am going to make sure your travels and everything is taken care of. His estate will also be handled properly."

"Thank you." She hugged me tightly. "You are a good man. I know how much my son appreciated and loved what you did for him."

"I know he did," I said, holding her.

"We can make our way over to the morgue now," the detective said.

The word "morgue" slammed my ears. I couldn't comprehend it. I lifted Tickman's mother from her chair and we followed the detective out the door. Shawty Mike met up with us to identify the body. We arrived and walked down the steps into the basement of the building, and Tickman's mother began to weep again.

We entered the cold room. They wheeled Tickman's body

from behind a sheet of plastic curtains. My heart pounded. A lump formed in my throat. My palms watered.

The coroner pulled back the sheet. Tickman's mother leaned over and kissed him on the forehead and then on the cheek. She was trying to speak through her tears as she caressed his face. "Yes, this is my son, this is my baby."

Then she walked toward the door. I reached out and hugged her. She clung to me. She pulled out a worn piece of tissue from her purse and slowly walked up the stairs of the morgue.

Kenya and I walked over to the iron slab of steel holding Tickman's body. I needed to see my love. I needed to touch him one last time. Kenya didn't stay long in the room. As soon as she saw him lying motionless on the slate, she turned and ran out crying. Tickman was like a big brother to her. They'd shared lots of intimate talks. They would laugh and play-fight. She kept him in check when he was acting up on the road or doing something he knew he shouldn't.

Kenya loved him.

I stood staring at Tickman's body. The tears flowed like an open faucet. They fell onto the white sheet covering Tickman. I touched his hands. They were cold. Lifeless. His face appeared peaceful. He looked like he was in a deep sleep. I put my head on top of Tickman's. I gently kissed him.

"I'm so sorry," I cried. "I wish I was there with you. Things would have been different. This would not have happened."

I stroked his hand. Then his head. I leaned in and kissed him one more time. "I love you very much. No one will replace you." Then I turned and walked out of the room, sobbing uncontrollably.

# FIFTY-FOUR

Tickman's body was flown back to New York and the funeral services were held at Emmanuel Baptist Church in Brooklyn, the church he grew up in as a little boy.

The service was crowded with family, friends, and celebrities. The police secured the streets because of the large turnout of fans. It seemed like everyone in Brooklyn was out to show their support and love for one of their own. They were blasting his music on car stereos and at the local businesses. Some teenagers opened their apartment windows and put speakers in them and blasted Tickman's music.

Cyn was broken up over the tragedy. She entered the church leaning on Big Mike. Her body was draped on his like a tossed blanket. She wore a simple Versace black dress—well, simple for Cyn—a black hat, and black gloves. She even wore a veil and large Versace shades.

Big Mike carried her up to Tickman's casket at the front of the church. She wailed and threw her body across the casket. Big Mike tried prying her off but she refused to let go. I rushed to the front and helped Big Mike to remove her. She threw her body back with her hands in the air, went limp, and fainted.

I caught her before she hit the floor. A few ushers rushed over with church fans. One ran and got some water. We eventually sat her in the pew, where she wept uncontrollably.

She had grown to love Tickman. He told me they shared no

intimate moments together, but I think she was hopeful, very hopeful they would be together romantically.

The tall broad elderly minister marched into the pulpit in his black robe. "I watched Tickman grow from a little boy into a man," he said. "I remember him being active in the church and being helpful with the other young people. He was a leader with the youth ministry and was well liked by everyone he came in contact with." His voice cracked and he wiped a tear from his eye. "He was so talented, and a God-fearing young man. And his life was cut short." I heard sniffling and crying throughout the church. People yelled, "Preach!" and "Amen!"

"Young people have to learn how to settle their disagreements and grievances better," he shouted. "We are tired of hearing about young people killing and fighting one another. We got to be in our children's lives. We got to help the young folk. We got to do better as a community, society, and world." The church erupted. People yelled, screamed, and cried out loud.

I refused to let the tears fall. I shook my head and held my head back. Forcing anything wet to stay inside. I would not cry in public. I needed to be strong.

I needed Tickman.

# FIFTY-FIVE

After the service we prepared to go to the cemetery. "Hey, Jasmine," I said, turning to her as we walked out of the church. "Could you take Tiffany home? I don't want her to go to the cemetery."

"I was thinking the same thing," she said. "Why don't you come home. I know this is hard for you."

"I can't. I need to be here for his mother and for Tickman."

"Okay." Jasmine gently stroked my face.

"I'll be home later." I kissed her on the cheek. Then I kissed Tiffany on the forehead. "See you later, princess."

"See you later, Daddy."

I got into my car and drove alone to the cemetery. The preacher performed the last rites.

Said the final words.

It was over.

Done.

After the burial I got into my car and drove to Tickman's house. I wanted to be in his space, to feel his presence. I wanted to smell him. Hear his voice on the answering machine. I wanted to lie in the bed where we made love. I just wanted to hold on to something that would remind me of his love.

I arrived and sat in the car, staring at the house. I was hoping I would see him, or some movement in the house. I hoped Tickman would walk out the front door and tell me to hurry up and come inside. But after twenty minutes, nothing. No sign. No Tickman.

I finally pulled myself together and used my spare key to let myself in. The house looked just as Tickman had left it. There were clothes strewn throughout because he'd packed at the last minute. He was rushing to get to the city to run some errands. He had to get to Sean John, A.T. Wares, and Gucci showrooms, because they were giving him clothes to wear on his tour.

I walked through the house slowly, creeping. I didn't want to disturb anything. I let my body guide me. I was not thinking of where I was going but of where my body wanted to take me.

I climbed the stairs and glided toward the master bedroom. The room where we last made love. I just stood in the doorway. I looked around the room, taking it all in.

I entered and walked to the unmade California King–size bed and lay down. I stretched my arms as far as I could across the bed. I rolled over and sniffed the pillows. I wanted to catch a whiff of Tickman's scent, which lingered on the pillow and sheets.

I hugged and squeezed the pillow as if I was holding my man. I began to cry. Tears flowed, staining the pillows. I lay in the bed alone, wishing my love was with me. I thought about how I should have gone to Indiana. If only I had one more day . . . one more hour, minute, or second. I just wanted to see his face. Touch him. Hold him. Losing my first love was burning inside me like a raging fire.

I fell asleep in the bed and woke up the next morning. I went through the house reminiscing about the good times we'd shared. I reflected on the day I signed him to the label. I thought about the times we made love. I thought about the trips and dinners. Everything seemed like yesterday. His death was surreal.

I began to gather things of importance. Things I knew needed to be taken care of. Important papers, bills, and checks, anything to help his mother. I picked up a few pictures of me and Tickman. I planned to take them to my house. I wanted and needed Tickman around me.

I checked throughout the house to make sure I did not leave anything. I picked up a last picture on the mantel of me and Tickman together on the beach in Miami. I ran my fingers gently across the picture and put it in my black leather duffel bag. I walked to the door and turned back. I glanced around the house and closed the door.

I packed everything in my car and drove home. As I was driving I thought about how I would move on with my life; how things could take a turn without a moment's notice; how one day you could be here laughing and living and the next you're gone.

This was a moment in time I wished I could play back and start over. This was permanent. I had to deal with it. My life was changing. I had no alternative but to change with it. I just hoped the change would be for the better.

I reached into the black leather duffel bag sitting next to me on the passenger seat and pulled out the picture of me and Tickman. I placed it on the dashboard and smiled, "I love you and miss you," I said.

I turned on the radio. The DJ was expressing his sadness over Tickman's death. Then he played Tickman's "Too Much Too Little." It was a rap song about loving someone.

Tickman had dedicated the song to me after he recorded it.

# FIFTY-SIX

Tiffany was running around the house playing with her dolls. She was growing fast and starting to speak. She would grab or tap me and Jasmine and point to whatever she wanted or saw. She loved being around me. Her face lit up and she smiled wide whenever she saw me.

She ran toward me as she realized I'd come through the door. I picked her up and kissed her all over her face. She laughed and squealed, trying to get out of my arms. I walked into the kitchen carrying her. Jasmine was preparing a snack for her. She was making peanut butter and jelly sandwiches and was cutting them into small servings. There was an apple and banana on the plate as well.

"Hey," I said.

"Hey, where you been?" she asked. "I've been trying to call you but your cell phone just goes straight to voice mail. I figured you were at Pop's or in the studio."

"Naw, I went to go get some things from Tickman's house."

"Oh, what did you get?"

"Just a few things. Some pictures, CDs, and paperwork," I said.

"Are you hungry?" she asked as she walked over and kissed me. She gave Tiffany one of the small sandwiches.

"Naw, I'm good."

"How are you doing?" she asked.

"I'm all right."

"I'm talking about are you *really* all right?" She stopped what she was doing and looked at me with concern.

"I'll be cool," I said and put Tiffany down on the floor. "I got a lot to get done today." I walked out of the kitchen and headed upstairs to the bedroom. "I'm going to take a shower and then go to the office."

"You got to call Tracey. She's been calling about interviews the radio and press people want to do," she yelled as I disappeared up the steps.

When I got upstairs I took off my suit and walked into the bathroom. I stepped into the shower and let the water massage my body. The hot water was soothing to my tired muscles. I got out of the shower and wrapped a towel around my waist. I went to the bathroom sink and stared at myself in the mirror. I shook my head and picked up my toothbrush and brushed my teeth.

I brushed my hair and then put lotion on my body. I walked into the bedroom and sat on the bed. My cell phone was vibrating. I sighed. I wasn't ready to do a lot of talking. I wanted to be alone. But in this business there is no time to be alone. It's work, media, press, interviews, exposure, and more work.

I checked my voice mail messages. Everyone in the business was calling to express their condolences. I heard Tracey's message. The newspapers wanted to do an interview. The radio stations wanted me to come on the air and talk about the state of Hip Hop and the tragedy of Tickman being gunned down. They all wanted exclusive interviews—*Rickey Smiley Morning Show*, *Frank and Wanda* in Atlanta, Michael Baisden, and *Coco, Foolish, & Mr. Chase* in Detroit.

Pop called. He said he needed to talk with me as soon as possible.

I dressed in one of my A.T. Wares navy blue sweat suits and white Nike sneakers. I called Tracey and told her I would do the interview with radio personalities Angela Yee, Charlamagne

Tha God, and DJ Envy of the *Breakfast Club* on Power 105. They had a strong Hip Hop–listening audience. I knew going on their show I could make an impact in speaking to young people about violence. I also told her I would go on MTV and BET to do special interviews.

I wanted to do the interviews soon. I didn't want to waste any time. I needed to communicate to the world how much we needed to pray for the individuals who did this horrible thing, as well as to pray for Tickman's family and the other families who lost loved ones during the tragedy.

I finally made my way downstairs. Jasmine was cleaning up behind Tiffany. The television was on in the family room. The children's program *Dora the Explorer* was on. Tiffany loved watching that show. She was sitting on the floor in front of the TV attentively watching the program. I walked over and kissed her on the forehead. Then I walked over to Jasmine in the living room. She had a bundle of Tiffany's toys in her arms.

"Hey, I'm going to head over to the office."

"We haven't spent any time with you. Are you sure you're okay?" she asked.

"I'm cool. I just got a lot on my mind."

"I know, and I am here for you so please don't shut us out." She walked closer to me.

"I'm not going to shut you and Tiffany out. This is something I know I got to deal with and go through. I still got the label to run and Southern Gent's album needs to be put out. Things got to go on. I just need some time to regroup and focus. It's hard when everybody is asking me if I'm okay." I walked to the front door and then turned toward Jasmine. "Hell, this shit is hard. I got to be strong to get through this. I've been through a lot of shit, but never burying a friend."

"That's what I'm saying," she said and walked over to me. "You got to let us who love you be of some type of help to you."

"It's a lot right now," I said, holding the doorknob. "I got to do these interviews and send a message to these motherfuckers about staying positive and hopeful when all I'm thinking about is killing those niggas myself."

She reached out and hugged me. I hugged her back. Squeezing her closer to me. I needed the comfort of someone who loved me. I needed to feel a body. Any body. Jasmine was soft, sweet. Her body was warm.

She breathed when I did. I felt my heart beating on her face as it lay on my chest. I reached down and kissed her. I pressed hard against her lips. She pulled closer to me.

I needed to release. I wanted to do it with my love, Tickman. Jasmine was in my arms. I pushed her away from me. Then I grabbed her hand and led her upstairs. As we walked by the family room Jasmine looked over to check on Tiffany. She was still sitting on the floor watching television.

I thrust her against the wall in the bedroom. I ripped off her top and skirt. I snatched off her panties. I pulled off my sweat suit jacket and white T-shirt. I yanked down my sweatpants and underwear. I was fully erect. I wanted to enter her badly.

She moaned loudly when I pushed my dick into her. I was forceful. I wanted to fuck, not make love. She moved and groaned as I thrust harder and harder into her.

I thought of Tickman as I fucked her. I thought of how I wanted to be with him. I thought of how it felt each time we made love.

Jasmine was screaming.

I was rough with her. She scratched my back. I pushed my body and dick into her more and more. My body began to jerk as I reached my climax. I almost said Tickman's name through a moan.

I pulled out of her. My dick still hard. My sweatpants around my ankles.

Jasmine went into the bathroom. I lay on the bed. I closed my eyes. Jasmine left the bathroom and went downstairs.

Thirty minutes later I emerged downstairs fully dressed. I walked over to Jasmine and Tiffany. They both were in the family room watching television. I kissed them and told Jasmine I would be back later.

# FIFTY-SEVEN

When I arrived at the record label everyone was working diligently. They were prepping for Southern Gent's album release. Some office workers were still grieving because they had come to know Tickman very well. They'd worked closely with him, especially the publicity/marketing and promotions departments.

Tammy, my new assistant, came into my office when I arrived. Kenya had referred her after she was promoted to VP of A&R. Tammy was not Kenya, but I saw the potential in her. She was a go-getter.

She got me up-to-date on a few contracts I needed to look over and sign. The office was so busy she didn't have much time to spend with me, as her phone was continuously ringing. "Get Tracey on the phone," I said. "Find out when I am scheduled to make my appearances on television and radio. And tell Kenya to come to my office."

There was a gentle rapping on my door. It was Kenya. She slowly strolled into my office. Her hair tied in a bun. No makeup. She had on jeans and a fitted top. She looked worn out. Tired.

"Baby girl, take some time off," I said to her.

"I'm good."

"No you're not. I know how much Tickman meant to you. I need you to get some rest and grieve."

"Work is helping me," she said. "I need to be here. And on

that note, Southern Gent's album is on schedule. The sponsors of the promotional tour want to move ahead with him."

"Thank you, Kenya. I am glad you are on top of things. But please take at least a few days off."

"I will. Thanks, Big A.T."

Once Kenya left my office Tammy let me know she had Tracey on the line.

"Hey, Big A.T."

"Hey, Tracey."

"So this is what's on the agenda. First you go over to MTV and BET for exclusive interviews. Your last interview is with the *Breakfast Club* and radio personality Angela Yee later in the afternoon. You are doing a full hour on their show. Your talking points are what's next for the record label, how you're coping with Tickman's death, the state of Hip Hop and violence, and Southern Gent's album. Then you answer calls from the fans."

"Well, do I get to eat and shit?" I asked. We laughed. I needed to laugh. I needed to lighten the mood. Everyone was in go, go, go, go mode.

"I set up for the fashionistas to come and style you for your television appearances," Tracey continued. "I will meet you at MTV. Let me know if you need anything else."

"Thanks, Tracey. I really appreciate all of this."

"You're welcome. Anything for you, Big A.T."

I had to mentally prepare myself, because it was going to be a long day. Answering many of the same questions. Reliving moments and remembering my friend. My lover. I had to do this for the fans, and because I, too, loved music. I had to keep making music. Pouring my energy and creativity into it. This would help me remain sane. I didn't know what I would do if I didn't have music to focus on.

Just as I was about to leave, Southern Gent came into my office. Kenya had been working with him on a few underground-mix CDs. He was growing in popularity and was being asked to join other rappers and DJs on their mix tapes.

"Sup, boss man," Southern Gent said.

"Hey, what's going on?"

"I'm coolin'. I'm jus' checkin' in on ya."

"I'm all right."

"You ain't been to da studio so I came to see ya."

"I know Kenya got everything under control. What you need? You working on the mix tapes, right?" I asked.

"Yeah, dem joints gon' hit da streets like fire."

"That's what I'm talking about."

"But I wanted to let ya know dat you gon' get one hundred ten percent of Southern Gent. I ain't slowin' down and I'm goin' to keep Tickman's memory alive in da music. He was my boy and I know it's different but I know we can do dis way bigger dan he dreamed. I'm lookin' to keep his legacy alive and do what I can wit' da music, you feel me?"

"I hear you." I smiled. "I'm not going to let his legacy or music die. He was a big part of Hip Hop and as long as I can keep his music and lyrics on the street and in the world for everybody, I'm going to do that. I'm also one hundred percent behind your project. We are going to take you as far as you want to go."

"Man, I appreciate dat." Southern Gent smiled. "I know you got a lot to think about and on your plate right now so let me know if I can help or do anything."

I walked from behind my desk and toward Southern Gent. I gave him some brotherly dap and patted him on his back. "Thanks for that. I appreciate and thank you for being a man and coming to me. You are going to go far in this business—just don't let anybody take advantage of you and your kindness."

"You ain't got to worry 'bout dat," Southern Gent boasted. "I'm from da South, and a nigga got heart, naw mean?"

"Yeah, I know what you mean." I laughed. I put my hand on Southern Gent's shoulder and we walked out of the office.

# FIFTY-EIGHT

Everyone in New York and across the country was tuned in to my exclusive interviews on MTV and BET. They planned to rebroadcast my interview throughout the week. But the largest audience was the *Breakfast Club*'s show. It was emotional for me. I almost broke down and started crying on the air.

Sensing I was overcome with emotion, Angela went to a commercial break. She was good in being tactful on the air with her interviews.

Listeners called in and told me how much they loved my music. They gave their condolences and talked about how Tickman's music was so powerful lyrically and poetically.

After the radio interview I drove to Pop's house in New Jersey. While I was en route, Big Mike and James called. They wanted to get together for drinks.

"Yo, we got some new prospects we discovered." Big Mike laughed.

"Thanks but no thanks. I'm not really in the mood," I said.

"Well, then you got to hear this story. Yo, James, tell him about the dude you fucked in your office and then caught him going through your Rolodex."

They both were in hysterics.

"Hey, Big A.T., you know how Big Mike always find these little street kids who want to get in the game, right?"

"Oh, boy," I said.

"Well, he found this one kat at Cyn's album release party.

He was there taking photos. So Big Mike was like, I haven't seen you before. You a new photographer?"

"The kid was like, 'Yeah. This is my first gig.' Then Big Mike tells him he is head of A&R at Def Jam. The kid's face lit up. Now, you know what happened next, right? Big Mike put the smackdown on him. Had the young kid sucking his dick and fucked him bananas. The kid thought he had an in. Big Mike sent the kid to me telling him I could also get him a lot of gigs taking pictures.

"Man, dude sucked my dick like it was the last dick on earth." James laughed. "Then I bent him over my desk and fucked him right there in my office. It was insane!

"After I finished I told him to have a seat and I went to the bathroom. When I returned the kid was going through my Rolodex writing down names and numbers. I threw his ass out.

"Then his young stupid ass starts calling people telling them he and I are good friends. He tells them he's a photographer, so they start sending him free promotional items, tickets, and invites to parties. He didn't know we got this game sewn up tight. I saw him at a party and dude almost shitted on himself when he saw me. I went over to him and said, 'Look, dude, if I hear you calling any more of my people telling them you know me, I will whoop your ass. You hear me?' He nodded and I walked off."

Big Mike was hooting and hollering.

"Damn, that's fucked up," I said. "Who was he?"

"James, what was his name?" Big Mike asked.

"Shit, I don't know. Mr. Good-dick-sucker-with-the-fat-ass." They both cried out laughing.

"Man, I keep warning y'all you're going to learn one day about fucking over these dudes," I said. "Somebody is not going to take too kindly to being played and they will retaliate."

"Big A.T., what are they going to do? Out us?" Big Mike said. They both continued laughing.

"Well, I'm going to meet Pop. Let's get together later this week. I do want to hang out and have some fun."

"Aight, no doubt," James said. "We're here for you."

"Thanks, man. I appreciate it."

When I arrived at Pop's we stood in the foyer staring at each other. I had not seen him since the funeral. There was no movement, no words spoken.

After a few minutes Pop gave me a big hug. I lifted my arms and embraced him. When we released I was beginning to cry. Pop stepped back and then turned and headed toward the kitchen. He wasn't a real emotional type of guy. I'd never seen him cry or get sad. I wondered if he'd cried for Tickman.

Pop returned with two glasses of Hennessy on the rocks. I was sitting on the sofa with my head in my hands.

"You all right?" Pop asked, handing me one of the glasses.

"Yeah, I'll be fine . . . I just got a lot on my mind right now."

Pop just stood in front of me, staring. He didn't know what to say or do.

"How are you doing, man?" I asked.

"I'm hurting, but hey, I'm strong and been through this before."

"I thought I was ready to talk about it, but after today and doing all the interviews, I realize I still need time," I said.

"Whenever you're ready, just let me know," Pop said. "I need to change clothes. I've been wearing this suit all day and I need to relax. You need anything?"

"Naw, I'm cool."

Pop walked up the flight of stairs to his bedroom.

I rose from the sofa and went into the kitchen to find some food.

"Hey, Pop, I see you don't believe in buying food," I yelled to him upstairs.

"What?" Pop said.

"Food, man, food. What you got in the cupboards or hidden somewhere? Damn, people would starve over here."

"Look in the pantry by the refrigerator, there should be something in there," Pop yelled.

I searched through the pantry but found it nearly bare. There was a half-eaten bag of potato chips, a half jar of salsa, lots of canned soda, and a variety of cookies.

Pop descended from upstairs dressed in blue jeans, a tan pullover polo shirt, and brown suede slip-on shoes. He grabbed his keys off the table in the kitchen and walked over to where I was standing.

"You should have told me you were hungry—I would have ordered something and had it here by the time you arrived. We can go and get something from this nice little Spanish restaurant not too far from here," Pop said.

"That's cool," I said.

As we headed toward Pop's Mercedes, I thought how lucky I was to have him in my life.

We drove to the restaurant laughing and talking about the good old days and how Hip Hop had changed. "You know what, Pop?" I said. "Sometimes I don't understand all the bullshit and violence in Hip Hop. I mean sometimes you love it and it's your life, then at moments you hate it because of what some knuckleheads do to destroy the hard work many of us put into it."

"I feel you, and you know I've seen it all," Pop replied. "We just got to keep doing what we do and hopefully all this unnecessary violence will end."

Pop pulled into the parking lot of the Spanish restaurant. It was a hole in the wall. There were only a few tables and we were lucky to get one. By the smell of the food, I was shocked it wasn't crowded. My stomach growled as soon as the scent hit my nose.

A short portly Spanish man rushed over to me and Pop. He and Pop exchanged a few words. "You haven't come in a long time, my friend," the Spanish man said.

"I apologize," Pop said. "I have been busy. I promise to stop in more often." Then Pop introduced us. The portly man smiled and laughed, shaking his finger at me, "I know who you are."

He grabbed two menus and ushered us to a table in the back

of the restaurant. He snapped his fingers and one of the waiters rushed over, carrying a bottle of wine along with two glasses for the table. "The wine is on me," the Spanish man said.

"Thank you," Pop said.

Then the man spun on his heels and made his way to the kitchen, speaking in Spanish.

"Pop, you get around." I laughed.

"Hey, I still got it."

"Why haven't you settled down by now with someone, Pop? Do you get scared sometimes people will question the fact you don't have a woman, no kids, and live alone?"

"At my age, I don't have to worry about it anymore," Pop said. "To some I'm just a bachelor living a fruitful life. I have the life most men would want. No kids, no woman, and no drama."

"I feel you on that," I said. "It's a lot of pressure nowadays. I mean in this business so many people will question you over something little that has nothing to do with you."

"It's the nature of the beast. Back in the day nobody was thinking about who was gay, down-low, or bisexual. We were all having a good time and having fun. The business was much more exciting and the parties were off the hook," Pop said.

"I can imagine. I know you had your share of fun." I smiled at him.

"Man, my share, your share, and a whole lot of other people's share." He laughed. "But it is different today. That's why I'm so hard on you. I want to make sure you stay ahead in this game and don't let anyone or anything stop you. We need more of us in the boardrooms, in the big offices, owning companies, and running shit. Being black and gay, bisexual, and down-low, we got double jeopardy. Unfortunately, the world ain't ready for an openly gay black man in the entertainment business."

"That's why we got to build our connections bigger and stronger," I said. "The more of us we help out to get in this game, the more of us will be in control of this."

"We are doing it," Pop said. "We've been pretty successful. Look at you, me, Clip-O-Matic, K-Luv, Big Mike, Chris, James, and the rest of them. For a long time there were no black, gay or bisexual men in the entertainment business on corporate levels. Many of them only held positions in fashion, and as publicists. If an openly gay man said he wanted to be in marketing, promotions, or A&R, folks would question him, asking what does he know about marketing and promoting rap and Hip Hop music. They put gay men in a small box and think we can only do certain things like dress someone, decorate a video, put together special events, or handle the press. Then they think if we did marketing and promotions we would go after the gay audience and it would threaten the artist's image with them having such a huge gay following," Pop said. "Some executives question that we may not know how to seek out artists and get them signed to the label. They think we may go out and get gay artists and the label is not ready for that, and neither is the world."

"But white gay men get away with that shit," I said.

"Yeah, because they own everything and they work together," Pop replied. "We don't work together and we don't own shit."

"True that. I guess we will have to wait for the day when a celebrity black man does it for us, huh?" I said. I wanted to gauge Pop's reaction. He knew I wanted to tell Jasmine about me.

I was ready.

I was tired.

It was time.

"Yeah, but that will happen when hell freezes over," Pop said, looking from his menu at me.

# FIFTY-NINE

The next several months came like a whirlwind, and with it my label and my artist, Southern Gent, soared.

When his album dropped, it debuted at number one on the *Billboard* charts. The album sold over four hundred thousand copies in the first week. I couldn't believe it. He couldn't believe it. The response from the fans was truly overwhelming. The girls loved Southern Gent. Everywhere he went he got mobbed by hysterical and overly excited teens.

To capitalize on his moment, we coordinated the Southern Player Promotional Tour. We sent Southern Gent to Philadelphia, D.C., Charlotte, Atlanta, Detroit, Chicago, Houston, and Dallas, and his last stop was going to be in Los Angeles.

I made arrangements to fly out to L.A. to meet Southern Gent. His show was at the House of Blues and had sold out two nights in a row. I wanted to help him celebrate the end of the tour. He'd been on the road for six months. Although I got daily check-in reports, I really hadn't focused on him.

I was still missing Tickman. My mind was racing about telling Jasmine everything about me. So much time had passed. I convinced myself I was going to tell her when I returned from L.A. No more stalling. I had nothing to lose. I'd lost important people in my life, people I loved.

My father.

And my lover, Tickman.

I no longer gave a fuck.

It was time to do me. Be me. Live for me. And take the consequences, be they what they may.

Big Mike and James came with me. They were looking at some new acts to sign, and we decided to make a fun-in-the-sun trip. Mix business with pleasure. I needed to have some fun, loosen up, and get my groove back.

My mojo.

Since Tickman's death I'd been working myself nonstop. Kenya, Tracey, and Pop encouraged me to take a break. So, I did.

Jasmine was upset I didn't invite her along. She wanted to join me and bring Tiffany. "Let's have a family vacation," she said.

"Not this time. I am going to be doing a lot of work. Lots of meetings. And, it's a boys' week. I haven't been with the crew in a while. I need to hang out and just have some fun."

"What about me? What about us?" she asked. "I've been here with you and taking care of your child. Don't we deserve some time with you as a family?"

*Oh boy.*

*Here we go again.*

*She keeps calling us a family. WE ARE NOT A FAMILY!! I should just tell her now. I should just get it over with.*

"Look, when I return we can do a family vacation, wherever you want to go. Just let me have this week with the boys." I gave her a hug, pulling her closer to me, letting her feel my erect dick.

"Whatever!" She pushed away from me. "We *are* going somewhere when you get back. No excuses!"

"No excuses," I said.

# SIXTY

We arrived in L.A. ready to party. First we headed to Roscoe's House of Chicken and Waffles on Sunset Boulevard and Gower to get something to eat. This was a ritual whenever we went to the West Coast. We had to stop in for some fried chicken wings and buttery waffles.

Then we headed to Rodeo Drive in Beverly Hills. I had accounts at Armani, Prada, and Gucci. When I arrived the salespeople made sure to bring out their best and finest for me.

I got shoes.

Pants.

Shirts.

Suits.

Belts.

Sunglasses.

Damn, it felt good to be catered to. I hadn't shopped in a long time. I had everything sent to my hotel.

Later that evening we gathered at the home of a family member, actor Shawn Phillips, from the popular television series *Friends, Lovers, and Life.* His secluded house in the Hollywood Hills overlooked the entire city. In the backyard were a heated full-length swimming pool and a basketball court.

He and a few actor friends were playing basketball when we arrived. Southern Gent took off his shirt and got into the game. I sat on a pool chair next to the pool. Big Mike was at the bar in the corner next to the underground barbecue pit. He was talking with Durty Souf, a rapper from Texas. He was signed to Def Jam South.

James was on his cell phone setting up a booty call with a local guy he knew named Gary. He walked over to me with his hand over the mouth of his cell phone. "You want me to hook you up with someone? I can tell him to bring his boy Keith. He would be perfect for you."

I was reluctant. Unsure. Maybe I wasn't ready.

"Shawn knows him. He is good people," James said.

I still wasn't sure if I was ready to be with a man. Even if it was casual. I hadn't been with another man since Tickman died. But I trusted Shawn's judgment. He wouldn't invite anyone who couldn't be trusted to his home.

"Okay," I said to James.

James told Gary to come to Shawn's house at nine o'clock and to bring his friend Keith. By that time everyone would have left. It would be just me, James, and Shawn at the house.

Southern Gent, Big Mike, and Durty Souf were going to hang out and then head to the studio to listen to some of Durty Souf's music.

After everyone left, I was feeling a little nervous. I couldn't stop fidgeting with my watch. The anticipation was getting to me. I drank a few beers and had some shots with Shawn and James. I was trying to calm my nerves, but I kept thinking about Tickman. It felt as if I was cheating. The guilt was getting to me.

The doorbell rang at nine o'clock. It was Keith and Gary. They were on time.

Shawn went to the door and let them in. He brought them into the guest room, where me and James were sitting watching television and listening to some music.

They walked into the room and introduced themselves. We gave each other daps. I immediately noticed Keith. He was my flavor. Very attractive. We were about the same height, but he was slimmer and slightly bowlegged. He had a smooth walk. It was like he was moving in slow motion, gliding across the floor. He had a bald head and no facial hair. He looked younger than his thirty years.

I could tell that at one time he had been in a gang. The tattoos and scars on his arms and hands were remnants of a rough lifestyle.

Keith kept staring at me.

I wasn't sure if he was trying to figure out if he knew me or if he'd seen my picture in the magazines, on television, or on the Internet.

"I have to do some reading of a script. I'll be in the den." Shawn excused himself and walked out of the room.

James and Gary struck up a conversation.

"Come outside by the pool with me," I said to Keith. I was shocked by my own demand. I was forceful, as if I was talking with someone who worked for me. Keith followed me outside. We sat in the pool chairs.

It was quiet. The lights on the bottom of the pool illuminated the area only slightly. Around the backyard the tea candles' flames flickered and danced in the night air.

I admitted to myself that I was attracted to Keith. But I was still cautious. I wanted to find out where his head was. What was his conversation? I needed to know if I hooked up with him did I need to worry about any consequences afterwards.

"Sup, man?" I said.

"I'm chillin'. Sup wit' you?" Keith replied.

"I'm cooling."

"Yo, check it," Keith turned to me and said. "I know who you are and you ain't got to worry about me putting you on blast."

"Oh word?" I laughed.

"That's my word, player. Besides, I've been with some other kats in your industry, so it ain't nothing new to me. I got my own shit to keep low too." He smiled and winked.

"That's good to know. So, are you from out here?"

"Born and raised. I'm a Cali nigga for life," he boasted and smiled. "You from da East, right?"

"Yeah, man, Brooklyn."

"I never been out there. I definitely want to come but I'm always busy dealing with work and my girl."

I smiled to myself. I liked the fact Keith had a girl. He had something at stake. We were in the same situation.

"You got to get out there at least once. You'll definitely like it."

"Yeah, I know. I keep trying, but something always comes up."

Keith wiped his forehead with his hand. "You want something to drink?" he asked.

"Yeah."

Keith went to the bar. A few minutes later he came back with a tray of Heinekens, a bottle of Courvoisier, and two glasses with ice.

"Yo, man, I didn't know what to get you so I just grabbed a few options." He smiled.

"That's cool," I said, laughing.

I took one of the glasses and filled it with Courvoisier. Keith grabbed the other glass and followed suit. We took sips from our drinks. The liquor was a contrast from the slight cool breeze in the air. It burned and was strong. But, it felt good.

My body temperature rose. Maybe it was the liquor. Maybe it was Keith.

"It's really nice up here in the hills," Keith said.

"Yeah, and it's quiet. This is exactly what I need right now," I said.

"So what a nigga got to do to help you relax even more?" Keith asked.

I smiled. I felt an erection coming. "A rubdown would be good right now."

Without a word, Keith got up and stood over me. He pulled off his white T-shirt. His muscular chest was filled with tattoos. A charging panther was on his right pec. On his left was a biblical scripture written in cursive. His hard six-pack abs displayed the symbol "LA" right above his pelvis.

Keith bent over and unbuttoned my shirt.

"Turn over so I can massage your back," he said. I unlatched the pool chair from the upright position. It became flat like a bed.

I turned onto my bare stomach.

My dick hard.

My body hot.

Keith straddled me and began rubbing my back. When he touched me, I jerked. I had not been touched by any man since Tickman. But it felt good. I liked it.

Keith handed me my glass. I gulped down the liquor. It burned my throat, my chest, and my stomach. My dick got harder. He continued rubbing my back. My shoulders. My lower back.

With each touch I let out a slight moan. He squeezed gently and then harder to help relieve the tension I was holding.

Now Keith was trying to take all the built-up stress I was holding on to. And with each attempt I let out a moan.

Louder.

Louder.

Keith became more sensuous with each touch. He slowly moved down my back. My dick was throbbing. Then he stood in front of me and slid out of his jeans and boxers, revealing his large hard caramel-colored dick. "Turn over," he said.

He unfastened my belt and pulled off my pants. My Ralph Lauren boxer briefs concealed my hard dick. Keith massaged and squeezed it. He leaned in and kissed me. His lips were soft. Tasted like candied liquor. He played with my nipples with his tongue and then found his way back to my mouth.

Keith then sucked and licked me from my neck to my lower stomach.

It was good.

Real good.

Phenomenal.

Keith's tongue was exquisite.

His kisses were gentle.

Passionate.

I touched Keith's head with my hands and guided him to my dick. Keith pulled off my underwear.

My dick was free.

Piercing the air.

Keith put it in his mouth.

He licked and sucked it from the shaft to the tip of the head. I moaned. Grinding each time Keith swallowed me. I didn't want him to stop. And he didn't.

He stroked his own dick and worked his magical tongue and mouth on mines.

Faster.

He slurped.

Faster.

He slurped.

Faster.

He slurped.

Yes. Yes. Yes.

My eyes rolled into the back of my head.

I was coming. I was coming hard.

My body jerked.

My dick pulsated.

"Oh shit! I'm about to come," I moaned. My body twitched and jerked.

Keith opened his mouth wider and engulfed my dick as I released. He caught all of my juices as we climaxed together.

I lay back, breathing hard and heavy under the night sky.

I felt free.

Weightless.

I wanted more.

The blood rushed through my dick as I thought about Keith's warm mouth wrapped around my dick. I began stroking myself.

Keith climbed between my legs. He grabbed my dick in his hands. He stroked me.

"You want some more?" he asked.

"Yes. I want more," I said. This was exactly what I needed, and Keith happily obliged.

# SIXTY-ONE

Through the lens of my camera I peered over the tall wooden fence that separated A-list actor Shawn Phillip's home from the outside world.

This was it. I had it.

The money shot.

Damn, I couldn't believe it. Big A.T. The homo. The fag. I knew he was down with Big Mike and James. Those mother-fuckers played me. Fucked me and used me.

Now I am going to fuck you.

No grease.

No lube.

No condom.

FUCK YOU!

With the pictures I would be a household name. This was an exclusive. My blog would be known the world over. My name everywhere.

There isn't anything wrong with what I do. I get paid for my witty and unadulterated pictures of celebrities in uncom-promising positions. Most of my photos are seen all across the country in supermarket tabloids and on some of the most popu-lar television gossip shows: *E! City Access. TMZ.*

I rapidly snapped the pictures of Big A.T.'s outdoor Holly-wood romp. I couldn't contain my excitement. I was giddy with joy. I knew these pictures would be worth millions of dollars. I would be the only photographer in the world to have graphic photos of an entertainment mogul engaged in sexual relations with someone of the same sex.

This would be the biggest break of my career.

After shooting two rolls of film, I quickly went back to the photo lab. I worked feverishly developing the photos. I knew I had some damaging photos. This would take my career over the top. The notoriety I would receive for the pictures would last a lifetime.

Developing the photos only took a few hours. I stared at the pictures, studying Big A.T. What made him so special? What did he have I didn't?

I hated their crew. I hated what they did to me.

I was young and dumb when I met Big Mike. He promised me entrée into the game. He only used me. He and James. For six months they fucked me raw. Passing me back and forth.

My plan was to take them all down, one by one. But I wanted to knock over their King first. It was nothing personal toward Big A.T. I knew once he was crippled and taken out of the game, the rest would be easy. It only served them right for what they did to me.

Besides, I owed it to my blog readers. They needed to know the real deal about these celebrities. How they use and take advantage of people.

I grabbed a large manila envelope and black marker. I put a few pictures in the envelope and marked it *City Access.*

On another envelope I wrote Jasmine Bourdeaux and put several pictures inside. I rushed to FedEx. Filled out the form and paid the cashier.

"Excuse me, Mr. Craig Johnson, but you didn't check how you want it sent," the young girl said.

"Priority overnight." I grinned.

I held on to the envelope for *City Access.*

I had other plans.

# SIXTY-TWO

JASMINE

While Big A.T. was in L.A., I did a lot of shopping for the house. I'd decided to make over the sitting room and the two bathrooms.

It was a project I knew would keep me busy as well as hone my home decorating skills. After I'd watched all the successful home makeover shows on HGTV, it hit me. I had a flair for style and décor. I had finesse. I loved shopping.

So I redecorated Big A.T.'s home. It was so drab. A leather sofa with a plasma-screen television and entertainment system. How boring is that? Does every guy in America think having a leather sofa and huge TV and stereo is decorating?

I jazzed up the place. I got rid of the sofa and replaced it with a black Westminster Chesterfield sofa. On the ends I put Louis XV side tables. In the hallway I added a cherrywood Chinoiserie console. I repainted the walls with rich greens, blues, and suede Ralph Lauren colors.

In the bedroom I specially designed the headboard from oak wood with a primer finish. The sixteenth-century cuts and moldings complemented the headboard. I placed an ottoman at the foot of the bed. Added new gold satin drapes to the windows and gold trim around the baseboards of the room.

Not to mention what I did for Tiffany's room when she was born. Everything was handcrafted and designed by me. All my friends wanted me to do their children's room after they saw Tiffany's.

Yes, it was the perfect career. I would become an interior designer.

Besides, it would allow me the opportunity to have my own successes. I enjoyed the money and perks I got because of Big A.T. I could walk into any store off Fifth Avenue and they'd know my name. I got front-row seating at all the fashion shows. Versace. Betsey Johnson. Carolina Herrera. Gucci. My picture splashed throughout the magazines. They called me a style icon and I always made the best-dressed list. And of course, the premieres and red carpet events.

It was wonderful, but I needed something to do to keep myself busy. Something I could have of my own, then my mother couldn't say anything to me. Her constant nagging wore me out. "When you're going to marry Big A.T.? How come he hasn't proposed yet?" It was so much effort going to her house or talking with her on the phone. "He can leave you at any moment. Then what are you going to have? Tiffany is not insurance."

My good friend Kim always had something to say. "Girl, stop playing house with him. You need a ring on that finger. I know these industry niggas. They ain't shit." I often had to remind her that just because she was burned by them it did not mean I would be.

I was standing in the bathroom musing over what to do with the room. Should I repaint? Should I take out the tub and replace it? What about the sink?

*Buzz.*

The sound startled me.

I went to the wall next to the front door and pushed the intercom.

"Yes?"

"Hello, Ms. Bourdeaux," the doorman said. "There is a package here for you. Would you like for me to send it up?"

"Yes, please send it up."

I figured it must be the color swatches I requested.

The doorman brought up the package. I took the FedEx envelope and went into the living room.

I flipped it over and noticed there was no return mailing address. The sender's information only had the name "Craig Johnson."

I didn't know a Craig Johnson. I checked to make sure the package was for me. Yes, it had my name as the recipient.

I tore open the package. Inside were sealed manila envelopes. I opened them.

My mouth fell open. My hands were shaking. My heart dropped into my stomach. I was in shock.

"No. Hell no!!!" I screamed. I looked at the pictures in horror. "No, not you, no, my God no!" The pictures were too much to bear. They were of Big A.T. and a man kissing. Some were of the man sucking Big. A.T.'s dick. The others had them naked and embracing.

I dropped the envelope onto the floor. I fell on my knees next to the pictures. I was crying hysterically. "Nooooo!"

I sat there for a good ten minutes, unable to stop the pain I felt in my heart. Everything I gave Big A.T. was emptying through my tears. I couldn't move. Every time I looked at the pictures they made me want to vomit.

Then everything crashed my mind. It fell into my brain. Every thought, visual, and word Big A.T. ever said. Why he never asked me to marry him. Why he never said he loved me.

I thought of the long nights, he was in the studio with Tickman. Their so-called business trips together. The arguments I had with Tickman. How he looked at me with disgust whenever I was around. The gifts they gave to each other. All the things I chose to ignore.

My chest heaved. I was unable to catch my breath. I didn't move from the floor. I refused to. I reluctantly looked at the pictures again. I hated to see them. I hated Big A.T. I hated myself for being naïve.

Anger replaced my tears. My heart was no longer filled with

love. I wanted to destroy him. I wanted to hurt him the way he hurt me. I wanted him to feel the excruciating pain.

"He will never see Tiffany again!"

I put the pictures of Big A.T. and his boyfriend back into the envelope.

I called Kim. She had told me to be wary. She'd warned me about these industry men. But no, I didn't listen.

"Hey, girl! I am so fucking mad right now," I said.

"Uh-uh. What's wrong?" Kim asked.

"You won't believe this shit. Oh my gosh! I can't believe I was so stupid."

"What, girl? What is it?"

"Big A.T. is fucking gay!"

"What!?!"

"Girl, he is one of them down-low niggas. I got some photos in the mail today of him with another man kissing and sucking each other's dicks."

"Girl, no! Stop! I knew it was something wrong with him. I just couldn't put my finger on it. Who sent you the pictures?"

"Some guy named Craig Johnson."

"Who is he? Why did he send you the pictures? How did he get the pictures?"

"Girl, I don't know. I don't know him. Fuck all the questions."

"Damn, Jasmine. That is fucked up."

"Hell yeah it's fucked up."

"Big A.T. is still in L.A.?"

"Yeah. I can't wait for him to come home."

"Girl, you got to put him on blast! That is some fucked-up shit. I told you about these industry dudes. They ain't shit. If I was you I would sell the motherfucking pictures and get paid."

"Fuck some tabloid money. I want *his* money, *his* life, *his* soul! He has fucked with the wrong bitch now, fucking black-ass nigger, talking about he loves his daughter, fuck that shit!"

"Oh shit, girl!" Kim yelled. "You got to get an AIDS test."

"Oh my gosh—Kim! That motherfucker jeopardized me and

my daughter fucking with another man!" I was on a rampage now. I started throwing my clothes from the drawer and closet into my Louis Vuitton suitcase.

"You got to make him pay. He betrayed you. He lied to you," Kim said. "That whole crew he hangs with got to be down-low too. They all are fucking each other."

I felt as if I was the last idiot on earth and everyone knew about Big A.T. except me.

"That bitch Kenya knows. I know she does. She's his fucking confidante. His little angel that does no wrong!" I said, pacing the floor. "They will all pay."

"And I bet he and Tickman was fucking," Kim said. "They were a little too close for me. You noticed how he acted after Tickman died? I don't know any man who would be that emotional and distraught."

"Too bad that motherfucker Tickman is already dead, because I would kill his black ass myself!" Then I said, "Kim, girl, I got to go. I'm going to take Tiffany to my mother's. I got some things to prepare for Big A.T.'s ass when he gets home."

"I'm here for you, girl. We can both whoop his ass!"

I quickly packed two bags. I stuffed some of my clothes in one, and in the other I just threw whatever shoes could fit. I planned to come back for the rest of my things before Big A.T. came home.

I grabbed some of Tiffany's things and stuffed them into another suitcase. I frantically rushed to get Tiffany ready. I put some photos in my Christian Dior bag, picked up Tiffany, and stormed out of the house. I took her to my mother's house, where I'd keep her until I devised my plan.

He wanted to play fucking games. Then we were going to play.

I had to make that son of a bitch pay.

Oh yes, he would pay.

# SIXTY-THREE

Big A.T. arrived from L.A. two days later. When he entered the house I was sitting on the sofa flipping through the latest issue of *Essence* magazine. They featured an article on me and Big A.T. talking about our relationship, his music, and what it's like being involved with a music mogul.

I was seething, because the article was a lie. A bullshit, bald-faced lie. He lied about how happy he was. How I was the inspiration to his music-making. I wanted to jump up from the sofa and smack him with the magazine.

But I couldn't. I had to make everything appear normal. Not let on so early and easy.

"Hey, baby," he said and kissed me on the cheek. I damn near jerked my head away. But I caught myself.

"Hey. How was L.A.?" I asked. I crossed my legs. My foot started shaking furiously.

"It was cool. You know, the usual stuff. Got a lot of work done. Southern Gent's promotional tour ended. It was a great ending at the House of Blues." He walked to the other side of the room, to the bureau, where his laptop sat. He dropped his luggage and placed some papers near the computer and walked into the kitchen.

I held the magazine in front of me. I clenched my jaws and shook my head. I watched him out the corner of my eye.

While he was in the kitchen I pulled the photos from inside the magazine. I got up from the sofa and laid them on the dining room table. When Big A.T. walked out of the kitchen and passed the table, he stopped mid-motion. He did a double take and stood staring at the photos. He dropped his glass of apple juice. It crushed into pieces as it hit the floor. Juice splattered everywhere. His mouth fell open. His eyes bugged.

"What, what . . ." He couldn't speak.

"Surprise, honey—look what I came across," I sneered.

Big A.T. was in total shock. What could he say? What could he do? He grabbed the photos off the table. He looked at me, confused and dumbfounded.

I slowly walked toward him in my black Christian Louboutins. I cocked my right arm back as far as it would go and swung as hard as I could. I slapped the shit out of him. Then I hocked up as much spit as I could and spat in his face. "You fucking faggot!" I yelled.

My spit sprayed all over his face. His eyes, nose, mouth, and cheeks were covered in my fluids. He wiped his face with his hands. I turned to walk away but Big A.T. grabbed me by the arm and spun me around. My beaded necklace swung around my neck. He raised his hand to hit me but quickly put it down.

I snatched my arm away. "That's right, punk. You don't have the balls!" I spewed and gathered my things off the table. I reached into my Chanel bag and pulled out a legal envelope.

"This is for you. Read it, sign it, and I'll pick it up later." I turned from him and walked toward the door. "By the way, I have taken all my things and your daughter's things and moved into an apartment. I'll be in touch."

# SIXTY-FOUR

BIG A.T.

I was traumatized.

Speechless.

Motionless.

My entire life flashed before me. I was frozen. I didn't know whether to run after her or find out what was inside the envelope.

It was a good five minutes before I moved. I kept looking at the door, expecting Jasmine to walk back through it. I closed my eyes, hoping it was a dream. I kept them closed. The photos replayed in my mind at full speed.

Like a time warp.

I staggered to the sofa, staring at the envelope. I was so upset tears streamed down my face. My vision became blurred. I wiped my eyes and opened the envelope. Inside was a contract.

*The terms of this contract are NOT NEGOTIABLE!* it read.

Jasmine wanted 60 percent of my income and savings. Two of the several brownstones I owned and ownership of the building I'd recently purchased on Park Avenue. She demanded the convertible BMW and she wanted part ownership of Change Up Records.

Then, it read, my daughter Tiffany would only be allowed to visit when Jasmine felt like letting her. If I did not comply with the terms, she was going to take the photos to the newspapers, magazines, Internet, and television stations.

I had seventy-two hours to make a decision. I couldn't believe what I was reading.

Me. Big A.T. being blackmailed. This shit was not real . . . not real at all.

*Either give up my life to her or she will expose it to the world.*

Everything went through my mind. I should have told Jasmine sooner. Much sooner.

Like before I fucked her.

Got her pregnant.

Damn!!

I missed my daughter. I wanted to hold her and tell her everything would be all right. I wanted to call my mom. She would've told me everything would be okay. I just wanted someone to tell me everything was going to work out.

I thought about Tickman. My love. The love I lost. I needed him to hold and comfort me. I missed him tremendously. The pain of that loss was unbearable now.

The only thing to do was call my lawyer, Seth Goldstein, and explain everything to him. He would know what to do.

Seth explained my options. "Well, the unfortunate part is that she has the photos. So regardless of what the outcome is, they can still end up in someone's hands in the media." I hated that answer, but it was the truth. "On the other hand," Seth continued, "we can have her arrested for extortion and sue her for the photos. Which means this whole mess ends up publicized."

I was too numb to think.

"Well, whatever we decide, we have seventy-two hours to respond before she takes matters into her own hands," I said.

Seth took a deep breath. "I have another alternative," he said. "This would take a lot of thought and could change your life forever."

I listened intently. My heart raced, thumping in my chest. I started fidgeting with my watch.

"You can go public yourself. This way you would save the disgrace of embarrassment and take control of the situation."

Did I like Seth's alternative?

Hell naw!

The thought of going public was not an option for me.

I put my head in my hands. I wanted to throw the phone across the room. I wished none of it was happening. I wished I wasn't fighting for my life. I wanted it all to go away.

"Look, think about it and get back to me as soon as possible," Seth said. "In the meantime, I will work on having Jasmine arrested for extortion. I need for you to fax me that contract ASAP."

"Now that is a good idea," I said. I knew it would piss her off. At that point, I didn't care because *I* was pissed off. Besides, with Jasmine behind bars I had more time to decide on what I wanted to do.

"Jasmine can easily make bail, considering this is her first offense," Seth said. "But it's up to the judge to decide what the bail will be."

"Okay. Thanks, Seth, I appreciate everything. I'm faxing over the contract to your office now."

"Don't forget to let me know as soon as possible what you're going to do."

"I will."

I ran over to the fax machine. I dialed Seth's fax and put the paper on the machine. I watched my life transmit as I pondered the best solution. It didn't take me long. As much as I didn't like the choice, I knew what I had to do. I was taking my life into my own hands.

I would go public.

Despite what Pop said. Despite what Jasmine threatened. Despite the fact that everybody told me not to do it. It was time for me to think for myself, not follow others' thoughts.

I would tell the world I had sexual relations with men. There would be no need to explain Tickman. Bringing him up would do nothing. He was already dead. He would not have to bear the burden.

I picked up my cell phone. I wanted to call someone to talk about my choice. But who? I tried to call Pop, but he was on a flight back to New York from L.A.

Big Mike.

Naw.

James.

Naw.

My mom.

Naw. I wasn't ready to have the conversation with her yet.

I called my baby girl.

"Kenya?"

"Hey, what's up?"

"A lot. I need to talk with you."

"What's going on?"

"Jasmine found out about me," I said.

"Found out what?"

"Me having sex with guys."

"Oh my God, how did she find out?"

"She got some really explicit photos of me with this guy in L.A."

"Fuck!"

"Yeah, fuck."

"What do you need me to do?" she asked.

"Just be here for me."

"You know I got your back."

"Yeah, but there is something else." I didn't know how to say it.

"Uh-uh. What is it?"

"I have to go public with my sexuality."

"What? why?" she exclaimed.

"She threatened me if I did not comply with her contract."

"'Contract?' That fucking bitch!" Kenya screamed.

"Calm down. It's all right. I guess I had to do it at some point or another." I paused. "I guess it's that time."

"But this isn't fair." I heard Kenya crying.

"You're right, it's not fair, but who said life was."

Silence.

Kenya's cries settled.

"You know what, Kenya, I have trusted you with a lot. Right now I'm going to need you to take care of a *whole* lot of business for me. You're going to be my right and left hand."

"Anything you need, just let me know," she said.

"I'm going to make an official public announcement. I need for you and Tracey to set everything up for tomorrow morning. I want every media outlet there. ABC, NBC, CBS, TMZ, and the show *City Access*. I'll let Tracey know what's going on and the damage control she will need to do. Right now Seth is working on getting Jasmine arrested for extortion. This will give us some time."

"Got it," she said.

"Thanks. So now get to work, you have a lot to do," I said.

"Gotcha. And hey, I love you," she said.

"I love you too."

I smiled to myself, because I knew I could count on Kenya. She could handle business.

That's why I made her VP of A&R: I believed in her. All the training I put into her would now prove its worth. I was shaping and molding a Queen.

# SIXTY-FIVE

A lot happened within a five-hour span. Kenya and Tracey called. The media had been contacted for the breaking-news press conference. Everything was set up for tomorrow.

Seth informed me that Jasmine had been arrested an hour ago for extortion. Her bail was set at fifty thousand dollars. Seth let me know that Jasmine was being detained until the next morning. It was just enough time.

Kenya, Tracey, and I laughed and talked about what the world was in for.

"Lawd, I can't believe this," Tracey said, laughing. "In all my twenty years of doing publicity, this is a first. I've had to deal with shootings, baby mama drama, and sex tapes. This right here is definitely going to be on every media outlet."

"I know," I said. "I can't believe I am really going to go through with it."

"You are not going through it alone," Kenya said.

"Have you told Pop, or any of the rest of the crew?" Tracey asked.

"I haven't. I already know how they feel about it. They would not be happy."

"Well, you know once you come out the media is going to want to know who else is gay. The question is going to come up. How are you going to handle it? Are you going to out others? Are you going to protect them?"

"I'm not outing anyone else. This is about me."

"But you know anyone you associate with, people are going to assume they are gay as well," Kenya said.

"She's right, Big A.T.," Tracey said.

Silence.

I didn't know what to say.

Would the crew disown me?

Would I be blackballed?

I hadn't thought it through.

Shit.

What the fuck was I doing?

"You sure you really want to do this?" Tracey asked.

"I got to. I'll handle things and cross the bridge when I get there."

"It's been a long day. I think you should rest and sleep on this," Kenya said.

"I agree. We'll talk in the morning at the Ritz-Carlton," Tracey said.

"Yeah, I need some rest. I got to clear my head," I said. "See you ladies in the morning."

After I hung up the phone, I realized I had not eaten all day. I ordered some Chinese food. I went into the kitchen, opened a bottle of Moët, and I poured myself a glass.

I went upstairs to the bedroom to wait for my food. I went into the walk-in closet. I moved the pictured frame of me and Jasmine off the wall. Behind it was my safe-deposit box. I twisted the knob right, then left, then right again. I opened it and pulled out some photos of me and Tickman.

I looked at them with new meaning, with wonderment and excitement.

I sat on the floor next to a row of Ferragamo shoes. I gazed at the photos. Reliving that time . . . that moment with Tickman.

"Hey, babe, I guess you already know what's going on," I said out loud. "I know if you were here we would be walking through this on some real tight shit. It would be thorough.

Damn, I miss you." I felt tears forming in my eyes. "The fight in your spirit. Your conviction of standing up for yours. That's what I loved about you. We would be handling it together. Me and you."

I stroked the frame and then gently kissed the picture.

# SIXTY-SIX

JASMINE

"Jasmine Bourdeaux, your bail has been posted," the officer yelled.

I heard a loud click and the cell I was sitting in opened.

Oh . . . my . . . gosh! I thought I was going to die. I had never been arrested before in my life. I damn near ran down the officer as I rushed through the door.

I was in that tiny piss-smelling cell overnight. I think I vomited at least three times. They gave me some stale bologna on some hard-ass white bread and orange-looking cheese. I tossed it on the floor. I wasn't going to eat any jail food.

I know I looked a mess, too. I couldn't do my hair or makeup. No shower, so I know I was reeking of funk and jail.

The officer led me to the property room to collect my things. For a brief moment I thought Big A.T. had bailed me out. Then the thought quickly diminished as I stood in front of the caged office waiting for my belongings.

He was the reason I was in jail. I was fuming. My blood was boiling. Hot enough to cook a full meal.

I can't believe he had me locked up for extortion. I was driving to meet Kim when the police pulled me over for speeding. Then the officer came back and said there was a warrant out for my arrest. "Are you serious? I've never done anything," I said to the policeman.

"You are Jasmine Bourdeaux, correct?"

I stared at the officer, still confused. "Yes, I am."

"I'm sorry but I'm going to have to take you in."

I think I said every curse word known to man.

I waited for my Chanel bag, diamond rings, and tennis bracelet. The precinct was awfully quiet. It was not busy and noisy like a police station should be, especially in New York.

I noticed that everyone's attention was focused on the large television in the corner of the waiting area. There on the screen was Tracey Chambers. She was reading a statement about Big A. T. Everyone's eyes in the room were transfixed on the television. The words coming from Tracey's mouth held everyone in a trance.

"On behalf of my client, Big A. T., I am issuing his official video statement to the press and the Hip Hop community," she said.

Big A.T.'s face appeared on the screen. He looked nervous. I saw some perspiration on his forehead.

"For many years I have hid my sexual orientation from my fans, the public, and my family. While I was yet with a woman, Jasmine Bourdeaux, I had been involved in an intimate relationship with a man for a number of years. I can no longer keep this secret hidden. I am a gay man." There was a brief pause. Everyone in the precinct gasped. I was mortified.

"Shhh, hush!" someone yelled.

"I make this announcement because I have been withholding this secret for many years and it has kept me in turmoil. I pray my fans and those who love Hip Hop will continue to support me and the many men and women who struggle and hide their sexuality on a day-to-day basis. I would like to express I am a man first and foremost. With whom I sleep should not be anyone's business. I am confident I have full support from many of you. Again, I pray my fans will continue to support not only me, but Hip Hop, which is about unity and empowerment."

The video ended and Tracey thanked the press for their time, then stated she would not be taking any questions.

I was stunned. I couldn't believe what I was seeing or hearing. "That motherfucking bastard," I said under my breath.

After I signed for my things I turned, and all eyes were on me. Every policeman standing in the station watched as I put on my Chanel shades and made my way to the front door.

Then I heard a husky raspy voice.

"Hello, Ms. Bourdeaux," the man said.

Startled, I turned and looked curiously at the short stocky man with large full lips. At his wide, forced and crooked smile.

"Hello, Odyssey, what are you doing here?"

"I am here to help a friend in need."

"Oh," I said.

"By the way, I'm sorry to hear about your friend, Big A.T."

"Ex-friend," I practically screamed.

"I see. Is there anywhere you need a lift to?" he asked.

"No. I mean someone just posted my bail and I will have a ride. Thanks anyhow." I turned and began walking again.

"No problem—that is . . . to your bail being paid."

I spun around with my head cocked to the side. "You?" I said and pointed at him.

"Yes, and no need to say anything further." He approached me with that crooked smile. "Let's get out of here. I fucking hate policemen."

Odyssey put his arm around me and ushered me through the station. Close by were an entourage of very large men who looked like bouncers at nightclubs. They surrounded me and Odyssey and led us out the door.

As we exited the station, the paparazzi were everywhere. Their cameras flashed. I shielded my face with my hand and put my head down. I heard the news media yelling and screaming for me to respond to Big A.T.'s statement.

Odyssey's bodyguards pushed through the chaos. A reporter from TMZ shoved his camera toward my face. One of the bodyguards pushed him away.

Another reporter thrust his microphone near my mouth.

"Ms. Bourdeaux, does this come as a shock to you? Reportedly you are the mother of his child," the reporter asked.

One of the bodyguards was about to grab the microphone until he looked at Odyssey, who nodded at the policemen, then back at the bodyguard.

We quickly entered the black Mercedes sedan with tinted windows. Once inside, Odyssey asked if there was anything I wanted to say to the reporters. "I'm not ready to speak with anyone at this time." He grabbed my hand and squeezed it.

Odyssey stepped out of the car and everyone became silent. "At this time, Ms. Bourdeaux is declining to comment until further notice. However, I would like to state that Big A.T.'s announcement is a betrayal to Hip Hop and his fans. He has deceived those fans and the woman who gave her life and love to him. Everyone should be utterly disappointed. I have nothing further to say, except that I wish Big A.T. the best in his future endeavors." As the camera flashes started again, and everyone yelled and screamed, Odyssey stepped back into the car and we pulled off through the swelling crowd.

# SIXTY-SEVEN

Odyssey stroked and caressed my hand during the ride. "Everything is going to be okay," he said.

He provided the right comfort. I felt betrayed and used. I needed to be told it would be okay. I needed someone to save the day.

While the Mercedes drove through the city, I told Odyssey I needed to get to my daughter. "She is in Westchester with my mother."

"No problem," he said. I provided Odyssey with the address and he instructed the driver to take us to Westchester.

When we arrived at my mother's home, Tiffany ran to the door. "Mommy! Mommy!" she yelled. I ran and scooped her up into my arms. I was so delighted to see my daughter. It was the first time we'd ever been separated.

"Daddy, Daddy, where's Daddy?" Tiffany cried.

"Daddy's not here, but I am. Oh, I missed you, baby." I hugged and kissed her.

"Well, well, well." My mother walked into the living room dressed as if she was going to a cocktail party, her hair teased and draping her neck. "You know, I am not a babysitter."

"Please. Not right now, Mother," I said. I'd refused to call my mother when I was arrested. I didn't want to hear her mouth. But she started anyway.

"You didn't want a doctor or lawyer, did you? You wanted to

hang with the hooligans. The thugs and gangsters," she sneered. "Well, look where it got you."

"Enough, Mother. I didn't come here to hear that. Could you please be on my side for once?"

"I raised you better than that, Jasmine. What happened? What did I do wrong?"

"Nothing, Mother. You did nothing wrong. I am my own woman. I can make my own decisions."

"Oh really? So you decided to go to jail?"

I shot my mother an evil stare. "Not in front of my daughter."

"Well, let's hope she learns from your mistakes so *she* won't end up in jail." My mother peered through the window. "Who is that in my driveway? Another one of those thug rappers?"

I grabbed Tiffany's clothes and backpack. I was rushing, trying to get out of my mother's house. "Come on, Tiffany. Let's go. Give Grandma a kiss."

Tiffany ran and leapt into my mother's arms and kissed her on the cheek. "See you, Nana."

She ran back and I clutched her hand in mine. "I'll call you later, Mother."

I was visibly upset when I returned to the car with Tiffany. My hands were shaking. I was breathing hard.

"Are you okay?" Odyssey asked.

"I'm fine. We can leave."

"Where do you want me to take you?"

I didn't respond. I was still furious with my mother's comments.

"Jasmine?" Odyssey said. "Where do you want me to take you?" he repeated.

"I'm sorry." I stared out the window. *Why can't I please her? Why does she hate me? Why is this happening to me?* I wanted to cry. I was about to break down.

"Listen, you are more than welcome to come to my home and spend some time," Odyssey said. "I have more than enough room. Besides, let me be a friend and take care of you."

"Yes. That will be fine," I said. I liked that idea.

Odyssey told the driver to head to his home on Long Island.

I was tired. I did not get much rest in jail. I refused to lay my head on that filthy mattress. The thought of the many people who'd slept on it was a turnoff.

I held Tiffany in my lap and rested my eyes, trying to catch a moment of sleep. The ride to Odyssey's house was quiet except for the brief moments he talked on the phone with his artists.

The Mercedes pulled through the large black metal gates leading up the winding road to his mini-mansion. At the end of the road his record label's name, "Dreams," was paved in the ground in black letters. In front of the house were several luxury cars, a few men were standing alongside them.

When we stepped out of the car, I thought I was in a dream. I felt like an African queen returning to her beautiful home with the servants ready to serve.

Odyssey escorted me into the house and my eyes lit up like a small star flickering in the sky. The house was immaculately clean. On the walls were oil paintings by Monet and Georgia O'Keeffe. Statues and ornaments were meticulously placed around the room. After I'd surveyed the entrance, an elderly dark stout woman hobbled over to us, her smile crooked like Odyssey's. He kissed her on the cheek and whispered something in her ear, he then turned to me.

"Jasmine, this is my mother, Coral."

I extended my hand. "Pleased to meet you, Coral." The woman opened her wide fleshy arms. "Oh, chile, give ole mother Coral a hug."

I smiled and embraced her.

"And who is this pretty little thing?" She reached her hand out.

"This is my daughter, Tiffany. Say hello, Tiffany."

"Hello," Tiffany said.

"Well, aren't you the prettiest little thing?" Coral said, patting Tiffany on the head. "Come on, you two. I'll show you where the guest room is so you can freshen up. And I'll put something on the stove so you can eat," she said with her crooked smile.

"Thank you," I said. Tiffany and I followed Coral up the stairs. Then I turned and said to Odyssey, "Thank you, too."

Odyssey stood at the bottom of the steps gazing at me as I ascended the spiral steps.

PRESENT DAY
THE STORY CONTINUES . . .

# SIXTY-EIGHT

The plane descends into the Las Américas International Airport in Santo Domingo, Dominican Republic. After three and a half hours in the air, I was bracing myself for reality.

My phone will be ringing off the hook. The media will be replaying the press conference on television.

There is one thing I want to do. I need to find out how my daughter is doing. I have to speak with Tiffany. I want to hear her sweet beautiful voice. I want to know if she is okay. I hate that I am going to miss out on coming home from a long trip and having my little girl run and leap into my arms.

I bring her a present every time I return. Each gift is a token of my love from the city I've just visited. Maybe when she's older she can visit those same cities and reminisce about the gifts I gave her. When I went to Philadelphia I brought back a crystal glass bell. Tiffany would ring that bell all night long. She loved it.

She would say, "Daddy, it makes a pretty sound, see?" and she would ring it for me.

I hear the bell.

It's distinct.

Then it gets louder.

Louder.

It's my cell phone. I anxiously pull it from my jacket pocket.

"Jasmine?"

"Hello, Big A.T."

Silence.

I don't know what to say next. I hear the agitation in her voice. She'd spat my name when she said it.

"Where's Tiffany?" I ask.

"She's here with me."

"Where are you? How is my daughter?"

"Hold on, Mister Confessional. I see you decided to handle things your way. Well, things are going to go my way now."

"What are you talking about?"

"You know what the fuck I'm talking about—that shit you pulled. You decided you'd get the upper hand and go public with your sad-ass forgiveness speech. Well, it doesn't work here. That shit does not work here! And then to top it all off you have me arrested for extortion. Oh, that's a good one. This is not over, do you hear me!"

"Jasmine, calm the fuck down," I say. I try to remain calm because I don't want to piss her off and have her not let me speak with Tiffany. "You left me with no alternative. I hope you didn't think I was going to hand over to you what I worked so hard for. Not just like that!"

"I helped you build what you got. I was there for you!" she screams into the phone.

"Jasmine, you were there but for all the wrong reasons. You wanted to prove something to your mother and your friends. Your concern was for you to invest in a future husband, and I cannot, did not, and will not be that for you."

I hope what I've said doesn't cause her to hang up. I wasn't trying to be mean. I just wanted to start telling the truth. No more lies. This is the new Big A.T.

I hear Jasmine crying softly into the phone.

"I loved you. I needed and wanted you," she says. "But I could not give you want you wanted. I feel so betrayed. How could you do this to me and your daughter?"

"I wanted to tell you so many times," I say.

"Why didn't you?"

"I don't know. I really don't know."

Jasmine continues crying.

"Can I speak with my daughter?"

After a few seconds, I hear my daughter's voice.

"Daddy, Daddy!" Tiffany screams.

My heart melts. It feels so good to hear my angel's voice.

"Hey, sweetheart. How is Daddy's little girl?"

"I miss you, Daddy."

"I miss you too, honey."

"Are you coming here?" she asked.

"We will see, honey. I'm trying to get there."

"I had some ice cream."

"You did? That sounds good, baby. I love you, honey."

"I love you, Daddy."

"I love you too, princess."

I hear Jasmine taking the phone from Tiffany.

"I have to go, and this is not over," she says.

"Jasmine, it is over. Let's just try to work something out."

"There is nothing else to be said or done, but you will pay."
She hangs up.

"Fuck!" I yell. "What the fuck does she want from me!?!" I
want to throw my phone across the airport.

I have to realize the relationship is severed. There is no
reasoning. I betrayed Jasmine. I hurt her.

But now I need to do something for the sake of my daughter.

# SIXTY-NINE

I wipe away my tears. I don't want Tiffany to see me upset.

I go into the bathroom and dry my eyes. *I am going to be strong. I am not going to let Big A.T. get to me.*

I come back into the room and pick up Tiffany. I squeeze and kiss her on the face. "Mommy loves you," I say.

"Everything okay?" Odyssey asks, standing in the door. His thick muscular body fills the space. His bald head is shining.

"Yes, everything is fine."

"Dinner will be ready in twenty minutes."

"Okay. Let me freshen up and we'll be down."

Odyssey's mother has made an enormous meal of oxtails, peas and rice, and cabbage. After dinner we're sitting and talking when I notice Tiffany falling asleep. I turn to Odyssey, sitting to my left.

"I would like to thank you for the wonderful time here at your home."

"No problem at all. It's the least I can do for such a beautiful woman." He smiles at me with his big crooked lips.

"I really have to go—Tiffany has been up all day, and I haven't had much rest myself."

"I understand, but there is plenty of room here and I would hate to have you go to an empty apartment all alone." His dark beady eyes dance. I know there is a story behind them but I am not sure if I want to know what it is.

"Thank you, but I wouldn't want to impose."

"It would be no imposition at all. I can have everything arranged for you to stay as long as you want." He strokes my hand, and a chill hits me in my spine.

*This is a beautiful home,* I think. *But there has got to be a catch. Of course there is—he's a man and I'm a woman. He's been flirting since he bailed me out of jail—yes, where Big A.T. had me put. I can't believe I was in jail. Not to mention this is all his fault. He's getting off easy and I have to start my life over. Maybe staying here wouldn't be such a bad thing. I could stay the night, get my head clear, and enjoy the attention.*

"You know, Odyssey." I gaze into his sleek eyes. "You're right. I deserve the best and I would not mind staying the night, just to get my head clear, if it's all right with you?" I smile at him.

"Perfect. Whatever you want, it's yours." He licks his large lips, lifts my hand, and kisses it. "I want your stay here to be most memorable, and if there is anything I can do, please do not hesitate to ask."

I gather Tiffany in my arms and take her up to bed. I undress and put her under the covers. I lean over and kiss her on the forehead.

I change into a black slip dress hanging in the closet. The dress clings to my body and reveals every curve from my breasts to my hips and ass. My nipples are erect from the soft satin rubbing them. I pin my hair into a bun to illuminate my face.

I saunter down the stairs. It's time to make an entrance. I tap on the door behind which I hear Odyssey talking with some men.

"Come in," his voice booms.

The faces on the men are priceless. The conversation halts. Their mouths drop. All eyes are on me.

I glide across the room toward the lounge chair in the corner. Odyssey stands and motions for the men to leave the room. "We'll continue this meeting later," he says. He walks over to me and nods his head in amazement.

"You sure know how to make an entrance," he says with his crooked smile.

"Thank you. I hope I did not interrupt your meeting?" I slowly cross my legs.

"No, not at all, we were just finishing up anyhow," he continues, looking at me in wonderment. "You are so beautiful. Big A.T. must have been a fool."

The statement hurts. It smacks me harder than when I hit Big A.T. I lower my head and take a deep breath. When I look up, my eyes begin to water.

"I'm sorry, I guess I'm being a little insensitive," Odyssey says. He kneels in front of me and places one hand on my lap as the other caresses my neck.

"Please forgive me, I did not mean to be so harsh, but you are a beautiful and delicate woman."

I refuse to cry. I do not want to think about Big A.T. now. I sniffle and reach for a tissue on the table next to me.

"I'll be all right," I say. "It's just this has been too much for me now. I can't believe I was that stupid. I was so blind."

"You're not stupid," he replies. "You were betrayed and he played you."

I feel the comfort in Odyssey's words, and I look into his dark eyes. I see softness and sincerity in them. They are speaking to me. He leans forward and kisses me gently on the lips.

"Come on, let's go for a walk. The fresh air will be good," he says.

We exit the study through the French doors and enter a radiant and beautiful garden. Flowers, shrubs, and trees dancing and living comfortably together. It is absolutely peaceful and serene.

Odyssey pulls me close to him, holding me by the waist as we walk through the garden. I feel at ease and once again like a woman. A real man holding me. It's something I missed. I walk closer to him so I can feel his hard thick muscular body, hear his deep vibrating voice, and smell his scent of cologne mixed with a sweet musk and soap.

We reach a bench along the trail and decide to sit. I take off my sandals and place my feet on Odyssey's lap. He takes my feet and rubs them tenderly. He caresses each of my toes with his large dark hands. Then he kisses the top of my feet. I lean my head back, enjoying the soft touches. I moan each time he squeezes them a little harder.

Odyssey releases my feet and pulls me into him. He holds my face in his hard rough hands. He kisses me. His large lips are a complete contrast to his hard exterior. They are soft and supple. I respond and return the kiss. I can't help it. I want him. A man. I feel warm inside, and this is the feeling I used to enjoy when I was with Big A.T.

Odyssey licks my lips and plays with my tongue. He nibbles on my ear and neck. He is making me feel good again. I am vulnerable, and he knows it. He plays with my mouth over and over again. He places his hands on my breasts and gently squeezes them. He caresses them and pulls on my nipples.

I am wet. My clit is swollen. I can't stop moaning from his touches and his kisses. It feels good to be held and coddled.

"Let's go in the house," he says. He grabs my hand and we get up from the bench and head toward the house. I let my sandals dangle in my left hand as I hold Odyssey's hand with my right.

Once inside I go to the room and check on Tiffany. She is sound asleep.

I stroke her hair. She looks like such an angel sleeping. "I am going to take good care of you. I will never let a man hurt you," I whisper. I kiss her on the forehead and ease out of the room, gently closing the door behind me.

As I exit the room, Odyssey is standing majestically in the hall. A smirk on his face. His eyes inviting.

He walks toward me and scoops me off my feet with his huge thick arms. He carries me over the threshold of his bedroom and lays me on the bed. He climbs on top of me. Again, he nibbles on my ears, neck, and breasts. He delicately bites my nipples. I let out a soft moan. Odyssey eases off my slip dress. He undresses, revealing his long black dick. He grabs my hand and places it on his intense erection. It throbs in my hand. I guide him to my wetness. I am burning with desire. Odyssey enters me and we make love, love, love.

# SEVENTY

BIG A.T.

I sit in the back of the taxi smelling the fresh Caribbean Sea breeze rushing through the windows. The swaying green palm trees reach high into the sky. The expansive bright sky is gloriously blue. The highway runs parallel to the Caribbean Sea.

For as far as my eyes can see there is nothing but clear blue water wrapping, stretching, and bending, rustling at the island's shores.

I ride through Santo Domingo, making my way to the beach house. On the way I see rustic houses, dilapidated buildings, and ancient brick ruins of a long-ago war.

The Dominican Republic feels like a country trapped in a time warp. Ten years behind America. Old cars no longer available in America rumble and putt through Santo Domingo. People dressed in bright reds, yellows, and whites so loud they scream. White shoes everywhere. Loud Spanish music blares from clubs, storefronts, and homes. No place is quiet.

I smile. It's worlds away from my superstar life.

The taxi finally makes it to the tri-level beachfront home. It belongs to my billionaire European friend. He invited me to his home when I first started producing. I'd worked with a good musician friend of his in Los Angeles, and he asked me to work with his Latin girlfriend. He brought me down on three different occasions. She had a voice, but making a record wasn't serious for her. It was a hobby. Just something to do.

When I exit the taxi, I hear the water rushing on the beach.

I inhale deeply. Exhale slowly. I get to the door and Consuela greets me with a big hug. A petite fair-skinned woman, she always has a smile on her face. Her dark eyes are like pieces of coal and dance when she speaks.

Consuela is the live-in maid. She loves when I come to stay—she has someone to cook for. And I love her food. She prepares so much food it's like she's feeding a large family. I walk through the door and the aroma of food consumes me. The smell snakes from the kitchen and throughout the house.

My stomach growls. I am hungry and want to eat a home-cooked meal.

"You go," Consuela says as she gently pushes me toward the stairs. "I cook you something good. You go change."

"Okay, Consuela," I say with a smile.

I settle into the bedroom. I unpack my bags and change into a pair of shorts and a T-shirt. I decide to take a walk on the beach—I want to clear my head and think. I walk out the sliding doors and across the deck. I look out into the never-ending waters. I climb down the stairs and head there.

It feels good to relax without anyone calling or being in my face.

No reporters.

No paparazzi.

No Jasmine.

Just me.

Eventually I will have to go back home to confront the many naysayers. I will have to talk to the press. But for now and for the next week, I need to build up my strength.

The media is a beast. I need all the power and conviction I can muster in order to tackle and slay it.

Walking the beach is refreshing. The rustling waters crash the shore. Men and women are relaxing and sunbathing. Life seems easy and simple for them. They don't appear to have a care in the world. They are just lying on the beach, letting the sun kiss their skin with its rays.

I sit down in the sand and look out into the ocean. My thoughts race and I see myself in front of the media. Then images of Jasmine, Tickman, Southern Gent, Kenya, Pop, my mom, and Tiffany.

I have to be a man and stand up for myself. I cannot let the media or anyone tear me down.

I feel like an army of one, strong and resilient. I've got to build a solid team to have my back, but I know that a lot of gay and down-low brothers will not come forward. They do not want to be exposed. Many of them have careers, wives, and families to lose.

I weigh my options. Who can I count on? Will Pop be there for me? Will Big Mike? James? Chris? Mark?

"Papi! Papi!" I hear Consuela yelling. She wobbles toward me, waving her hands. "Come eat!" I stand and head to the house. When I get inside Consuela leads me to the dining room. I sit at the head of a table made for twelve, amazed at all the food covering it.

There are pots and pans of rice and beans.

Grilled marinated chicken.

Shredded pork.

Fresh vegetables.

Dominican teas and punch.

Fresh bread.

Homemade sauces.

And desserts.

Consuela piles something from each pot onto a plate and puts it in front of me. "Now eat. You need to be strong." She smiles.

I don't hesitate. I dive into the plate, savoring each bite. My taste buds are dancing. My stomach is rejoicing. Food prepared from the hands of love soothes my soul.

After the second plate, I tell Consuela I am full. "I will eat more later. I promise."

"Good. Good. I glad you like."

I go upstairs to the bedroom to rest. I am stuffed. My stomach is full. I got the itis seriously. Time for a nap. I stretch across the huge king-size bed with fresh white linens. The room is bright white, like the majority of the rooms in the house. Next to the bed is a nightstand with a lamp and telephone on it. I roll over and reach for it. I need to call Kenya. I am curious about what is happening at home.

"Hey, Kenya," I say. I start fidgeting with my watch.

"Hey, you there yet?" she asks.

"Yeah, I've been here for a few hours. Anything going on?"

"You are the major news. It has exploded and everyone is talking. The phones have not stopped ringing."

"Mmm," I moan.

"The news has been running the video you did all day. The radio stations have been talking about it. And it's all over the blogs!"

"What are they saying?" I ask. I don't want to know, but I do.

"Some are shocked and saying what's going to happen to Hip Hop," she says. "Some people are saying they don't care and why are we so consumed about somebody's sexuality anyway. A lot of people are trying to see who else is going to come out of the closet. They are throwing names out there of who else may be gay. But for the most part, you got a lot of support. A lot of people are saying how brave you are."

"Whoa!" I sit up on the bed. "That's crazy. I wasn't expecting to hear this."

"This is a whole new day and age. People are not as shallow as they were ten and twenty years ago. I think we have become more tolerant today," Kenya says.

"I don't know, Kenya. We'll see when I get back who's going to be there and who's not. Besides, I don't know if a lot of the brothers in the family are going to be supportive. They got their careers and families. Now I got to protect their secrets. This is a heavy burden. I clearly didn't think of them before I decided to come out. I was just trying to protect myself, and now I'm getting the feeling it's going to be larger than that."

"Well, a couple of organizations called to show their support: Gay Men of African Descent, Gay Men's Health Crisis, and GLAAD."

"I don't know if I want to be the gay poster child. I mean it's cool they support me, but I don't think a lot of straight men want to know that gay organizations are going to be breathing down their backs and demanding they put every gay man on in the industry."

"I think you may be the one to make the change in the industry. It just may be you who makes the world see black gay men in another light. You're not a stereotype of the typical gay man we see on television and in the movies. I think you can put another face to what gay looks like," Kenya says.

"Maybe you're right. I don't know, though. I sense it's going to be a long road ahead. What else is going on?" I ask.

"Let me see." She pauses, and I hear her rummaging through some papers.

"I found this hot new artist named Wizard. I want you to meet him and hear his music. He's from Harlem and he's hot like fire. He's been showcased on BET and has been blowing up the battle-rhyme scene."

"Well, I trust you, Kenya. You're over the A&R department. If he got fire like that, then e-mail me some of his tracks. I can listen to them down here."

"Okay. I will do that as soon as we're done talking. Oh yeah," she continues, "Southern Gent is going crazy not knowing what's going on. He feels neglected right now, so I think you should call him as soon as you can."

"I'll call him as soon as I get off the phone with you."

"Your assistant Tammy gave me the new designs on your upcoming fall menswear line. They need your approval. And, the developer of the new hotel in Atlanta is waiting to get the go-ahead too."

"Damn, I forgot all about them. Okay, e-mail the photos of the menswear line, and I'll call the developer in Atlanta to get things moving. By the way, I need for you to handle the new vodka deal. Let them know I am interested and I want you in on the deal. I would love for you to be a part of it."

"Wow, thanks, Big A.T., I appreciate it . . . , uhm, by the way, have you heard from Jasmine?" Kenya asks.

"Yeah, I talked to her as soon as I landed. She's waging a war right now and I'm trying to keep it cool."

"You should have seen her coming out of jail, looking crazy." Kenya laughs. "She looked a hot mess."

"They showed her coming out of jail?" I say, shocked.

"Yeah, it's all over the news, too. She had the nerve to be all up under Odyssey. What the fuck is that all about?"

"What!?!" I yell. "What do you mean?"

"They show them leaving the police precinct together. I thought you knew."

"Naw, I didn't know. She didn't say anything about Odyssey to me. How in the hell did she hook up with that nigga? She knows I don't like him. This shit is getting way out of control. The two of them together, I know they are plotting some old scandalous shit. I know I got to watch my back now." I am pissed.

"You are absolutely right," Kenya says. "He's shady and she's just a mess."

"I'm telling you, Kenya, this shit is about to get real ugly."

"I know," she says. "I know."

"All right, baby girl, I'm going to make some other calls," I say.

"Wait. Hold on. Pop and Southern Gent just walked in."

Pop comes on the phone.

"How the hell you going to do some crazy shit like this and not tell me? What the fuck were you thinking?" Pop laughs.

"What's up, Pop?" I'm not sure if his laugh is genuine or sarcastic. "Your ass was out of town so I didn't have a chance to get with you about it. I had to do something and I needed to do it fast."

"This is a mess," Pop says.

"I know."

"Now the whole family is in jeopardy. You got a lot of these niggas scared as hell. They're calling me asking what's going to happen now. The want to know if you are going to out them. I told them to sit their scary narrow black asses down and shut the fuck up. This isn't about them and if they are that damn scared then they *need* to worry." Pop laughs.

I sigh. I feel relieved. Pop has my back.

"Man, Pops, I don't know what I would do without you." I smile.

"Well, we got to think of the next few steps. And what the hell are you doing in the Dominican Republic?"

"I needed to get away. I had to get somewhere and be alone. My next few steps are going to be crucial," I say.

"The Dominican Republic? You could have gone to Miami or L.A. And if you really wanted to hide you could have gone to Minnesota or Idaho. But the Dominican Republic? Is there somebody down there you went to see?"

"There you go. There is no one down here. I like being in Santo Domingo. It's calm, quiet, and relaxing. A good place for me."

"Well, I think you are going to like to hear some good news. We are coming down there."

"'We'? Who is 'we'?" I ask.

"Me, Kenya, Southern Gent, and Tracey."

"Why are you coming here?"

"Oh yeah: Big Mike, James, and Chris are also coming."

"Hold up, hold up. What's going on?"

"We are not going to let you go through this alone. We are your family and we are going to help you whether you like it or not. Besides, Southern Gent has something very important to tell you and it's best he tells you face-to-face."

"What?" I ask. I am curious to know what he has to tell me. "Put him on the phone."

"Okay, hold on. But, listen, we should be there tomorrow. I have the travel agent making the arrangements right now," Pop says.

"Okay, cool. I look forward to seeing everyone. Now put Southern Gent on the phone."

A few seconds go by. I am anxious to know what Southern Gent has to tell me. The suspense is killing me.

"Sup, boss man?" he says.

"Hey, what's going on? What do you have to tell me?"

"Man, like Pop said, it's best I tell you face-to-face."

"You wanna leave the label? You want to move on?" I ask.

"Naw, it ain't dat," Southern Gent says. "I'm down fo' you. You done a lot fo' me and I ain't gonna bounce like dat."

"Then what is it?"

"Look, man, we gon' be down dere tomorrow and I know you would appreciate me tellin' you den."

"All right, I guess I have to wait," I say. I'm disappointed.

"I'll tell you dis one thing; Dis entertainment game is about to explode even more, boss man. I heard dat Jasmine got some pictures of you. But dere is a videotape out dere wit' niggas sexing on it. I think dat's why niggas is goin' crazy right now. Some of dem niggas is thinkin' dey about to get exposed 'cause dey think she got a copy of da tape too," Southern Gent says.

"So you mean to tell me that there is chaos in the industry because there is a sex tape and everybody thinks they are on it? Wow!" I say.

"Yeah, dis tape got some niggas on it doin' some of everythang at a sex party dat went down a few years ago. Some dude taped everythang."

"How do you know about it?" I ask.

"One of my boys was dere and told me all about it," Southern Gent says.

"Damn, so now we got to worry about a tape floating around. This shit is way out of control right now."

"But dat ain't what I got to tell you. I'll talk wit' you about da other thang when I see you."

"There's more?!?" I say, shocked.

"Yeah, it's more. But here's Pop and I'll see you tomorrow, boss man."

I hear Southern Gent handing the phone to Pop.

"We got to get a new game plan," Pop says. "This drama is better than the soaps. Everybody is waiting to see who's going to make the next move and come out. But as long as we play our cards right, you are going to come out on top once again."

"From your mouth to God's ear," I say.

"I heard myself." Pop laughs. "Well, I'm about to get out of here so I can pack and get to the airport tomorrow. We got a lot to talk about when I see you."

"Thanks, Pop, I appreciate it. Let me know what time your flight gets in and I'll meet you all at the airport."

"Will do. Here's Kenya."

"So I guess I'll see you tomorrow," she says.

"Yeah, but make sure to let Tammy know that she is to call us and check in every hour."

"I'm already on top of it."

"Good. I know I can depend on you to handle business."

"By the way, happy birthday," Kenya says.

"Thanks, but we'll see how happy it is tomorrow when it comes. It will be a very interesting birthday, that's for sure."

"Yes it will."

I hang up the phone smiling.

I am filled with excitement—and anxiety. I am glad the family is coming to join me. But I'm also a bit worried about what Southern Gent has to tell me.

I roll onto my back. I put my hands behind my head and stare into the skylight. The sky is bright, blue. Not a cloud anywhere. It's a beautiful clear day. If only I could get my mind to be just as clear.

I close my eyes and drift off to sleep. Maybe this is all a dream. When I awake I will be in my own home . . . in my own bed . . . in New York.

# SEVENTY-ONE

I get a good whiff of food cooking. I force open my eyes. I look at my watch. What felt like a quick nap turned into me sleeping until eight the next morning. The sleep did me well. I roll over and sit on the edge of the bed. *Happy twenty-fifth birthday to me.* I sure didn't feel older. But, hell, what man can say he brought Hip Hop to its feet at twenty-five?

No one. No one but me, that is.

The test now is to keep Hip Hop on its feet with only a few battle scars.

I climb out of the bed and walk over to the entertainment center. I put in Southern Gent's CD. I'm starting my birthday celebration early.

The music blares from the wireless speakers as I walk into the bathroom. It's more like a palatial spa. The heated tiles warm my feet as I cross to the walk-in shower. I turn the gold knob and the six shower heads spew water from the wall. I step inside and rinse the past twenty-four hours away.

After I shower and dress I head downstairs. I follow the sweet-smelling scent into the kitchen. Consuela is singing and dancing through the kitchen as if it's a Spanish disco. She shimmies and shakes as she stirs the pots.

She glides over to me smiling. "I am preparing a special dish for you."

"Thank you for taking care of me," I say. "Today is my birthday. I have some friends coming from New York."

"Today is your birthday. Oh, yes, yes, yes!" Conseula gets even more excited. "Okay. I make you a cake. It's a celebration." She jets around the kitchen, speaking fast in Spanish. Then I hear her say, "I have so much to do." She prepares a plate of food for me. "Okay, you eat. I go to the store to shop for food."

I sit and again eat the food slowly. I want to savor each bite. The food is delicious. I've missed home-cooked meals, especially my mother's. She is an amazing cook. She loves cooking from scratch. She doesn't use processed or canned foods. When I was a kid she always made sure I got fresh vegetables, fruits, and meats. To her, it was lazy for a woman to always make instant food. That was one thing she didn't like about Jasmine. "How can she keep a man and not know how to cook?" my mom would say. "I hope she don't think them looks are going to last forever. She better learn how to cook." Jasmine couldn't boil rice without burning it. I grew tired of her sandwiches and so we simply ordered out every night.

When I finish eating, Consuela clears the table and rushes out of the house to get to the grocery store. I go back upstairs to my BlackBerry. I figure this is the best time to check the messages I've received. I am a little reluctant because I don't want to spoil my birthday with any negative messages.

I scroll through the text messages. I notice that a few were sent from Southern Gent telling me he needed to speak with me as soon as possible. I also got texts from Pop, Big Mike, Chris, and James. Each message asking where the hell I was and what the hell was going on.

As I continue checking the messages, I notice that many are from people whose names I do not recognize. They are from anonymous users saying they support me and are proud of me. They encourage me to keep my head up and not let this get to me. They admire my courage and ability to stand up for myself. I smile as I read them.

Then I notice the signatures in most of the messages. They are from various down-low brothers in the industry.

My smile fades as I read a few calling me a "homo, booty bandit, and faggot." These messages say they hate fags and that homos need to stay out of the industry, that this business is not for homosexuals, that niggas like me are the reason for HIV/AIDS being spread in the black community.

I sigh and delete the messages. I knew that everyone was not going to be supportive, but I am not going to let that keep me from my love of making music.

The last message is from Kenya: The crew has made their flight. They arrive at six. This gives me time to start my own celebration. I put several CDs in the stereo changer. Shawty Mike. Tickman. Lil Wayne. Drake. Biggie. Jay-Z. Kanye. Ne-Yo. Beyoncé.

I pump up the volume, then go downstairs to the lounge room. I walk across the white plush bearskin rug over to the fully stocked bar. I pour me a glass of vodka with a splash of seltzer.

I grab a full bottle from the mini-refrigerator. Then I put five bottles inside, enough for the crew when they arrive. I take the bottle and my drink outside on the deck. I sit in the patio chair under an umbrella facing the Caribbean Sea.

The music echoes outside. I take a sip. "Ahhh." Yeah. *Happy birthday to me!*

# SEVENTY-TWO

I'm at the airport, anxious, ready to get the party started with the family. Nothing will bring me down. I purposely haven't watched the news, checked the blogs or my BlackBerry. I am on a mental vacation.

I go inside the terminal. I see Kenya. She breaks into a sprint and leaps into my arms.

"It is so good to see you." Kenya smiles and throws her arms around my neck.

"Oh, baby girl, it is good to see you too."

We release each other and Pop and Southern Gent rush over. More hugs and smiles.

Then Big Mike runs over and grabs me. He starts screaming, "Oh my gosh, oh my gosh, it's really you," touching me all over my body and planting kisses all over my face. I push him away. The crew is doubling over in laughter.

Tracey strolls over with her dark Gucci shades and her Gucci bag clutched in her hand. "Hey, Big A.T." She flings her black mane behind her back. We hug and she gives me an air kiss. Only Tracey.

Everyone puts their bags into the awaiting taxis and climb in. When we arrive at the beach house everyone gasps. "Now this is a beach house," Big Mike says.

"Wow!" Kenya puts her hand over her mouth.

"Man, dis is dope," Southern Gent says.

They walk through the doors shaking their heads in wonder-ment. "This is absolutely beautiful," Tracey says. "I wouldn't mind living here."

"Now that is a plasma television." James points at a large screen covering an entire wall.

"Hey, everyone, I want to introduce you to someone," I say. Consuela enters the room with her warm bright smile and gives everyone a hug. "Welcome to my country!" she says.

"What smells so good?" Pop asks.

"My specialty," Consuela says. "Now relax. Dinner is almost ready."

"Damn, Big A.T., you got it good," Big Mike says. "This is the motherfucking life right here."

"Yeah, man. I think I'm going to come down here more often," James says, walking to the sliding balcony doors that face the sea.

"How many bedrooms are there?" Tracey asks.

"Eight, with eight and a half baths."

"Damn!" everyone says in unison.

"We all get our own room," Southern Gent says.

"Yes," I reply. "So there are two bedrooms on this floor, three on the second level, and three on the third floor. You can take your bags and grab a room. I am on the third floor."

Everyone gathers their bags and makes their way through the house.

"Yo, who wants something to drink?" I ask as everyone exits to their rooms.

Everyone responds that they need a drink. I go behind the bar and open two bottles of champagne. I take out the vodka and rum. I set the glasses on the bar and put ice in each.

When everyone returns, I click on the stereo.

"Let's get this party started." Big Mike starts shaking his booty.

"Boy, you are so crazy," Kenya says.

"Man, its good seeing y'all," I say.

"It's good to see you too. Happy birthday and happy coming-out-of-the-closet," Pop says. Everyone laughs.

"Shit, he didn't come out of the closet, he fell out of it," Chris says, laughing.

"Hey, where are the boys?" Big Mike asks.

"Damn, this ain't about you," James says. "This is about us being here for Big A.T. This isn't the time for that."

I look over at James. Were those his words coming out of his mouth? James? Being serious?

"Aw, nigga, I know you ain't talking," Big Mike says. "You probably got some Dominicans lined up here for some action."

Everyone laughs.

"Yeah, I do, and guess what; I got somebody for you, you, and you." James points to Pop, Southern Gent, and Chris.

Tracey enters the room wearing a long flowing sundress. She swings her hair as she saunters to the bar.

"It is so good seeing you," she says. "I'm glad you got away, because New York is a zoo right now. My phones have not stopped ringing."

"Well, with you, Tracey, I know we got this situation on lock," I say. "I'm glad you're on my team. It's important to know I have solid friends who have my back."

"I don't see you as just another client. You are my friend." She smiles and blows me an air kiss.

"Help me give these drinks out," I say to Tracey. We put the drinks on a platter and she carries it out from behind the bar.

I grab a glass and walk over to Southern Gent. He is standing by the window looking out at the sea.

"It's beautiful, isn't it?" I hand Southern Gent the glass.

"Man, dis is awesome." Southern Gent smiles. "I ain't neva been out da country, and to come to a place like dis, yo, dis is what's good."

"Yeah, it is good. We all need a good getaway sometimes," I say.

"Can we go somewhere to talk?" Southern Gent asks.

"Sure, let's go outside on the beach."

I open the sliding doors and we step outside. The warm sea breeze hits our faces. We climb down the stairs toward the water.

"Don't go too far," Pop yells. "We want to make a toast for your birthday. And Consuela says dinner will be ready in twenty minutes."

"We'll be right back," I say.

Me and Southern Gent walk along the shore barefoot. The warm water rushes against our feet. We stop and face the sea. The sun is beginning to set. An orange glow glares from its rays and dances on the water.

"What's up?" I turn to Southern Gent.

"I'm good, but all dis craziness is gettin' to me," he says.

"Don't worry about it. I am going to make sure nothing happens to you and your career."

"I appreciate it, but I ain't worried 'bout me. I'm worried 'bout you and what dis industry can be about. I know I am new to all of dis, but I've been around niggas and know how dey feel about gay shit."

"I already know. I know how people can be and what they say about the gay lifestyle. Many times when I heard people saying something negative about gay men I should have spoken up, but I kept my mouth closed because I was afraid. I was too focused on making music and climbing to the top," I say.

Southern Gent scoops up some stones and throws them into the water.

"Boss man, dere is something I need to tell you. I had to tell you face-to-face, 'cause dis ain't something to say on da phone," Southern Gent says.

"What's up? Talk to me."

"Remember when I told you 'bout da dude from Brooklyn who came to my hood in North Carolina?"

"Yeah, I remember," I say. "You moved to New York

because of him. He was going to hook you up with some deal or something like that."

"Yeah, dat's it. Well, dat nigga is Odyssey's cousin," Southern Gent says.

My face drops and I turn and look at Southern Gent.

Without missing a beat, he continues, "I moved in wit' him when I came to New York. I met Odyssey once when he came to our apartment in Brooklyn. Dude was like, Odyssey is my cousin and he is a big rapper here in New York. He told Odyssey 'bout me and he came through to check me out. Odyssey told me 'bout his label and dat he was lookin' for new talent. He said he would get back to me in a few days. Well, we got evicted from da apartment. I didn't see neither of dem again. I tried to get in touch wit' Odyssey to see if he was fo' real 'bout signing or hookin' me up."

"Why didn't you tell me this before?" I ask.

"I was so caught up and excited 'bout dis opportunity, I didn't want to fuck it up," Southern Gent says. "Man, I'm sorry."

"Naw, it's all good," I say and put my hand on Southern Gent's shoulder. "You got talent and you're a quick learner. You are an asset to the industry and to the label. I am glad to have you as part of the family and as a friend."

"Thanks, boss man."

"So is that what you had to tell me?"

"No, it's not," Southern Gent says and takes a deep breath.

"Okay," I say.

Southern Gent looks down and then turns and faces me.

"Well, dere's dis girl in my hood at home in North Carolina name Kiwanda. She's a few years older than me and I know her sister really good. Kiwanda was a video dancer. A real good dancer. She moved to New York when she was like twenty-one or twenty-two. Something like dat. She was in all da videos. She was da first person to move out da hood and do somethin'. But like three years later she came back. Everybody was buggin' because she looked different. She lost a lot of weight and she looked really different."

I listen intently.

"When she moved back she had a nice crib and a new BMW, but she was always sick. Some days she would be real cool and laughing, and da next, she would be laid up. She couldn't move. She wasn't workin' or nothin' so da rumors started. One was she had an older man who was payin' her for sex and takin' care of everything. Well, one day when we was chillin' at da house, Kiwanda told me and her sister everythang. She told us dat she met dis dude name Odyssey. He was dis big rapper in New York and she danced in his video. Dey kicked it for a minute and started seein' each other on da regular. She moved in his house. One day she went to da doctor because she thought she was pregnant. The doctor told her dat she was not pregnant, but dat she should take a HIV test. When she took da test she found out dat she was HIV positive. She knew she had got it from Odyssey because he was da only nigga she was fuckin' around wit'."

I do a double take.

I'm mortified.

Shocked.

Stunned.

I can't believe my ears.

"I know dis sounds crazy and all, but I know it's true. She called him right den and told him she needed some money. He sent it to her Western Union." Southern Gent continues, "Odyssey sent her back home and promised to take care of her financially if she kept her mouth shut. She signed some type of confidentiality contract wit' him. She can't say nothing 'bout him and how she got HIV."

I don't say a word. I am not sure if I really heard Southern Gent and the words "HIV" and "Odyssey" come out of his mouth.

"Man, dat's why I didn't want to tell you over da phone," Southern Gent says.

"Are you sure? I mean . . . ," I don't know what else to say.

Southern Gent turns and with a serious look on his face he says, "I am one hundred percent sure."

I put my head in my hands. I start shaking my head. "No, no, no," I repeat.

Kenya told me that Jasmine left the police station with Odyssey. I wonder now if they've been sleeping together all along. If Jasmine has been exposed to the virus. If I've been exposed to the virus. I think about my daughter. My head begins to ache. I close my eyes. Things are falling apart . . . crumbling right in front of me. My whole world has just turned upside down.

"I'm sorry to tell you dis during all dat you are goin' through. But when I seen Odyssey wit' Jasmine, and then hearing 'bout your press conference and you tellin' everyone 'bout you, I felt I had to say somethin'," Southern Gent says.

"Man, you did the right thing. I really appreciate this, but I got to make sure this is all true. This is not the time to be assuming or guessing," I say.

"Well, Kiwanda is my homegirl's sister and we're real close. They don't live too far from my family. I can get in touch wit' her," Southern Gent says.

"Good. Good," I say. I turn and face Southern Gent. I put my hands on his shoulders.

Southern Gent steps closer to me and opens his arms. With the sun fading and the night lights of Santo Domingo illuminating the sky, we embrace.

# SEVENTY-THREE

When me and Southern Gent enter the house everyone is drinking and dancing in the living room. The music is blaring. The party has begun.

James walks over and hands us each a glass filled with champagne.

"It's a celebration!" James sings. "It's your birthday, it's your birthday. We gon' party like it's your birthday, and we sipping on Cristal like it's your birthday." Everyone raises their glass in the air and continues dancing.

Consuela steps into the living room with her warm smile. Big Mike grabs her hands and twists her around. They do the bump and she starts to salsa. Everyone screams in excitement.

"Okay, okay," she says, laughing. "Time to eat now."

She leads us into the dining room. The table has been set. We bring the bottles of wine, champagne, and liquor with us.

We take our seats and everyone gawks at the display of food. Consuela has really set it off.

Shredded pork with garlic sauce.

Roasted chicken in bamboo leaves with coconut milk.

Grilled fish.

Rice and beans.

Roasted potatoes with onions.

Fresh sweet corn.

Cut tomatoes.

Fresh lettuce.

And homemade bread.

"Now this is a spread," Big Mike says.

"Okay, I am bringing Consuela back with me," Chris says.

"Well, before we eat let us pray," I say. We hold hands around the table. Everyone bows their head.

"I am thankful for this occasion and being able to see another birthday," I say. "I have been blessed beyond measure, but today has a special meaning. I am here with my family of friends, who have been supportive and encouraging. I am blessed to have friends like these. I am thankful for this meal and for the love Consuela put into making this happen. I don't know what the future holds for me, but God, I know everything is in your hands and part of your plan. Just give me the strength to be courageous and strong. In the name of Jesus I pray, amen."

"Amen!" everyone says.

"Let's eat!" James yells.

All I hear is the sounds of grunts and "mm, mm, mm" as the food is passed around.

"I am going to marry Consuela," Big Mike says.

Everyone laughs.

"Oh my gosh. This food is so good!" Tracey says. It is the first time I have ever seen Tracey take more than three bites of food.

Just as we are finishing, Consuela brings out a vanilla butter crème cake with "Happy Birthday" written on it.

"Yay!" James and Big Mike scream and clap.

Everyone lifts their glass and sings "Happy Birthday."

"You getting up there in age," James jokes. "We are going to have to start setting you up with senior citizens."

Pop glances over at James. "We older men have something you younger men want—and by the looks of it, you need some of it." Pop slowly moves his hand over his crotch. Everyone breaks out in laughter. James runs over to Pop and jumps in his lap. "Take me, big daddy, take me."

"Well, I'm looking to find me a fine Dominican man. So can

we get ready to go out to the club?" Tracey says. "I need some loving right about now."

Everyone's head jerks in unison toward Tracey. "What?" she says. "Don't sleep on me. I can get freaky when I want to." She starts gyrating and shaking her butt. We all laugh.

"It's not that we didn't think you were freaky," Big Mike says. "We just thought you had a man who was keeping you right."

"I had to get rid of that fool. He was too controlling and overprotective. I don't have time to be trying to convince any man about what I'm doing and where I'm going."

"Hello!?!" Kenya says. "Girl, these men today, I swear they think they can keep a hold on you. We are businesswomen who have our careers. We don't have time to take care of ourselves *and* you."

"Girl, I swear I'm going to get me a rich white man," Tracey says.

"What, you don't already have one on reserve?" James says.

"I'm trying to give the brothers a try, but their insecurity is getting the best of them," Tracey says. "I don't need an insecure man. I need a strong black man. A man who can put it on me and have my back when I need him. I need a man who can hold his own financially and don't have to beg and borrow from me."

"Okay!" James says. "That's the type of man we are all looking for."

Everyone breaks out in laughter.

Tracey, Kenya, Chris, Big Mike, and James get up from the table and head to the lounge to finish drinking and dancing. Me, Pop, and Southern Gent go outside and sit on the patio.

Pop pulls out a cigar and lights it. The moon's reflection dances on the water. A gentle breeze tickles my skin.

"You know we got a lot to deal with when we get back," Pop says, looking at me.

"Yeah, I was thinking about that," I say.

"The first thing is to get you in front of the media and

have the public sympathize with you," Pop says. "Tracey can make you out to be a media darling, but we have to handle this right."

"I'm not worried about it too much," I say. "It's my baby girl Tiffany I am concerned about. I know Jasmine is going to put up a fight for custody and child support. I am bracing myself for that."

"She's going to get everything she wants, you know that," Pop says. "Basically you made it easy for her."

"I know, but I don't care about the money. I just want to make sure I get some type of custody or visitation with Tiffany. I am willing to fight too," I say.

"I know a brother who is good with these types of cases. I'll get you his information."

"Thanks, Pop. I really appreciate everything."

"We also got to think about Odyssey and how we are going to handle this," Pop says. "It won't be easy to get him to confess. We also can't confront him, because the girl signed a confidentially agreement. Technically, we don't know shit about him."

"This shit is tricky," I say. "Our hands are tied. But no matter what, I'm going to confront Jasmine about it. I don't want her caught out there. She deserves to know about that dirty-ass nigga."

"You sure you want to open that can of worms with her right now?" Pop asks.

"I got to tell her. She is still the mother of my child. And what if she has been sleeping with him all along while she was with me? Fuck, man. That means I got to get tested."

Pop puts his hand on my shoulder. "Look, Big A.T., you don't know if she's been sleeping with him or if she just met up with him. Don't assume anything. But I do agree you need to get tested."

I put my head down and let out a deep sigh. "When shit happens, it really comes down, doesn't it?" I pick up my drink and gulp it down.

"We're here for you," Pop says. "And don't let this put a damper on our party. It is your birthday. Come on." Pop stands up and rubs my head. "Let's have a good time. We'll work everything out over the next couple of days."

I let out a chuckle and follow Pop and Southern Gent into the house, where the party is clearly well under way.

# SEVENTY-FOUR

The next afternoon, after everyone has awakened, Pop calls a meeting. He wants to go over the plan for when we return home to New York. He wants to make sure his investment, empire, and family of brothers are going to be protected. He's also concerned about me. "I don't want you to go through this alone," he says. "I don't want you to feel like we're going to abandon you."

Tracey has a major plan. She knows the press can be fickle. If you ignore them, they attack you. They will print the most devious and destroying things they can find out about you. They will bring you down.

"First and foremost, you are doing an exclusive interview with Scott Jaredson of *City Access,*" Tracey says.

"We are dating, so that's not a problem," Chris says.

Everyone's head jerks toward Chris.

"What?" he says.

"Who knew?" Big Mike says, shrugging.

"You are scheduled to go live on the air with him as soon as you return," Tracey continues. "I will also reach out to the network of brothers who work throughout the industry, but more importantly, those with the press. They will help in writing your story for the papers, magazines, and blogs. Their savvy wordplay will help you gain sympathy.

"The next interviews are with the *Today* show, *Good Morning America*, MTV, and BET. You are doing exclusives for the networks. You will talk candidly and directly to Hip Hop fans. You will discuss your desire to be happy and to love, but more importantly to make music your fans can enjoy.

"You're going to do an exclusive interview with Karu F. Daniels with AOL Black Voices and Natasha Eubanks with YBF. And also with Clay Cane at BET.com, and Emil Wilbekin over at Essence.com.

"I'm also lining up some interviews for you to talk with bloggers. They've been extremely supportive of your career, and you know they have a huge following. So, you're going to talk with Necole Bitchie, Hello Beautiful, H-Listed, Bossip, Panache Report, Global Grind, Rap Radar, All HipHop, and Gyant Unplugged.

"We also know that community involvement is a key element for any celebrity. I am going to get you out and about in the communities. You will set up foundations, camps, and scholarships with the local schools. You will make guest appearances with other celebrity artists. You will create a scholarship to help underprivileged high school seniors to attend college. You will also help to build a community center and dedicate it to a local activist in the community.

"You will do some work with the gay organizations. They are key allies. You will do appearances at events and get on their boards. Trust me, if you get the gays to support you, the rest of the world will follow."

"Damn!" Big Mike says. "You are thorough as hell."

"This is what I do." Tracey swings her hair behind her back.

Tracey has many connections. Community organizations love her. She is their point of contact for major Hip Hop celebrities. She makes things happen, but she also gets many of the black leaders to succumb to her beauty, poise, and power. Tracey has whipped many leaders with her prowess. They will do anything for her. She has them in the palm of her hands.

Listening to Tracey's plan seems like a lot of work, but I

need to rebuild my name, my brand. I am ready for the challenge. I have to get the public's sympathy.

The black community is the most forgiving community. Working the white community is a different beast. I will have to use the connections Pop and I have in elitist societies to help me out. They can provide me with access to philanthropic causes. I will join their boards and help raise money. I will become a spokesperson for one of their causes. The plan is perfect, precise.

Hell, it's like Pop told me early on, "This is the entertainment industry. Everything isn't what it seems anyway." The distraction will get everyone's attention off my sexuality. People will focus on my work, my commitment to the community and to children. Everybody loves the kids. I have to keep the fans distracted. I have to keep moving.

I knew I could depend on the help of the gay and down-low brothers who work in the media, and with community organizations, as well as leaders and board members at various institutions.

I've always been impressed with Pop. He manages to keep his sexual life out of the media and papers. His work has always been the focus of any press about him. He is a master manipulator. He learned from the "old boys' network." They taught him to keep everyone guessing. "Never let them know what you are up to," they say. "Just do it and then move on to something else."

If people start talking about one thing, you bring up another. Change the topic. Talk about another cause and how it is affected by what they think is the major cause.

If they are talking about the negativity in Hip Hop, you talk about the positive things it has done for the community. You get them to see how music has changed and helped so many young men from the ghettos and projects. You talk about the many jobs that have been created because of Hip Hop and how black people are benefiting from it.

And I have been one of those persons responsible for helping

a lot of black people benefit from it. The many people I've hired
with my record label.

My clothing line.

My real estate ventures.

Yes, it's time for me to reclaim my life.

I am ready to get back to New York.

To take back my empire.

# SEVENTY-FIVE

CRAIG

My plan is working perfectly. I have the entire entertainment industry on pins and needles. I'm in control. Man, it feels good.

I am holding off on posting the photos of Big A.T. on my blog. I want to make it a complete package with his photos and the sex tape I have.

Oh yes. That's me.

I hear that all the men are nervous, especially Big Mike and James.

They came to the down-low sex party I gave at my house a few years ago. I'd just moved to New York from Chicago. One of my boys used to work at Atlantic Records. He wanted to introduce me to everybody because I was the new fine dime-piece, and of course they would all want a piece of me.

I hid cameras all throughout the house, especially in the bedrooms. I wanted to capture all the action going down that night. And, boy, did I get some great shots of everybody going at each other. Dicks in mouths. Dicks in asses. Dudes who had girlfriends and those who were married being the biggest bottoms at the party. Oh, this is just too good.

If Big Mike and James hadn't have fucked me over like they did I probably wouldn't be doing this.

Naw, yes I would.

# SEVENTY-SIX

## BIG A.T.

Being back home in New York is bittersweet. There is no place like New York, but I have the overwhelming task of creating my new life and facing the world.

When I walk through the door, there is silence all through-out the house. It is lifeless. There is no one here to greet me. No Tiffany, no Jasmine. I am by myself, starting anew. I sigh heavily.

I walk into the living room and place my bags on the floor near the sofa. I sit down and glance at the pictures of me, Jasmine, and Tiffany on the table. It's a picture of us at Tif-fany's first birthday party. We're all smiles and hugging. Happy times.

I reach over the end of the sofa and grab the phone to check the voice mail. It is full with messages. There are calls from producers, rappers, and singers I've worked with, as well as record label executives and other celebrities. They were all calling to show their support and offer themselves if I needed anything. It feels good to hear there are people by my side.

I get up from the sofa and walk over to the entertainment center. I turn on the stereo and Hot 97 radio DJ Funkmaster Flex's voice booms through the speakers.

"Yo! What's up, New York! So I've been asking everyone to call in about Big A.T.'s announcement. That's my mans and I still got love for him, no homo. But I want to know what's on your minds. What is the state of Hip Hop? What does this mean for music? Can Big A.T. regain his power as one of the leading producers in the game?"

Yeah, this is going to be very interesting. Tomorrow is going to be busy. It's go, go, go. I will be moving nonstop until the press dies down because as of right now, I am the topic of the day. Unfortunately, there are no other pressing or major news stories happening in the world.

It's all about me.

Fuck!

Pop promised me fame and the world. Now I have them. But how unfortunate the situation, and now I have to make the most of this time.

Tracey has set my schedule. Everything starts tomorrow. I will be making the rounds to all the networks, doing interviews. I am doing a press junket with the media. This will allow all newspapers, magazines, and blogs the opportunity to question me in one large-group setting.

I then go to Harlem, Brooklyn, Queens, the Bronx, Long Island, and Staten Island. I will do photo ops with the community leaders there who support me. I plan to shake hands, smile for the cameras, and make donations to the many programs in those communities.

I grab my bags and take them upstairs. When I walk into the bedroom I look at the bed where Jasmine once lay. I miss her being here.

I drop my bag and turn off the lights and head back downstairs. I walk over to the stereo and plop in a CD. I got to feel some bass. Some treble. Hear some instruments.

Southern Gent's new single, "Ain't Nothin' But a G," thumps through the speakers. It is going to be released later this week. This is the song that's going to put me back on top. I am sure of it.

# SEVENTY-SEVEN

I rush out of my condo and hop in the back of the black sedan. I have to be at *City Access* studios at ten. The show will air this evening. This is phase one of Tracey's plan.

Tracey is in full publicist mode. When she is like this, she is not to be fucked with. She is short and quick with people. She demands respect. And she gets it.

Tracey and Pop meet me at the studio. When we walk inside the building the producers and network president come out to introduce themselves. "We support you," the president of the network tells me. He smiles, revealing his coffee-stained teeth. "We are happy you chose us to tell your story." He extends his hand.

"Thank you for your support," I say. I shake his hand. "I really appreciate everything you all are doing."

"I am also glad you are supportive, but for me and my client's assurance I need to see the questions and get a copy prior to the interview." Tracey pushes her mane back. Her Birkin bag dangles in her hand.

"I will get them for you right now," the producer says.

A pimply-faced boy escorts me and Pop to the green room. Tracey follows the producer to get copies of the questions.

"You ready for this?" Pop asks me.

"I don't have a choice now," I say. "I got to go through with this, and I only know it'll make me stronger."

"Not only stronger, but wiser and smarter," Pop says and

winks. "This is your opportunity to get the world to fall in love with you, and I am sure you won't have a problem with that."

I smile, but inside I am nervous and anxious. I want it to be over quick. Fast. Hell, I want everything to just be over. The entire country is talking about gay this and gay that. Who will be the next celebrity to come out of the closet? Is this the end of my career?

A well-manicured pretty boy comes into the green room. It's Scott Jaredson. He has a nice glow to his dark skin. His curly hair is cropped close. He's very slim and small but has a strong presence. We smile at each other when he enters. Scott closes the door behind him.

"I'm glad you are doing this with me," Scott says in his broadcaster voice.

"Man, just make me look good." I laugh. I am still nervous.

"I got you, but I want you to know I have to make it look like I am really interrogating you. I still have to do my job as a journalist."

"I understand. You got a job to do."

"Well, I also want to give you this." Scott hands me a manila envelope. "I got it in the mail. It was addressed to me, but it had no sender information on it."

I open the envelope. It is the photos of me and Keith in Los Angeles. The same photos Jasmine had at the house.

"What the fuck!!" I yell.

"I know, man," Scott says. "I didn't show them to anyone. No one even knows I have them."

"Man, I really appreciate this," I say.

I am pissed. I know Jasmine has something to do with this. She is out to get me. She is trying to destroy my career, my life, everything I've ever achieved. I put the pictures back into the envelope.

"I figured I'd give them to you. I don't have any use for them and I don't plan on mentioning it. But if I were you I would try to find out who else has these photos or if they are circulating anywhere," Scott says.

This is exactly the extra stress I do not need. Not right now. My heart starts to race. I want to punch something or someone.

"Now I know this isn't going to be an easy ride." I shake my head.

"We'll get to the bottom of this shit," Pop says, standing and walking over to the table. He grabs a bottle of water. "Whoever this motherfucker is, they don't know who they are fucking with."

"You got my support," Scott says. "Anything I can do just let me know. I'll also keep my ears and eyes open with other journalists in the media. We do talk, and I am sure if someone else got these pictures they will let me know."

"Thanks, Scott," I say.

We sit and talk while we wait for the studio to let us know it's time for the interview. Scott does his best to keep me cool. In a few minutes I will be sitting on the stage with him, just the two of us. I will have to answer the tough questions. I will have to explain to Hip Hop and the world why I decided to come out. I will have to talk about my sexuality in front of millions of viewers.

Tracey enters the room with the producer. "They will be ready in ten minutes," she says. Scott stands and shakes my hand. "You will do fine." He and the producer exit the room. Tracey has the final questions of the interview. We look over them. She preps me on how to answer and what to say. She gets me ready as best she can. The rest is up to me.

I walk onto the set and sit opposite Scott. He flashes a smile at me. My mouth becomes dry. My palms start to sweat. I rub my hands on my jeans. I pick up the glass of water sitting on the stand next to my chair. I drink all of it. I am thirsty and I need to keep my mouth watered.

The makeup artist rushes over and dabs some gloss on my lips. The production assistant refills my glass with water. He walks away, then turns and leaves the pitcher next to me. I smile.

Although this is a ten-minute exclusive, I know in the world of television it's a long, long time. The set falls quiet. Scott inserts his earpiece to hear the producers in the booth. He smiles at me. "You ready?"

"Ready as I'm going to be," I say.

The stage manager starts the countdown. Five.

Four.

Three.

Two.

And then points to Scott.

"Thank you, Big A.T., for joining us," Scott says.

"Thank you for having me," I say.

"Well, I guess we should start with the shocking announcement you made last week. Are you gay?"

My heart is pounding. My insides are twisting and turning. I fidget with my watch.

"Yes, I am gay," I say. "But, let me be clear. I am a man. I don't put labels on myself. I am so many things that it would be hard to put me in a category or box. I am a musician, a producer, a businessman, a father, a son, and a friend."

"But why come out? Why disclose your sexuality?" Scott asks.

"I've thought about it for a while. I have struggled with this for some time now. It was a hard choice for me to come out publicly and disclose my sexuality, but there was something more and deeper at the core. There was my integrity, my word, and what I am committed to," I say.

My mouth is dry again. I take a drink and then I continue.

"I love making music. I love seeing my fans' faces light up when they hear a song I did. It makes me happy to hear them singing along and dancing to the beat. I was once like them. I was once a fan, but now I am a creator in this industry. I knew what it felt like to look up to the people in this industry and want to be like them. We get so caught up in what we see on television we forget they are real people, everyday people who have problems, issues, and challenges. I want to let my fans know I am still human. I still struggle. I have problems. I want them to see me, all of me. I know my fans will see and appreciate me for that. I am certain in the long run it won't matter who I sleep with, but rather, that I am a productive citizen in the world and helping others along the way. But I also felt it was important for other gay men and women to see someone like them in Hip Hop. It was time that people saw an openly gay black man in Hip Hop, and hopefully we'll stop the gay-bashing and bullying."

"There are a lot of people who say it will be hard for you to regain your fan base after this. Will you quit making music?" Scott asks.

"I will never stop making music. Music is who I am. I love doing what I do. I can't imagine doing anything else. I plan on continuing to produce for many artists. I have gotten a ton of calls from artists and record labels to work on their projects. People know me for making great music. They want to continue working with me. I am getting a lot of support from the recording industry. I can truly say I have a lot of friends, and their support."

I'm more comfortable. I make eye contact with Scott. I feel myself being natural. I feel powerful, vigilant. My life is coming back. I can feel it pumping through my veins and in my blood. My spirit is dancing and singing. I feel good.

"You disappeared after your announcement. Where did you go and why did you leave with so many unanswered questions lingering?" Scott asks.

"I needed a break. I needed the time to think, reflect, and be with myself. I knew I would have to go through this alone. I mean, I have my friends and family, but no one knows this experience or has dealt with anything like this on this magnitude. Think about it. How many prominent high-profile black men would come on national television and discuss their sexuality for the whole world to judge them? Especially someone from the Hip Hop community. Not too many. So I had to take the break to be prepared. It allowed for me to be responsible as a man," I say.

"What do you think this means to Hip Hop? Is Hip Hop ready for something like this?" Scott asks.

"Well, I guess we are all going to find out now. I think this is a huge milestone for Hip Hop. I think true fans of the music will not only welcome me, but embrace others who are different in many ways. This is something powerful. I mean really, think about it. Here is an opportunity to accept someone not based on the color of their skin, or their sexuality, but on the content of their character. My fans, friends, other artists, and business associates all know me and love me. Nothing has changed about that. Nothing has changed about me. I am still the same person. I am still the same guy who can be funny and serious. I still love. I get hurt and angry just like everyone else. I am no different from anyone out there listening and watching this. Hip Hop is about community. It's about culture and style. It's about unification. We are all one in this."

"Do you think other male artists or celebrities will come out and follow suit?" Scott asks.

"I can't answer that," I say. "I don't know what other male artists or celebrities will do. I can only be accountable for me and my family."

"Do you know of other closeted men in the industry?" Scott asks.

"I am sure there are. But I just focus on making music and keeping my fans happy."

"Are you currently dating and if so, who?" Scott asks.

"Right now I am only focused on me. I am not ready to be involved with someone at this time," I say.

"What would you like to say to your fans?" Scott asks.

I turn and look into the camera. "I would like to say to my fans to please be here for me. I ask you to please forgive me if any of you feel I have misled you in any way. I am a man and I am human. We all have faults and demons we have to deal with. I am dealing with mine. I know that a lot of you have been very supportive, and I appreciate it. It means a lot to me. I ask each one of you to be patient with me. God is still working on me. And, regardless of anything, I am proud of who I am. I am not ashamed and I am no longer going to hide. I also want to let any young person or adult out there know that if you are dealing with something you feel you can't handle, find someone to talk to. I know how hard it is to struggle with something. You can't do it alone. Talk to a friend, loved one, or anyone. You don't have to go through it alone."

"Thank you again, Big A.T., for your time. This has been truly an amazing interview and again, I appreciate you coming to speak with me," Scott says. He reaches over and shakes my hand.

"Thank you, Scott. I appreciate everything you and *City Access* have done to make this interview happen," I say.

And just like that, the interview is over.

# SEVENTY-EIGHT

Tracey gives me a big hug as I exit the set. Pop pats me on the back.

"You did a great job," Pop says.

"Oh my gosh!" Tracey squeals. "You were so relatable. So endearing and compassionate. You definitely sold yourself to the audience. Everyone watching it is going to eat it up."

I am proud of myself. As nervous as I was, I got through the interview. What seemed insurmountable is now over. I am on to the next challenge. I am on to conquer the next set of interviews with the press. I am excited.

Instead of taking the black sedan to the onslaught of events for the day, I decide to ride with Pop and Tracey. This way we can talk and Tracey can prep me for the upcoming questions. But I have an important stop to make. I have a doctor's appointment with Dr. Levinstein for an HIV test. As much as I want to ignore it and stay on high, I have to take this test.

Pop pulls in front of Dr. Levinstein's offices on Seventy-seventh Street and Park Avenue.

"You want me to go inside with you?" Pop asks.

"Naw, I'm good," I say. I don't want anyone around if I get some unfortunate news. And, if it comes to it, I will choose to die a lonely death rather than have anyone witness me suffer and deteriorate from an incurable disease.

I walk inside and the nurse greets me. "I will let Dr. Levinstein know you are here."

Dr. Levinstein comes through the door separating the waiting area from the examining rooms. He motions for me to come with him. We go through the doors and I follow him into the first room. Dr. Levinstein closes the door behind us.

"I am glad you are doing this," Dr. Levinstein says.

"Yeah, me too," I say. Although I really am not thrilled to be here.

"A lot of people don't get tested. When they do, in some cases, it's too late."

I hope this is not me. I pray I am not in that boat.

*Please, dear God, please let my test come back negative,* I silently pray. *From now on I promise I will always use a condom. I will do whatever I need to do.*

"This won't take long." Dr. Levinstein takes a swab and places it in my mouth. He twists and turns it on the inside of my jaw. Then he places it in a tube. "I'll be back shortly," he says and steps out of the room.

I take a deep breath and let out a long sigh. In a few minutes I will know my fate. I will know my HIV status. I wonder what I will do first if I am HIV positive.

Will I tell anyone?

Will I live with the secret?

I think about death and dying. I am too young to die. There are things to be done I have not done. I have to be here for Tiffany. I need to see her graduate from high school and college. I want to give her away at her wedding. I want to see my grandchildren.

Dr. Levinstein comes back into the room. He has the same blank look he had when he walked out of the room. I am scared. The doctor knows something. I can tell. I can see it in his face.

"Well, Big A.T.," Dr. Levinstein says. My heart is in my throat. I'm breathing heavy. "You tested negative for the HIV virus."

"Whew!" A huge smile spreads across my face.

"However, this does not let you off the hook, young man,"

Dr. Levinstein says. "You still have to make sure you continue to practice safe sex. You have to make sure to protect yourself. HIV can be contracted through unprotected sex and from risky sex behaviors. I have to warn you of that because I am your doctor."

"Thank you, Dr. Levinstein," I say. "This is a big relief."

"Let's keep it negative." He smiles at me.

"I promise I will."

I walk out of the doctor's office with another victory under my belt. Everything is working in my favor. The odds are on my side. This is a good thing. A damn good thing.

When I get in the car I put my head down and shake it in disbelief. "Damn, damn, damn," I keep saying. Pop and Tracey stare at me. They don't know what to say.

"I'm negative." I lift my head, smiling.

"Don't play like that," Tracey screams. "I was about to really start crying and mess up my makeup." She pulls down the visor and checks her face in the mirror.

"You had us going." Pop smiles. "That was a good one."

"Man, I am feeling really good," I say. "I was really worried today. Getting that test is scary, but I'm glad I did."

"Good," Pop says. "You got to get tested. It's the only way to stay healthy and to know your status. Besides, this is your moment. This is your shining moment," he says and starts the car. We make our way to the press junket at the W Hotel in Times Square.

My cell phone buzzes. I pull it out of my pocket.

"Hey, Southern Gent. What's going on?" I say.

"Hey, boss man. How you doin'?"

"I am having the best day. A real good day."

"Dat's good. I wanted to let you know dat I got in touch wit' Kiwanda's sister."

"Oh, that's what's up. This is more good news for the day."

"Unfortunately, I got bad news. Kiwanda died two months ago from AIDS."

Damn. This is not the news I was expecting.

"Her sister said she tried calling me when she died, but I was on da road. I didn't check my messages. My bad."

"Naw. It's all good. Don't worry about it. I am sorry to hear about your friend's death."

I am disappointed. Aside from my sadness over a young girl's death, I know it's going to be difficult to prove anything against Odyssey now.

"I am really sorry," Southern Gent says. "I should have come to you before and said something, but I didn't."

"Really, Southern Gent, don't worry about it," I say. "Thanks for calling for me, though."

"Aight. I am on my way to da studio now."

"Okay. I'll stop by and see you later."

I tell Pop and Tracey the bad news.

"This is not good," I say. "I've got to tell Jasmine. She can be in danger."

"It won't be easy," Pop says. "But this has become a huge priority. And regardless of what's going on between you two, this needs to be handled."

"Yeah, I know." I slump in the backseat. "Damn, I hope that nigga didn't give her anything." I stare out of the window and begin fidgeting with my watch.

# SEVENTY-NINE

## CRAIG

Just like the rest of the world, I was glued to the television watching Big A.T.'s exclusive on *City Access.*

After the show went off, I couldn't believe how bogus it was. It was clearly staged. I know Tracey coached him on what to say. She is the top public relations rep in New York. But I'm not convinced by Big A.T.'s answers.

I am more pissed they didn't show the photos I sent Scott Jaredson. I thought for certain they were going to air them.

It's all good, though.

I teased my fans on my blog about the photos. The traffic to my blog was off the chain. I got over one million hits in one day.

I know Big A.T. and the crew are doing damage control, but I haven't unleashed the real fury yet.

# EIGHTY

BIG A.T.

The alarm clock jolts me from my sleep. It's eight in the morning. Another full day of activities. Yesterday was incredibly busy. I have never spoken so much in one day in my life.

I was exhausted. I didn't come home until three in the morning. After the interviews Pop, Tracey, and I went to Ashford & Simpson's open mic at the Sugar Bar on Seventy-second Street. When we walked in, the place erupted in cheers. People were clapping, whistling, and cheering for me. Many fans came over and shook my hand. They told me they loved me and would continue to support me and my music. All the love they showed felt good.

Throughout the night fans continued to send drinks to the table for me, Pop, and Tracey. My head is still spinning from all the drinks I consumed.

I get out of bed and open the curtains. The sun blares into the room. I squint as I look out the window down onto Park Avenue.

I walk into the bathroom and get a glass of water from the sink. The taste of alcohol is still in my mouth. I brush my teeth. I want that taste out of my mouth.

I go back in the room and grab the remote for the television. I push the Power button. My face is splashed on the screen. They are talking about my exclusive interview with *City Access.* The headline reads: **Hip Hop Celebrity Big A.T. Talks About His Sexuality.**

I smile and click the television off. I go downstairs to get the morning paper from my front door. When I open the door and pick up *The New York Times,* there I am on the front page. My picture. Not a bad-looking picture at that. It's one of my publicity shots. I am wearing a navy blue suit and red tie. The color photo is appealing. This is good. Image is everything.

Women will look at it and like me. They will think about me sexually. They will desire me and feel sorry for me. Men will like my posture and conviction. I stood bold and proud. I looked as if I would not be defeated. Black men like seeing another black man facing white America without any fear. I look fearless.

I need to remain fearless, because today I am meeting with Jasmine and her lawyer. This will be the first time we will see each other since my trip from L.A., when she stormed out of the house and demanded half of my empire. The wounds are still fresh. Deep. The bitterness and anger still prevalent. I know Jasmine has not recovered from the blow.

Our lawyers have been talking all week about the terms of the child support and custody. We reached an agreement. We will have to sign the paperwork. It will make it official. We will be in each other's lives forever. I dread it. I know Jasmine hates it. There is nothing we can do about it. This is all about Tiffany now.

I start preparing for the meeting, which will happen in a few hours. After the lawyer's office I plan to go by my office. I need to check in on my upcoming projects with Ms. Freeda and Wizard, along with my two new acts: a rapper named Jook Boy and the girl group FINE.

Then I have to meet up with Tracey and Pop. We're going to Harlem for a dedication ceremony. I am presenting a check to the Harlem YMCA and the Harlem Children's Zone for their young people's programming.

Just as I am getting ready, Kenya calls.

"Hey," she says.

"What's up, baby girl?"

"I spoke with Funkmaster Flex and DJ Clue about Southern Gent's single. They are excited about it and said they would play it tonight."

"Damn, that's good news."

"I've also got a few club DJs who said they were going to start pumping it at the clubs. I definitely think this song is going to put Southern Gent on another level," Kenya says.

"I put everything into this song," I say. "This is one of them joints that's going to be a classic in Hip Hop."

"I got to admit, this is some fire."

"Come on now, baby girl, you know me. You know I'm going to put it down." I smile.

"I ain't sleeping on your skills, but I got to admit this is classic, Big A.T."

"Thank you."

"Are you ready for your meeting with Jasmine?" she asks.

"Yeah, I'm getting ready now."

"Keep your cool, because she is going to trip and probably call you every name in the book."

"I know, I know," I say. "Everything is going so well I'm not going to let this spoil anything."

"Good. I'm glad to hear that from you."

"Look, I'm stopping in the office so I will see you later. I am also planning on coming to the studio tonight. What time will you be there?" I ask.

"We got the studio booked from midnight until eight in the morning."

"Cool. I'll probably come through around one or two. I got some things to do with Pop and Tracey and then I'll be there."

"All right, I'll see you later," she says.

# EIGHTY-ONE

The streets are crowded with cars, and I am running ten minutes late. Shit. I call to let my lawyer know I am stuck in traffic and nearby.

I finally make it to the law offices on Broad Street. The receptionist quickly ushers me into the conference room. When I walk in I see Jasmine, her lawyer, and my lawyer. I apologize and cross the room. I walk behind the long conference table and sit opposite Jasmine.

She looks stunning, more beautiful than ever. Her long hair is spiraling down her back and across her face. Her perfume dances through the room and tickles my nose. The fire red dress hugs her body. The top of the dress is a leather corset. It's cut low. Very low. Revealing her cleavage. Her breasts are perky. The dress does little to cover them.

She is hot!

The meeting begins. The lawyers do most of the talking. They discuss the arrangements of the contract. Then our lawyers speak with us individually.

I will get visitation of Tiffany every other weekend. I have to return her home to Jasmine by no later than eight in the evening after my visits. I will get to be with her every other holiday. I will also be allowed to spend Christmas and her birthday with her no matter where she is. I am required to pay fifty thousand dollars a month in child support. I am also responsible for Tiffany's health care, school tuition, nanny, and other expenses related to her well-being. This is what Jasmine and I have decided will be best.

As the lawyers review the documents, I ask if I can have a moment alone to speak with Jasmine. She agrees. We can be alone to talk for five minutes. That's all she will grant.

Once the lawyers step out of the room, I smile at her. I try to loosen up the tension in the air.

"You look beautiful," I say.

Jasmine doesn't respond. She stares blankly past me.

"Look, I don't want to make this out to be some bitter and slandering fight between us. I want the best for Tiffany just as much as you do, but I need for you to stop trying to destroy my name and reputation."

She gives me an evil stare.

"The pictures you had at the house—did you send them over to Scott Jaredson at *City Access*?" I get up and walk toward her.

She still doesn't say anything.

"Did you send the photos, Jasmine?" I ask, again looking into her eyes.

"Get the fuck out of my face!" she says, gritting her teeth.

I step back. I take a few deep breaths. *This can get ugly,* I say to myself. I don't need anything else to go wrong. Not now.

"You come in here and think you can demand respect and some answers because you got your wealthy faggot-ass friends helping you. You have some mighty big balls. You think I owe you an explanation after all this shit you put me through. I don't owe your black nasty faggot ass anything," Jasmine says, pointing her finger at me.

I cringe. Each word is filled with spite. And each hits me hard, like a bullet tearing through my flesh.

"You owe me. You owe me, damn it!" She slams her hand on the table. "You owe me the time I put in this relationship. Can you give me back those years? Can you give me back my love? What about everything I've done for you, huh?" She rises and walks up in my face. "I was there while you were building all this shit. I was the woman who had your back when Tickman died. I stood by your side. I was there when you needed someone to talk too. Now you want to have the pity party? Poor Big A.T. Well, what about me? What do I get out of this?"

I knew this was coming. This tongue-lashing is exactly what I deserve. I will let her vent. I will let her get it all off her chest so that hopefully we can move forward.

"What you get out of this I can't tell you," I say. "There is no consolation prize. There is no reward for being a great girlfriend. Sometimes we have to walk away with a broken heart. We have to settle for the pain and deal with it. That's what I'm doing right now."

"I was more than a girlfriend to you. I gave you everything. I gave you a daughter," she says. "I am hurting. I didn't ask for this. I didn't ask for any of this." She throws her hands in the air.

"Jasmine, I didn't mean to hurt you," I say. "It was not intentional at all." I turn and walk toward the chairs. I sit. "I want us to work this out and at least be friends—if not for us, then for the sake of Tiffany. She deserves to have a father in her life. I just want to be that for her. I'm sorry for all of this," I say and look at her.

Jasmine starts to cry. She covers her face with her hands.

"I don't need this shit," she mumbles through the tears.

"You don't," I say. I rush to her and grab her in my arms.

"I'm so sorry," I whisper in her ear. Jasmine pulls me closer to her. She feels good in my arms. I miss her.

Then I release her and take a step back. I hold her face in my hands. I gently wipe away her tears. "I look a mess now," she says. I hand her my handkerchief. She dabs her eyes and wipes her nose.

"No, you're beautiful," I say. I take a deep breath and let it go. It's time to confront her about Odyssey. It's time for me to say something. This is the moment. "There is something I need to tell you."

She looks up at me. Her eyebrows furrow.

"How long have you been sleeping with Odyssey?" I ask.

"What!" She steps back from me. "How dare you ask me something like that? And what makes you think I'm sleeping with him?"

"I saw the video footage of the two of you leaving the police station. I figured something must be going on. You never mentioned him before."

"Exactly!" She crosses over to the other side of the table. "And why do you care who I'm sleeping with? You weren't concerned when it was you who was sleeping around with other men." Her voice starts to escalate. She's getting angry again.

"Well, if you're sleeping with him there is something you should know." I sigh. She tilts her head and purses her lips. "Odyssey is HIV positive. A very good source told me. He gave it to a girl he used to mess around with. He made her sign a confidentiality agreement and paid her to keep silent. He sent her back home, and my source just found out that she recently died from AIDS. If you've had sex with him, you should get tested. I already did, and my results are negative."

"Are you fucking serious?" She spits. "Really, Big A.T.!?!" She starts pacing back and forth. "Now you want to play Mr. Fucking-Captain-Save-Me. You were the one fucking other men while we were together. You're the one who's on the down low. I don't know what the hell you were doing with those men. And now you want to come in here and tell me the man you hate and have a problem with is HIV positive because of what? Because you're jealous?" She throws her hands in the air. "Because you don't want to see me happy? Or is it, perhaps, that he's more of a man than you'll ever be?" She glares at me.

I march toward her. I'm angry. Pissed off that she would accuse me of being jealous of Odyssey. "Jasmine, I'm telling you the truth." I stop before I reach her and take a breath. "Look, I really want you to be happy. I want the best for you. I also hope that if you knew someone I had fucked was HIV positive you would tell me. And I wouldn't take it so lightly and flip it back on you as being angry, bitter, and jealous. So, for your sake and my daughter's sake, I suggest you get tested." I walk back to the chair I was sitting in. "And, for the record, Odyssey will never be more of a man than me. He's not even half the man I am."

I'm breathing fast and hard. I shove the chair into the table. The lawyers walk back into the room. Jasmine is standing next to the window with her arms folded.

"Can we get this over with?" She walks over to the table.

The lawyers give us the contracts to peruse. We sign them, making it all final. Whether we like it or not, Jasmine and I will have a relationship.

# EIGHTY-TWO

JASMINE

I can't fucking believe what Big A.T. told me about Odyssey. Was he for real? Why would he lie about something like that? To say that someone is HIV positive is a serious accusation. And, dear God, I can't deal with this shit right now.

Why me? What did I do to deserve this? There is no logical explanation. At least nothing I can come up with.

I can't even think straight, and I don't even want to think about how many times Odyssey and I had sex that night. Damn it! I have no one to blame but myself. No amount of vulnerability or yearning should have let me slip like that.

One thing I know I have to do is get myself tested. I'm not taking any chances. I have to be around for my daughter. I can't imagine dying so young and not seeing my daughter grow up.

And I refuse to let my mother think she is right about the men I've dated. If it was her choice I would be married by now to some wealthy doctor or lawyer playing happy housewife. I am not her or my sisters' woman. I am my own woman. I will bounce back, and I don't need a man to do that.

Signing the papers and knowing my daughter will be taken care of provides me some comfort—not comfort in love, or emotions, but in there being some financial stability for Tiffany.

I sit in my car in the parking lot for a good fifteen minutes before I decide to drive up the Henry Hudson Parkway to my mother's house. As I'm driving I make a detour and turn onto the Cross Bronx Expressway and then the Brooklyn-Queens

Expressway toward Long Island. I need to see Odyssey. It's important we have a talk. I need to confront him and find out if what Big A.T. said is true.

I pull into the long driveway and park in front of his mini-mansion, and Odyssey steps outside. He has that crooked wide smile on his face. His bright white T-shirt and sneakers are a sharp contrast to his dark skin. His thick arms and big chest are snuggled neatly inside the T-shirt.

He opens the driver side and I step out. "Whoa!" Odyssey says and takes a step back. "Damn, Jasmine, you look amazing."

"Thank you." I smile. I turned heads today, especially Big A.T.'s. That was my goal. To let him know what he is missing, and that drama or no drama, I got it going on and will do it with my head held high.

Odyssey leans forward and I gently turn my head to the left. His lips land on my cheek.

"What's up? I gets no love?" Odyssey asks with his arms open wide.

I feign a smile.

Odyssey reaches for my left hand. I reluctantly give it to him and place my right hand on top of his.

"Odyssey, we need to talk," I say.

"Well, let's go inside," he says.

"No. I would rather not."

"Oh?" He has a stunned look on his face. I pull my hand away.

"I have to ask you something, and I need for you to be really honest with me."

He looks at me perplexed. "What's up?"

"I am just going to be straight with this," I say. I put my hands on my hips and cross my legs. "Are you HIV positive?"

He stares at me with a blank look on his face. He takes a step back and shakes his head. "Am I what?" he says.

I fold my arms across my chest. "I asked if you were HIV positive. I need to know."

"What the fuck! Hell naw! Why you asking me some shit like that?"

"Someone told me that you were and I need to know. I don't like playing Russian roulette with my life. I have too much to live for."

"Who the fuck told you that?"

"It doesn't matter who told me. What matters is if you are or not."

"I told you no."

I stare into his eyes. I observe his body language. He puffs his chest. He clenches his fists. He starts gritting his teeth.

"Big A.T. told you that shit, didn't he?" Odyssey points his finger at me. "He's trying to get back with you? He's gay!" Odyssey spits.

"What are you talking about?" I shake my head. "He's not trying to get back with me." I lean against my car. "Look, Odyssey, right now I need some time to be alone. I really need to focus on me and my daughter. I've been so caught up in everything happening around me that I clearly have not been thinking straight."

Odyssey slumps next to me. "I do understand. What that nigga Big A.T. has done to you is not right. He fucked up and now you feel guilty about it. And now that nigga running around lying on me saying I'm HIV positive. That's how those gay dudes are, especially those down-low dudes. They manipulate and deceive people. Big A.T. took advantage of you and now he's trying to add my name in that bullshit. I'm going to fuck that nigga up when I see him. That's my word!" Odyssey pounds his right first into his left hand.

"Please don't do anything. I don't want this to get out of hand." I place my fingers on Odyssey's face and caress it. "Promise me you won't do anything?"

He stares into my eyes. He sighs and then says, "I don't appreciate that nigga lying on me like that. But, I'm going to keep it cool for you."

"Thank you," I say.

Odyssey puts his arm around my shoulder. "You are beautiful and deserve the best. You deserve a good man. I can be that man for you if you give me the chance."

"I don't feel running into another man's arms right now is what I need. Just give me some time to be alone."

Odyssey kisses me on my left cheek. "No problem. But I want you to know I am here for you."

"Thank you. I need a friend." I stroke his massive arms and then his face.

Odyssey opens the car door and I get inside. He leans in and again kisses my left cheek. "I'll be here waiting for you."

I smile and start the car. Odyssey takes a few steps back and I drive off. I glance in the rearview mirror and see him standing in the driveway with his hands in his pockets. His huge body fades as I wind out of view and onto the road.

# EIGHTY-THREE

The days, weeks, and months come and go. It's a whirlwind. I am all over the city. Each moment of my day is planned to the minute. Tracey created a tight schedule. I don't spend too much time in one place. She set it up so I will not be interrogated by anyone. I am in and out. Then on to the next event, location, or meeting.

I rarely see my office or staff. I communicate with Kenya via cell, e-mail, or text. She is basically running the office in my absence. At night I am in the studio checking on Southern Gent, Wizard, FINE, Jook Boy, and Ms. Freeda.

I am also still producing for many other big names in the business who need music for their albums.

Then I have Tiffany every other weekend. I have to be Daddy and full of energy for her. It really takes everything in me to care for a four-year-old bundle of joy and spirited little girl. Whenever I go pick her up at Jasmine's mother's house, I don't schedule anything six hours prior. I need to rejuvenate myself.

Besides, when I get to Mrs. Bourdeaux's house I have to deal with attitude and sarcasm. Jasmine's mother really doesn't like me. And Jasmine refuses to change the pickup and drop-off location for Tiffany.

"I don't want to see you. I need time for me. I need time to get over this," Jasmine told me. So, for the past five months I have not seen Jasmine. Our communication is via texts or messages through her mother. I was really hoping we would work out our differences. I've left message after message. She won't return any of my calls. I guess she does need time.

It's weird, but I do miss her. I miss her company, conversation, laugh, and concern for me. Yet, that does not fulfill who I am. I need and love being with men.

Plain and simple.

But I am hoping her not speaking with me will end soon, because I can only take so much of her mother. She is working my last nerves. But I smile. I speak politely. I don't engage in her sarcasm. I run in, get my daughter, and bounce.

I don't need any extra stress in my life. Not right now. I already feel like a zombie. All this shit is taking a toll on my body. I eat sporadically. The food does little to nourish me. I've lost fifteen pounds. I am drained emotionally and physically. I've stopped listening to the radio and watching television altogether. I barely have time. Besides, when I do hear or get a glimpse of what they're talking about it's too much. It's all about me. What I'm doing. Who I'm seen with. Will my career be saved?

They can't get enough. I hate it. The newspapers did polls on how many gay men were in Hip Hop. Everyone was an expert in speaking on the subject. Television shows did specials about homosexuality within the entertainment industry, and especially black culture. No matter where I turned something was on the radio, television, or Internet about me. Tracey had warned me this would happen to me.

"Don't listen to the media," she said. "You may have a lot of supporters, but there will be some negative press and comments. It will cause you to have a breakdown."

Many days and nights I find myself happy at times, then depressed and sad, then back to joyous, and then angry. I feel like the lone black gay man who came out in Hip Hop. Yes, a very heavy burden. Something I was not equipped to carry. But I troop forward. Keeping myself busy.

After the initial burst of support, there has been no one I

can really, deeply talk to about what I am experiencing. Not Pop. Not my mother. Not any of the family. In the beginning, I got calls of support from Ellen DeGeneres, Rosie O'Donnell, Wanda Sykes, Elton John, and Lance Bass. They all told me they were proud of me. "Yes, you will feel like you are the voice of all black gay men, and the black gay community," Ellen said. "But be your own voice. Find your own cause and be your own champion."

I appreciated her reaching out. But how do I apply this to Hip Hop, a homophobic culture where ego, machismo, and street cred are the determining factors of your manhood?

Many of my associates did shy away from me. Some producers and artists stopped calling. They didn't want to be guilty by association. It hurts to have people you've worked with for years turn their back on you. But I learned they were not my true friends. They were just like many other people I met in this business: When you're hot and the world is riding your jock, they want to ride with you. As soon as some shit goes down they are out, running wildly to the next hot thing or jumping off your bandwagon and onto the new pimped-out bandwagon.

Pop kept encouraging me when this started happening. He kept calling me The King.

"This is your kingdom," he said. "You are in a war right now. Don't let your enemies see you weak. A weak king will soon fall."

Well, fuck, if I am King, then where is my army?

I try motivating myself over and over again, but I am really tired. Maybe I will feel better after church. I am scheduled to be at Abyssinian Baptist Church in Harlem for the nine o'clock service. I don't think I can do it. My body and mind are wrestling with each other. My mind is active, but my body refuses to move.

I lay struggling with sleep that calls me to stay in the bed. My cell phone rings. It's Tracey. "You're meeting me at church at nine," she says. "This is a good look for you. You're doing a photo op with Reverend Calvin O. Butts the Third."

"Okay, Tracey," I mumble.

"You better be there. You're making a donation of fifteen thousand dollars for their scholarship fund. And you're doing it in front of the congregation at the beginning of the service."

"I'll be there, Tracey."

If I can just get out of bed and make it uptown I will be all right. But I am really exhausted. I'm tired of justifying who I am. I'm sick of everyone making such a big deal about my sexuality. I am at the point where I don't feel like being bothered with anyone. I don't want to shake hands, smile, or sign another autograph. I just want my life back. The way it used to be.

I force myself out of bed and drag my body into the shower. I slowly get dressed.

I put on my underwear.

Then take a rest.

I put on my socks.

Then take a rest.

I put on my pants.

Then take a rest.

I put on my shirt.

Then take a rest.

I am not in a hurry.

At the church, people are dressed in their Sunday best. They are smiling, chitchatting, and wishing one another morning blessings. As I sluggishly walk to the front doors, everyone is reaching out to shake my hand. "We thank you for coming. We appreciate everything you're doing for our young people. You are welcome here," they are saying to me.

I also heard some women say things like, "Yeah, that's him. You know, the one who said he was gay. I'm going to pray for him."

I spot Tracey and one of the ministers. They usher me

through the crowd as it swells around me. We make our way toward a flight of stairs and come to a row of offices. The young minister knocks on the last door on the right. He steps inside and two minutes later he and Reverend Butts come out.

"This is Big A.T.," the young minister says.

"Well, it is truly a pleasure to meet you, young man," Reverend Butts says. He extends his hands. He's much taller than I expected. His smile is very warm and inviting. I feel the presence of the Lord around him. "Thank you for your generous contribution to our young people. This is truly a blessing," he says.

"Let's get some photos before service begins," the young minister says.

Reverend Butts and I stand next to each other. He puts his arm around my shoulder.

*Snap.*

*Snap.*

*Snap.*

The photographer snaps a few photos of us smiling. "Thank you." He finishes and checks his camera.

The young minister helps Reverend Butts with his long black robe. I hear the organ being played.

"You will come down in the procession following the reverend and the rest of us," the young minister says. "You and Tracey will sit in the first pew, next to the first lady and the other ministers' wives."

While we are waiting to follow the procession, my cell phone rings. It's Pop. The ministers in front of me turn around. An usher rushes over. "You have to turn off your cell phone. We are about to go downstairs."

"No problem." I smile and put it on Vibrate.

As we start walking my phone starts vibrating in my pocket.

It's Pop calling back.

"Shit," I say to myself.

I put my hand over my mouth. But no one heard me. I look up to the sky and mumble, "Sorry, God." My phone keeps vibrating. I answer it. Tracey turns and gives me a stern look. The usher puts her hands on her hips and rolls her eyes at me.

"Hello," I whisper.

"Hey, where are you?" Pop asks.

"At church. What's up?"

"You haven't seen the news?"

"No. Why? What's up?" My heart starts to race. I wonder what they are saying now about me.

"A riot broke out in Detroit this morning." Pop is laughing. "General Motors and Chrysler announced they are laying off seventy-five hundred people in the city."

"That's what you called to tell me? They are always laying off people. That's not news," I say.

"Yeah, but the layoffs are effective immediately and they are moving out of Michigan. GM and Chrysler will no longer be based in Detroit."

"Okay, I am not following," I say.

"You are no longer the focus of the news. This shit is bigger than you!" Pop lets out a cheer.

My eyes brighten. I can't believe my ears.

"They are burning everything in Detroit as we speak," Pop says. "It's all over the news. CNN, ABC, CBS, and NBC. There is nothing else on. Man, you should see it. There are black people everywhere, running around, looting, shooting, breaking into buildings, and setting things on fire. They are acting a fool."

I smile widely. I am elated. My fate has changed.

"Thank you, God," I say and point toward the sky.

"Man, you just got one of the biggest breaks," Pop says.

Pop is right. The media is on to the new hot topic of the day. They will forget about me. I am officially yesterday's news. No one will care any longer about me or my sexuality. I can go about my business of making music. I can continue building my empire.

The King lives!

Everything in the world is all right. I click off my phone and hug Tracey. I take my spot back in line. I smile, poke my chest out, and march defiantly into the sanctuary as the choir's angelic voices sing "Stand" by Donnie McClurkin and filter through my relieved soul. I think I just might join church today.

# EIGHTY-FOUR

JASMINE

It has officially been one hundred eighty days, seventeen hours, thirty-two minutes, and fourteen seconds since I've last spoken to or seen Big A.T. Each day I mark the calendar with a big red X. It is my symbol of freedom and regaining who I am.

It's weird not talking to Big A.T. on a day-to-day basis, or him coming through the door and Tiffany running and jumping into his arms. I miss those moments of his hugs, kisses, and jokes. When I think about them I break down and cry. But, with each day it gets easier. I have learned that after being involved with a celebrity it's harder to live your own life.

To make sure I maintain a sense of who I am and what I am doing, I don't allow myself any interaction with Big A.T. The only contact we have is through text messages and my mother. Each month Big A.T. makes sure the child support payments are on time. So I really don't need to see or speak with him, and right now I don't have anything to say to him. One day I will get to the point of talking with him and even seeing him. But for now I need my space.

Odyssey calls every other day to check in on me. After a month I stopped taking his calls. Now he sends texts and leaves voice messages.

After I confronted him at his house about his HIV status, I wasn't completely convinced he was telling me the truth. The way he responded and how his body twitched and he diverted his eyes from mines, I felt he wasn't being forthright.

I went and got an HIV test a few days later. It was the most fearful thing I'd ever experienced in my life. My heart began to race the moment I walked into the doctor's office. My hands were shaking uncontrollably and I couldn't fill out the paperwork. I was a mess. But I'm glad I did it. I know my status, and thank God, I'm HIV negative. I plan to stay negative and use condoms at all times. I can't believe that I let myself be careless and sleep with Odyssey without a condom. That was very foolish of me.

After that episode I knew it was time to put folks on an extended break out of my life. I had to reevaluate a lot, and a lot of that introspection was for my own self-development and growth.

I even put Kim on a hiatus. That's my girl, but I don't need her telling me about Big A.T. and what he's doing.

It didn't matter anyhow, because the newspapers, magazines, radio, and news always had something to say about Big A.T.

I got a few calls from *Vanity Fair, Essence,* and other media outlets, but I declined all their interview requests. I really don't want to relive the hurt and pain I felt. I don't think any woman should have to go through what I've been through.

I've applied and got accepted to design school in Los Angeles. That part of my dream has not died. I still love decorating and watching HGTV all day.

I'm just contemplating on whether or not Tiffany will adjust to the move. We have no family in Los Angeles, but it will be a great opportunity to restart our lives in a new place with no people to interfere. I can begin anew. Start fresh.

I've been thumbing through the Fashion Institute of Design & Merchandising's catalogue for a week now. I've even picked out my classes for the fall semester. I don't know why I haven't sent in my tuition deposit. I made the check out and it's been sitting on the dining room table. I should just get up and drop it in the mail. Send it and be done with it. Make it final, and then I wouldn't be mulling over my decision.

As I'm deciding on whether or not I should take a marketing class, my phone rings. It's from an unknown caller. I hate when people call me and block their numbers. I generally don't answer the call because it's most likely a reporter wanting to do an interview.

After several rings it finally stops. The person doesn't leave a voice message. A minute later the phone rings again, and again it's an unknown caller. After four rings I sigh and answer. "Hello?"

"Hello. I am looking for Jasmine Bourdeaux."

"Who's calling?" I ask. I don't want the person to know it's me just in case it's a reporter.

"This is Jan Summers from the Bravo Network."

"Uhm, this is Jasmine. How may I help you?"

"Oh, hello, Ms. Bourdeaux. I'm so glad I got you. As I said, I'm Jan Summers with the Bravo Network. I am the executive producer for *The Real Housewives* franchise."

I sit up, a little confused, wondering why she is calling me.

"Hello?" she says.

"I'm here."

"I know you're probably wondering why I am calling you?"

"Yes, I am."

"Well, we've been following the story of you and Big A.T. and find it very fascinating. We find it so fascinating that we would like to extend an invitation to you to be the new housewife for our New York show."

My mouth drops open. The brochure I was flipping through falls off my lap and onto the floor. I almost drop the phone.

"Wait a minute. You want me to be on the show?" I say in disbelief.

"Yes. We think your story is powerful, and—"

I cut her off. "You do know that I am not married."

"Yes, we know. We want to give you the opportunity to show the world how you are rebuilding your life post–Big A.T. We are truly sorry for what you've experienced, but your story has a very unique twist that I am certain will be a big show bonanza. We can guarantee you will get a lot of camera time because of your experience and how you're starting over. Besides, I am certain there are many women who are in your shoes after a tragic split, and those women will relate to you. Also, *most* of the women on the show are not married. They are recently divorced, or have been in relationships with powerful men and live a certain affluent lifestyle."

"Okay. Wow. I am in shock right now," I say.

"I know this may sound overwhelming right now and you may need time to think about it, but we are gearing up for the next season in a few weeks. We are willing to pay you an appearance fee of seventy-five thousand dollars per episode for twelve episodes, with an option for renewal after the season. So if you would like to be on board, we would love to have you. However, I will need an answer by next week."

I'm still sitting with my mouth open and shaking my head. It feels like a dream. I look down at my catalogue. The words and logo of the Fashion Institute are blaring up at me.

I look around my apartment; unpacked boxes are scattered throughout. I've never really settled into this apartment. It has always been a transitional place. If I were to move to Los Angeles, I would have to go through the whole moving process again.

"Ms. Bourdeaux, are you still there?"

"Yes, I am here. You know what?" I say as I glance over at Tiffany playing on the floor with her dolls. "I will do the show." I smile. My heart is racing. I am giddy with excitement. "You can consider me the new real housewife of New York."

# ACKNOWLEDGMENTS

I would first like to give thanks to my Father in heaven. I've been truly blessed to use the talents provided me to make a living, and be called an author.

To my aunt Prisicilla Bradford, uncle Andrew Dean, and uncle John Williams, and my aunt by marriage, Amanda Williams. Thank you for your continued love and support. To my sister, Sheritta Gerald, and nephew, Mitchell, and my huge extended family of cousins and in-laws. Thank you for all your love, hugs, smiles, and encouragement.

This book is in memoriam to Grandma Pearl; my mother, Blanche Gerald; my brothers, George and Jevonte Gerald; and my aunt, DeLisa Dean. I always feel their presence.

To my brilliant and talented editor, Todd Hunter—I cannot thank you enough for your patience, time, and humility. What a writer's dream to have an editor who encourages, empowers, and helps shape creative minds. I truly am grateful for your eye, care, and insightful conversations.

My deepest gratitude to my publisher, Atria Books, and Judith Curr. Let's go to the top! And a very special thank-you and big hug to a DIVA and fabulous editor, Malaika Adero. You're beautiful and brilliant beyond words. To the FAB PR team who hold me down every time, Yona Deshommes and Christine Saunders. Where would I be without you ladies? My gosh, you know I got love for my two DIVAs! And, to the rest of the Atria/Simon & Schuster family who helped to put this book together, I graciously thank you!

To my mellow and ever-so-patient agent, Marc Gerald. I thank you for your persistence and encouragement. To Sasha Raskin, you go above and beyond. I cannot thank you enough your professionalism and kindness.

Thank you to my frat brother and big brother, Larry Johnson, and his wife, Monique, and their triplets—Kennedy, Kyler, and Chase. You don't know how many times you've saved me. Our conversations, your insights, your undying love: I cannot tell you how I'm glad to call your family, MY FAMILY. To my other frat brother and big brother, Marc Metze, and the Metze family—Samantha, Miriam, Miles, and Adam. Thank you for always standing by my side. For believing in me and reminding me who I am and my purpose. I love you, brother!

Special thank-yous to: Ernest Montgomery (thank you for being a best friend); the Permel family—Chris Beal (My "sis"— let's make a movie!), Ron, and Jenai Beal; Karu F. Daniels; JL King; Lori Read; Gil Robertson; Marlynn Snyder (love you, brother); Marlon Gregory; Lloyd Boston; Maurice Jamal; Emil Wilbekin (a powerful role model); Kevin E. Taylor; Rubin Singleton; Melody Guy; Janaya Black; Rod Gailes; William Lyons; Anthony Montgomery (Monaga); Stanley Bennett Clay; James Earl Hardy; Patrick Riley; Anthony Harper; Jerald Cooper; Russell Motley; Dwayne Jenkins; Charles Pugh; Peter Holoman; Fred T. Jackson; Tyrus Townsend; Leslie "Buttaflysoul" Taylor; Troy Johnson; Jeff Johnson; Lynette Holloway; Marcia Pendleton; Shirita Hightower; Felisha Booker and the Dynamic Producer family; Ailene Torres; the Dent family—Keisha, Stephen, and Stephen Jr.; Tananarive Due; Tamara Francois; Sydney Margetson; Lydia Andrews; Brian St. John; Adolfo and Sara Vasquez; Tu-Shonda L. Whitaker; Victoria Christopher Murray; Marva Allen; Carol Mackey; Abida Abrams; Deborah Bennett; Big Ced; Smokey Fontaine; Tonya Tait, Jennifer Howard, and Karen Johnson—my brunch DIVAS!; Sabrina Lamb; Desiree Cooper; Deborah Gregory; Myra Panache;

Paula Renfroe; Nikki Webber; DeMarco Kidd; Nicole Childers; my Fisk University family and the classes of '91, '92, and '93; Yasmin Coleman and the APOOO Book Club; Ms. Tamika Newhouse and the African-Americans on the Move Book Club; and Nikkea Smithers and the Readers With Attitude Bookclub. A special shout-out to all the book clubs who've shown me love and supported me. I appreciate each of you and I'm looking forward to coming to your meetings. So you better send me an invitation! And to all my friends in cyberspace, I appreciate your comments, friend requests, and continued support.

To all the men in Men's Empowerment—you all are so dear to me and I thank you for your patience and encouragement.

If I forgot anyone, please forgive me. You know how you have touched my life.

A very special shout-out to: *Essence* magazine (essence. com), AOL Black Voices, Interactive One/Hello Beautiful, and *Juicy* magazine. Thank you for allowing me to share my writings and voice with the world. I thank you graciously for giving me an outlet.

To all the bookstores: Outwrite Books, Our Story Books, Afrocentric Bookstore, Basic Black Books, Robin's Bookstore, A & B Books, Brownstone Books, Hue-Man Bookstore & Cafe, Alkebu-Lan Images, Howard University Bookstore, Shrine of the Black Madonna Bookstore, Urban Knowledge, Truth Bookstore, Karibu Bookstore, African American Literature Book Club (aalbc.com), and Black Expressions Book Club.

And, last, but not least, to all the urban media outlets that provide us with the real scoop—Gyant Unplugged; YBF; Media Takeout; Bossip; What's the T; Panache Report; HListed; Media Outrage; Straight From The A; Necole Bitchie; AllHipHop.com; Gawker, *Frank and Wanda Morning Show*; Michael Baisden; *Coco, Foolish & Mr. Chase*; Frankie Darcell; *Steve Harvey Morning Show*; *Tom Joyner Morning Show*; *Rickey Smiley Morning Show*; *Big Boy's Neighborhood*; Angela Yee; DJ Envy; and Charlamagne Tha God.

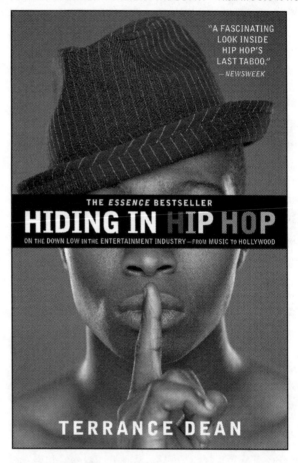

Printed in the United States
By Bookmasters